NEW YORK TIMES BESTSELLING AUTHOR

KEVIN J. ANDERSON

THE FUNNY BUSINESS

BEWARE: SILLINESS AHEAD

The Funny Business by Kevin J. Anderson
WordFire Press
wordfirepress.com

Ebook ISBN 978-1-68057-500-2
Trade paperback ISBN 978-1-68057-501-9
Dust Jacket hardcover ISBN 978-1-68057-502-6
Case Bind hardcover ISBN 978-1-68057-503-3
This collection copyright © 2023 WordFire, Inc.

"Introduction" copyright © 2023 WordFire, Inc. First publication.

Additional copyright information at end of book

All rights reserved. No part of this book may be reproduced or transmitted in any form or by any electronic or mechanical means, including photocopying, recording or by any information storage and retrieval system, without the express written permission of the copyright holder, except where permitted by law. This novel is a work of fiction. Names, characters, places and incidents are either the product of the author's imagination, or, if real, used fictitiously.

This book is licensed for your personal enjoyment only. This ebook may not be re-sold or given away to other people. If you would like to share this book with another person, please purchase an additional copy for each recipient. Thank you for respecting the hard work of this author.

Cover painting and design by Miblart
Kevin J. Anderson, Art Director

Published by
WordFire Press, LLC
PO Box 1840
Monument, CO 80132
Kevin J. Anderson & Rebecca Moesta, Publishers

Join our WordFire Press Readers Group for free books,
sneak previews, updates on new projects, and other giveaways
Sign up at https://eepurl.com/c_lmZP

CONTENTS

Introduction	v
Frog Kiss	1
Special Makeup	9
Memorial	19
Bump in the Night	21
A Dan Shamble, Zombie P.I. Adventure	
Quest Prize	41
Paradox & Greenblatt, Attorneys at Law	43
Eighty Letters, Plus One	57
With Sarah A. Hoyt	
Short Straws	69
The Sacrifice	77
TechnoMagic	79
Age Rings	89
Letter of Resignation	91
Rude Awakening	93
The Fate Worse than Death	99
(with Guy Anthony de Marco)	
Time Zone	107
Dark Carbuncle	109
(with Janis Ian)	
Tea Time Before Perseus	119
Santa Claus Is Coming to Get You	121
Cold Dead Turkey	127
A Dan Shamble, Zombie P.I. Adventure	
Loincloth	145
(With Rebecca Moesta)	
Grumpy Old Monsters	155
The Original Comic Scripts (with Rebecca Moesta)	
Previous Publication Information	269
Also by Kevin J. Anderson	271
About the Author	275
Autographed Copies	277

INTRODUCTION
THE LAST LAUGH (AND THE FIRST LAUGH)

In my career I've written plenty of tragic stories, killed a lot of characters ... some in particularly unpleasant ways (and a lot of them didn't deserve it!). I've started wars, destroyed planets, even (no kidding) tried to unravel the fabric of the universe itself.

But that doesn't mean I'm not a funny guy. I do have a lighter side.

I've written plenty of stories that are clever, witty, subtly amusing ... or twisted, dumb, and slapstick.

I gathered the best of them here in this book, covering a range of humorous science fiction, goofy fantasy, twisted horror.

Some of them turn classic tropes on their heads. You'll read about dragon slayers and virgin sacrifices, just trying to make the best of it. You'll see vampires in peril (one idea that I thought was so good, I wrote two different versions of it).

Some are short and sweet with surprise endings that'll make you snort, or at least blink in surprise. Because humor is often best when it's fast and punchy, I added selections of flash fiction, exploring just how short a story can be and still evoke a situation and a punchline. (The shortest one I could manage was "Letter of Resignation" at 13 words, not including the title.)

There are classic time-travel twists, the darker side of a rock comeback tour (co-written with Grammy Award-winning legend Janis Ian). I've got a riff on Jules Verne's *Around the World in Eighty Days*, a story about an alien magician stranded on Earth (which was commissioned by David Copperfield himself).

You'll read the very first vignette I ever published, "Memorial," when

I was a Junior in high school, and "Short Straws," a revision of the very first story I ever sold for pay ($12.50), which is the inspiration for my fantasy caper series *The Dragon Business*. I added two representative stories from my popular Dan Shamble, Zombie P.I. series, one of which has never before been collected. There are even two Christmas stories.

As a special treat, we close out the book with the complete original scripts from our hilarious four-issue comic series for IDW, *Grumpy Old Monsters*, coauthored with my wife Rebecca Moesta. We adore those loveable monster characters and their wild adventures. These have never before been published, and the comics themselves are long out of print, but you can still visualize see the story in your mind.

So let's get down to *The Funny Business*. You'll laugh, you'll groan, you'll feel guilty, but deep down inside you'll admit you were amused.

—Kevin J. Anderson
Monument, Colorado
March 2023

FROG KISS

He had gotten used to it by now. The frog tasted cold and slimy against his lips, with a taste like brackish water, mud, and old compost. But Keric gave it a dutiful smack on its mouth, hoping that it wouldn't suddenly turn into the fat old king, who had also been enchanted, along with several more desirable members of the royal family.

But the frog just looked at him, squirmed, and then urinated on Keric's palm. Nothing. Again. He took a dab of red pigment from his pouch, smeared it on the frog's head, and then tossed the creature through the trees and marsh grass. He listened to it plop in another pool. Another one tried and failed.

Around him, the sounds of thousands of frogs croaked in the dense swamp, loud enough to drown out the whine of mosquitoes, the constant dripping of water, and the occasional belch of a crocodile.

Sweat and dirty water ran in streaks from his brown hair, down his cheeks, and avoided the frog slime around his mouth. He had caught and tested more than three dozen frogs already, but it would be years before he could find them all—and that was only if any members of the frog-cursed royal family remained alive in the deep swamps. A crocodile splashed somewhere out in the network of cypress roots and branches. Somehow Keric couldn't imagine the brittle old Queen Mother deigning to eat flies, not even if they were served to her by someone else.

When the evil wizard Cosimor had taken over the kingdom less than a year before, he had followed the traditional path of sorcerous usurpers by capturing the entire royal family and transforming them into frogs and then turning them loose in the sprawling, infected swamps of Dermith.

Cosimor had intended to tax the kingdom to its death, drive the subjects into slavery, and generally keep himself amused. But less than three weeks later the wizard had died choking on a fish bone—no vengeful curse, that; simply poor cooking. Now the kingdom had been left without any rulers, not even the incompetent but somehow endearing royal family.

Keric, who lived in a hut on the fringes of the Dermith swamps, trapping muskrats and selling the fur in the noisy walled town, had decided to try to find the royal family in its exile, free at least one of them with a kiss, and then count on his reward. A palace of his own, perhaps? Gold coins stacked as high as an oak tree? Fine clothes. He pulled at his dripping, mud-soaked rags. Yes, fine clothes first. And then perhaps the hand of one of the princesses in marriage?

He spat drying slime away from his lips. But first he had to catch the right frog—and they all looked alike!

He slumped down on a rotting log covered with Spanish moss, then looked across at the piled undergrowth to see a bloated old bullfrog sitting under a drooping fern. Plainly visible on the frog's back were three equally spaced dark blotches, just like the supposed birthmark carried by every member of the royal family! Was this the old king, then? The fat duchess, the king's sister? It didn't matter to Keric—the frog sat right in front of his eyes. It had always taken him too long to see what was right in front of his face.

He didn't want to hesitate too long. Keric shifted his body forward and then lunged, splaying out his mud-caked fingers. He skidded through a spiderweb, needle-thin fronds, and dead leaves, but the bullfrog squirted away from him. He scrambled and grabbed again.

He didn't see the girl until she leapt out from the bushes in front of the bullfrog, opened up the mouth of a large squirming sack, and swept the frog inside. The bullfrog made a croak of alarm, but then the girl spun the sack shut. "Got him!" she said, giggling. Then she sprinted away through the underbrush, leaving only disturbed willow branches dangling behind her.

"Hey!" Keric shouted and jumped to his feet. He ran after her, flinging branches out of the way. He splashed through puddles of standing water, squished on sodden grass islands, and ducked his head in buzzing clouds of mosquitoes. All around, the other frogs continued their songs. "That one was mine!"

"Not anymore!" He heard her voice from the side, in a different direction from where she had disappeared. He looked in time to see her running barefoot down a path only she could see. Barefoot!

Keric ran after her. He found himself panting and sweating. He had grown up in and around these swamps. He considered himself an exceptional woodsman in even the deepest parts of the morass. He could outrun and out-hunt anyone he had ever known. But this girl kept going at a pace he could not hope to match. He stumbled, he missed solid footing, he splashed scummy water all over himself.

"Wait!" he shouted. He heard only the crocodiles growling.

"If you'd look over here, you'd have a better chance of seeing me!" She laughed again.

He whirled to see her across a mucky pool, not twenty feet from him. Without thinking—since he was wet and filthy anyway—he left the path and charged across the way. "Give me my frog!"

Keric tried to run with both feet, but each step became more difficult as the ooze sucked at his boots. He had to get the bullfrog with the three spots. He *knew* it was somebody from the royal family. The girl probably didn't know what she had. Maybe she wanted to eat it!

He sloshed onward, but before he had gone halfway across the pool, he felt the muck dragging him down. He sank to his waist and found he could not take another step. He continued to submerge in the ooze. "Oh no!"

From the spreading cypress tree over his head, he heard the girl's voice. "You should be more careful out here in the swamps. Plenty of dangerous things out here. Crocodiles, water moccasin snakes, milt spiders bigger than your hand, poison plants." Keric looked up to see her sitting on one of the branches, holding onto the frog sack with one hand and munching on a dripping fruit in the other. "But you really have to watch out for that quicksand. That's especially bad."

"Would you help me out of this?" He looked at her. He had sunk up to his armpits and felt the cold muck seeping into his pores. The mud crept to the tops of his shoulders. Keric had to lift his head to keep his chin out of the ooze. "Um, please?"

"I don't know. You were chasing me." She finished her fruit and tossed the pit down. It splashed beside him.

"I'll tell you what you've got in that sack of yours."

"It's frogs."

"No, if you'll just let me kiss one of them I'll show you something magic!" He had to talk rapidly now. The quicksand had reached his lips.

"Oh, you mean *that*! Sure, I've got the whole royal family here." She reached in and pulled out another frog, this one sleek and small. It also had the three identical splotches. "You don't think you were the only one to get the idea for finding the frogs in the swamp, do you?"

Actually, Keric *had* thought he was the only one to think of that. Once again, the obvious was staring him in the face.

"But you were going about it all wrong," the girl continued. "You kept trying to kiss them out here in the swamp. Now tell me, just what would you have done if the frail and arthritic Queen Mother had appeared? Or one of the dainty princesses who would squeal at the sight of a beetle? How would you get them back? Makes more sense to me just to carry the frogs in a sack, go back to town, and then change them all back. Reward would still be the same, maybe more for saving them the journey."

Keric had to lean his head back to keep his nose and mouth above the surface. "Will you please help me now and give me advice later!"

She shrugged. "You haven't asked me the right question yet."

"What is the question?"

"Ask me what my name is! I'm not going to risk my life to rescue a total stranger."

"What's your name? Tell me quick!"

"I am Raffin. Pleased to meet you." She paused. "And what's your name?"

"I'm Keric! Help!"

She tossed a vine down that struck near his face. Keric grabbed at it, clawing at the slick surface of the vine with his mucky hands. But he managed to haul himself forward, toward the near edge of the pool of quicksand. He heaved himself out onto the soggy ground and shivered. He had lost his left boot, but he had no intention of going back to get it.

When he looked up at the tree, Raffin was gone.

After dark, when Keric remained cold and clammy but unable to light a fire, he saw an orange light flickering through the tangled branches. He followed it to Raffin's fire, then crept close to where he could see.

She sat humming to herself and holding four sticks splayed in the flames. Little strips of meat had been skewered on the wood and sizzled in the light. The bound bundle of royal frogs sat beside her. "Come closer and sit down, Keric. You're making enough noise at being quiet."

Angry, Keric came out of his hiding place and strode with confidence into her firelight. Finally, he sighed and shook his head. "I thought I was good in the swamps, moving silently, always knowing my way. I can't believe I am being so clumsy around you."

Raffin shrugged. "You *are* good. The best I've seen. But I'm better."

Her long pale hair must once have been blond but now had taken on the color of fallen leaves and dry grass. Her eyes looked startlingly blue within the camouflage of her appearance. Raffin had washed most of the grime from her face, arms, and hands before preparing her food.

Keric didn't want to imagine what he looked like himself.

Raffin took one of the sticks out of the fire and blew on the sizzling strips of meat. "Frog legs, filleted." At his shocked expression, she laughed. "No, just normal frogs. Don't worry. Would you like some?"

Keric swallowed. "I haven't eaten anything all day."

"Say please."

"Please. Uh, I mean, Raffin, may I please have some?"

"Of course. You're my guest. I saved your life. Do you think I'd refuse a simple request like that?"

He took the stick she offered and ate the crispy meat right off the bark so he wouldn't have to touch it with his dirty fingers. "What are you doing out here all alone in the swamps?"

"I live out here. Don't worry, I can take care of myself."

Keric could believe that. He guessed she was only a couple years older than himself.

"But I don't mind company once in a while." Suddenly, Raffin appeared shy to him. "Just listen to those night sounds, the frogs and the humming insects. Why would anyone want to live in the town?"

Keric frowned and ate the last piece of meat. "Then why are you trying so hard to get the royal frogs?"

"Because you are. I've been watching you for days. It's been fun. Besides, I have dreams of getting a prince of my own."

They talked for much longer after that, but Keric could get no better explanation from her. He felt the weariness from the day sapping his strength, making him drowsy. He interrupted what she was saying. "Raffin, I am going to sleep."

He saw her smile as he let his eyes drift shut. "Make yourself at home."

When Keric cracked his eyes open again an hour later, his body screamed at him just to keep sleeping. But he couldn't. He had something much more important to do.

Raffin had stayed beside the fire, which now burned low and smoky, still driving the mosquitoes away. She lay curled up on the ground, her cheek pillowed on her scrawny arms. She looked very peaceful and vulnerable. Keric frowned, but then thought of palaces and princesses and fine clothes.

The fire popped as two logs sagged, and Keric used the noise to cover his own movements as he crept to his feet. She had left the sack containing the royal family sitting unguarded on the other side of the camp. He shook his head, wondering why she had made it so easy for him.

He picked up the sack and slipped out of the firelight, starting to run as soon as he got out under the moonlit trees.

"Keric!" she shouted behind him.

He stopped trying to be silent. The marsh grass whipped around him as he picked up speed. Willow branches snapped at his eyes. He kept splashing in puddles or flailing his hands at large, flapping night insects.

"Keric, come back!"

He didn't answer her but started to chuckle. He could make it out of the swamp to his hut. He would go immediately into the walled town and kiss all the frogs, even the old Queen Mother, and bring them back before Raffin could find him.

He used all his forest skills to weave his path. He couldn't hear her following, but then he doubted if he would. She was too good for that.

Keric looked behind him as he ran, seeking some sign. Raffin did impress him with her knowledge of the swamps. She could teach him many things. He decided he would share his treasure with her anyway, once he got it, but for now he wanted to succeed on his own, to impress her that his own survival abilities weren't so trivial either.

He tripped on the tail of the first crocodile and could not stop himself until he had stumbled into a cluster of the beasts. Once again, he had been looking in the wrong place and missed what was right in front of him.

The crocodiles hissed and belched at him. Keric cried out. He could count at least seven of them, startled out of their torpor and suddenly confronted with something worth eating. An old bull scuttled toward him, looking as large as a warship. It opened its mouth so wide that Keric felt he could have walked inside without ducking his head.

He turned and searched for a way out. Hissing and snapping their enormous jaws, the crocodiles moved in. The old bull lunged. Keric leaped back, caught his heel on the long body of one of the smaller reptiles, and sprawled backward. Even the smaller crocodile chomped at him. Keric dropped his sack of royal frogs.

He scrambled to his hands and knees, looking for an escape. The moonlight made everything dim and confusing. He thought he saw a flashing orange light behind a sketchy web of cypress roots, but he concentrated only on the nightmare of wide, fang-filled jaws.

Raffin appeared and struck the snout of the nearest crocodile with her roaring torch. "Get away from him!" The beast hissed and grunted as it lurched backward. Keric blinked in amazement. In her other hand, Raffin held a pointed stick that she jabbed at the remaining crocodiles.

The beasts backed away. The enormous bull stood his ground and let out a deep growl from somewhere at the bottom of his abdomen.

Keric crawled to his feet, too stunned and frightened to be much help.

Raffin faced the bull's charge and shoved her torch at her attacker. The crocodile hissed and snapped at her, but she was quick with the end of her torch, touching the burning end to the soft tissue inside the reptilian mouth. Keric heard the sizzle of burning meat.

With a defeated roar, the bull backed away and then, in a final gesture of frustration and spite, he lashed out with his long snout and snapped up the tied sack of royal frogs. The frogs made a combined sound like someone stepping on a goose. The giant crocodile crunched down with his jaws, chomped again, then swallowed. After a satisfied grunt, the crocodile crawled out of the clearing and splashed into the water.

"I told you to be careful out in the swamps," Raffin scolded Keric. "Do I have to watch out for you all the time?"

Keric sat stunned. "They're all gone! In one gulp, the whole royal family!" He shook his head. "I never meant for that to happen."

Raffin took hold of his hand and pulled him to his feet. "The kingdom will do fine without them. They weren't particularly worth rescuing." She stared at him, but he continued to sulk. "Hey, it was fun while it lasted."

"No, I meant my reward. The gold, the fine clothes, the palace—"

"And what would you do with all that stuff?" She looked at him, then tugged at his old, mud-caked tunic. "Fine clothes? Are you seeking what you really want, or just what you think you're *supposed* to want? What other people tell you to want isn't always right for you."

Keric lowered his head, sighed deeply. He looked at himself and realized she was right. "If I had a palace, I suppose I'd just track mud in it all the time."

Raffin giggled. "It's not so bad out here, you know."

"But what about my princess?"

Raffin flicked her hair behind her shoulders and looked angry for a moment, then spoke in a very shy voice. "You could stay in the swamps." She paused. "With me."

Keric looked up at her and listened to the frogs and the night insects. One of these days he was going to learn to notice the things right in front of him.

SPECIAL MAKEUP

The second camera operator ran to fetch the clapboard. Someone else called out, "Quiet on the set! Hey everybody, shut up!" Three of the extras coughed at the same time.

"*Wolfman in Casablanca*, Scene 23. Are we ready for Scene 23?" The second camera operator held the clapboard ready.

"Ahem." The director, Rino Derwell, puffed on his long cigarette in an ivory cigarette holder, just like all famous directors were supposed to have. "I'd like to start today's shooting sometime *today*! Is that too much to ask? Where the hell is Lance?"

The boom man swiveled his microphone around; the extras on the nightclub set fidgeted in their places. The cameraman slurped a cold cup of coffee, making a noise like a vacuum cleaner in a bathtub.

"*Um*, Lance is still, *um*, getting his makeup on," the script supervisor said.

"Christ! Can somebody find me a way to shoot this picture without the star? He was supposed to be done half an hour ago. Go tell Zoltan to hurry up—this is a horror picture, not the Mona Lisa." Derwell mumbled how glad he was that the gypsy makeup man would be leaving in a day or two, and they could get someone else who didn't consider himself such a perfectionist. The director's assistant dashed away, stumbling off the soundstage and tripping on loose wires.

Around them, the set showed an exotic nightclub, with white fake-adobe walls, potted tropical plants, and Arabic-looking squiggles on the pottery. The piano in the center of the stage, just in front of the bar, sat empty under the spotlight, waiting for the movie's star, Lance Chandler.

The sound stage sweltered in the summer heat. The large standup fans had to be shut off before shooting; and the ceiling fans—nightclub props—stirred the cloud of cigarette smoke overhead into a gray whirlpool, making the extras cough even when they were supposed to keep silent.

Rino Derwell looked again at his gold wristwatch. He had bought it cheap from a man in an alley, but Derwell's pride would not allow him to admit he had been swindled even after it had promptly stopped working. Derwell didn't need it to tell him he was already well behind schedule, over budget, and out of patience.

It was going to take all day just to shoot a few seconds of finished footage. "God, I hate these transformation sequences. Why does the audience need to *see* everything? Have they no imagination?" he muttered. "Maybe I should just do romance pictures? At least nobody wants to see everything *there*!"

❧

"Oh, God! Please no! Not again! Not *NOW*!!!" Lance couldn't see the look of horror he hoped would show on his face.

"You must stop fidgeting, Mr. Lance. This will go much faster." Zoltan stepped back, large makeup brush in hand, inspecting his work. His heavy eastern European accent slurred out his words.

"Well, I've got to practice my lines. This blasted makeup takes so blasted long that I forget my blasted lines by the time it comes to shoot. Was I supposed to say, 'Don't let it happen *here*!' in that scene? Hand me the script."

"No, Mr. Lance. That line comes much later—it follows 'Oh, no! I'm transforming!'" Zoltan smeared shadow under Lance's eyes. This would be just the first step in the transformation, but he still had to increase the highlights. Veins stood out on Zoltan's gnarled hands, but his fingers were rock steady with the fine detail.

"How do you know my lines?"

"You may call it gypsy intuition, Mr. Lance—or it may be because you have been saying them every morning before makeup for a week now. They have burned into my brain like a gypsy curse."

Lance glared at the wizened old man in his pale blue shirt and color-spattered smock. Zoltan's leathery fingers had a real instinct for makeup, for changing the appearance of any actor. But his craft took hours.

Lance Chandler had enough confidence in his own screen presence to carry any picture, regardless of how silly the makeup made him look.

His square jaw, fine physique, and clean-cut appearance made him the perfect model of the all-American hero. Now, during the War against Germany and Japan, the U.S. needed its strong heroes to keep up morale. Besides, making propaganda pictures fulfilled his patriotic duties without requiring him to go somewhere and risk getting shot. Red-corn-syrup blood and bullet blanks were about all the real violence he wanted to experience.

Lance took special pride in his performance in *Tarzan Versus the Third Reich*. Though he had few lines in the film, the animal rage on his face and his oiled and straining body had been enough to topple an entire regiment of Hitler's finest, including one of Rommel's desert vehicles. (Exactly why one of Rommel's desert vehicles had shown up in the middle of Africa's deepest jungles was a question only the scriptwriter could have answered.)

Craig Corwyn, U-Boat Smasher, to be released next month as the start of a new series, might make Lance a household name. Those stories centered on brave Craig Corwyn, who had a penchant for leaping off the deck of his Allied destroyer and swimming down to sink Nazi submarines with his bare hands, usually by opening the underwater hatches or just plucking out the rivets in the hull.

But none of those movies would compare to *Wolfman in Casablanca*. Bogart would be forgotten in a week. The timing for this picture was just perfect; it had an emotional content Lance had not been able to bring into his earlier efforts. The country was just waiting for a new hero, strong and manly, with a dash of animal unpredictability and a heart of gold (not to mention unwavering in Allied sympathies).

The story concerned a troubled but patriotic werewolf—him, Lance Chandler—who in his wanderings has found himself in German-occupied Casablanca. There he causes what havoc he can for the enemy, and he also meets Brigitte, a beautiful French resistance fighter vacationing in Morocco. Brigitte turns out to be a werewolf herself, Lance's true love. Even in the script, the final scene as the two of them howl on the rooftops above a conflagration of Nazi tanks and ruined artillery sent shivers down Lance's spine. If he could pull off this performance, Hitler himself would tremble in his sheets.

Zoltan added spirit gum to Lance's cheeks and forehead, humming as he worked. "You will please stop perspiring, Mr. Lance. I require a dry surface for this fine hair."

Lance slumped in the chair. Zoltan reminded him of the wicked old gypsy man in the movie, the one who had cursed his character to become a werewolf in the first place. "This blasted transformation sequence is going to take all day again, isn't it? And I don't even get to *act* after the first second or so! Lie still, add more hair, shoot a few frames, lie still, add more hair, shoot a few more frames. And it's so hot in the soundstage. The spirit gum burns and ruins my complexion. The fumes sting my eyes. The fake hair itches."

He winced his face into the practiced look of horror again. "Oh, God! Please no! Not again! *Um* ... oh, yeah—don't let it happen here!" Lance paused, then scowled. "Blast, that wasn't right. Would you hurry up, Zoltan! I'm already losing my lines. And I'm really tired of you dragging your feet—get moving!"

Zoltan tossed the makeup brush with a loud clink into its glass jar of solvent. He put his gnarled hands on his hips and glared at Lance. The smoldering gypsy fury in his dark eyes looked worse than anything Lance had seen on a movie villain's face.

"I lose my patience with you, Mr. Lance! It is gone! Poof! Now I must take a short cut. A special trick that only I know. It will take a minute, and it will make you a star forevermore! I guarantee that. You will no longer suffer my efforts—and I need not suffer you! The people at the new Frankenstein picture over on Lot 17 would appreciate my work, no doubt."

Lance blinked, amazed at the old gypsy's anger but ready to jump at any chance that would get him out of the makeup trailer sooner. He heard only the words, "it will make you a star. I guarantee that."

"Well, do it then, Zoltan! I've got work to do. The great Lon Chaney never had to put up with all these delays. He did all his own makeup. My audiences are waiting to see the new meaning I can bring to the portrayal of the werewolf."

"You will never disappoint them, Mr. Lance."

Without further reply, Zoltan yanked at the fine hair he had already applied. "You no longer need this." Lance yowled as the patches came free of his skin. "That is a very good sound you make, Mr. Lance. Very much like a werewolf."

Lance growled at him.

Zoltan rustled in a cardboard box in the corner of his cramped trailer, pulled out a dirty Mason jar, and unscrewed its rusty lid. Inside, a brown oily liquid swirled all by itself, spinning green flecks in internal currents. The old man stuck his fingers into the goop and brought them out dripping.

"What is—whoa, that smells like—" Lance tried to shrink away, but Zoltan slapped the goop onto his cheek and smeared it around.

"You cannot possibly know what this smells like, Mr. Lance, because you have no idea what I used to make it. You probably do not wish to know—then you would be even more upset at having it rubbed all over your face."

Zoltan reached into the jar again and brought out another handful, which he wiped across Lance's forehead. "*Ugh!* Did you get that from the lot cafeteria?" Lance felt his skin tingle, as if the liquid had begun to eat its way inside. "*Ow!* My complexion!"

"If it gives you pimples, you can always call them character marks, Mr. Lance. Every good actor has them."

Zoltan pulled his hand away. Lance saw that the old man's fingers were clean. "Finished. It has all absorbed right in." He screwed the cover of the jar back on and replaced it in the cardboard box.

Lance grabbed a small mirror, expecting to find his (soon-to-be) well-known expression covered with ugly brown, but he could see no sign of the makeup at all. "What happened to it? It still stinks."

"It is special makeup. It will work when it needs to."

The door flew open, and the red-faced director's assistant stood panting. "Lance, Mr. Derwell wants you on the set right now! Pronto! We've got to start shooting."

Zoltan nudged his shoulder. "I am finished with you, Mr. Lance."

Lance stood up, trying not to look perplexed so that Zoltan could have a laugh at his expense. "But I don't see any—"

The old gypsy wore a wicked grin on his lips. "You need not worry about it. I believe your expression is, 'Knock 'em dead.'"

༄

Lance sat down at the nightclub piano and cracked his knuckles. The extras and other stars took their positions. Above the soundstage, he could hear men on the catwalks, positioning cool blue gels over the lights to simulate the full moon.

"*Now* are you ready, Lance?" the director said, fitting another cigarette into his ivory holder. "Or do you think maybe we should just take a coffee break for an hour or so?"

"That's not necessary, Mr. Derwell. I'm ready. Just give the word, see?" He growled for good measure.

"Places everyone!"

Lance ran his fingers over the piano keyboard, "tickling the old ivories," as real piano players called it. No sound came out. Lance couldn't play a note, of course, so the prop men had cut all the piano wires, holding the instrument in merciful silence no matter how enthusiastically Lance might bang on it. They would add the beautiful piano melody to the soundtrack during post-production.

"*Wolfman in Casablanca*, Scene 23, Take One." The clapboard cracked.

"Action!" Derwell called.

The klieg lights came on, pouring hot white illumination on the set. Lance stiffened at the piano, then began to hum and pretend to plink on the keys.

In this scene, the werewolf has taken a job as a piano player in a nightclub, where he has met Brigitte, the vacationing French resistance fighter. While playing "As Time Goes By," Lance's character looks up to see the full moon shining down through the nightclub's skylight. To keep from having to interrupt filming, Derwell had planned to shoot Lance from the back only as he played the piano, not showing his face until after he had supposedly started to transform. But now Lance didn't appear to wear any makeup at all—he wondered what would happen when Derwell noticed, but he plunged into the performance nevertheless. That would be Zoltan's problem, not his.

At the appropriate point, Lance froze at the keyboard, forcing his fingers to tremble as he stared at them. On the soundtrack, the music would stop in mid-note. The false moonlight shone down on him. Lance formed his face into his best expression of abject horror.

"Oh, God! Please no! Not again! Don't let it happen *HERE*!!!" Lance clutched his chest, slid sideways, and did a graceful but dramatic topple off the piano bench.

On cue, one of the extras screamed. The bartender dropped a glass, which shattered on the tiles.

On the floor, Lance couldn't stop writhing. His own body felt as if it were being turned inside out. He had really learned how to bury himself in the role! His face and hands itched, burned. His fingers curled and clenched. It felt terrific. It felt *real* to him. He let out a moaning scream—and it took him a moment to realize it wasn't part of the act.

Off behind the cameras, Lance could see Rino Derwell jumping up and down with delight, jerking both his thumbs up in silent admiration for Lance's performance. "Cut!"

Lance tried to lie still. They would need to add the next layer of hair and makeup. Zoltan would come in and paste one of the latex appliances onto his eyebrows, darken his nails with shoe polish.

But Lance felt his own nails sharpening, curling into claws. Hair sprouted from the backs of his hands. His cheeks tingled and burned. His ears felt sharp and stretched, protruding from the back of his head. His face tightened and elongated; his mouth filled with fangs.

"No, wait!" Derwell shouted at the cameraman. "Keep rolling! Keep rolling!"

"Look at that!" the director's assistant said.

Lance tried to say something, but he could only growl. His body tightened and felt ready to explode with anger. He found it difficult to concentrate, but some part of his mind knew what he had to do. After all, he had read the script.

Leaping up from the nightclub dance floor, Lance strained until his clothes ripped under his bulging lupine muscles. With a roar and a spray of saliva from his fang-filled jaws, he smashed the piano bench prop into kindling, knocking it aside.

Four of the extras screamed, even without their cues.

Lance heaved the giant, mute piano and smashed it onto its side. The severed piano wires jangled like a rasping old woman trying to sing. The bartender stood up and brought out a gun, firing four times in succession, but they were only theatrical blanks, and not silver blanks either. Lance knocked the gun aside, grabbed the bartender's arm, and hurled him across the stage, where he landed in a perfect stunt man's roll.

Lance Chandler stood under the klieg lights, in the pool of blue gel filtering through the skylight simulating the full moon. He bayed a beautiful wolf howl as everyone fled screaming from the stage.

"Cut! Cut! Lance, that's magnificent!" Derwell clapped his hands.

The klieg lights faded, leaving the wreckage under the normal room illumination. Lance felt all the energy drain out of him. His face rippled and contracted, his ears shrank back to normal. His throat remained sore from the long howl, but the fangs had vanished from his mouth. He brushed his hands to his cheeks but found that all the abnormal hair had melted away.

Derwell ran onto the set and clapped him on the back. "That was *incredible!* Oscar-quality stuff!"

Old Zoltan stood at the edge of the set, smiling. His dark eyes glittered. Derwell turned to the gypsy and applauded him as well. "Marvelous, Zoltan! I can't believe it. How in the world did you do that?"

Zoltan shrugged, but his toothless grin grew wider. "Special makeup," he said. "Gypsy secret. I am pleased it worked out." He turned and shuffled toward the soundstage exit.

"Do you really think that was Oscar quality?" Lance asked.

༺༻

The other actors treated Lance with a sort of awe, though a few tended to avoid him. The actress playing Brigitte kept fixing her eyes on him, raising her eyebrows in a suggestive expression. Derwell, having shot a perfect take of the transformation scene he had thought would require more than a day, ordered the set crew to repair the werewolf-caused damage so they could shoot the big love scene, as a reward to everyone.

Zoltan said nothing to Lance as he added a heavy coat of pancake and sprayed his hair into place. Lance didn't know how the gypsy had worked the transformation, but he knew when not to ask questions. Derwell had said his performance was Oscar quality! He just grinned to himself and looked forward to the kissing scene with Brigitte. Lance always tried to make sure the kissing scenes required several takes. He enjoyed his work, and so (no doubt) did his female co-stars.

Zoltan added an extra-thick layer of dark-red lipstick to Brigitte's mouth, then applied a special wax sealing coat so that it wouldn't smear during the on-screen passion.

"All right you two," Derwell said, sitting back in his director's chair, "start gazing at each other and getting starry-eyed. Places everyone!"

Zoltan packed up his kit and left the soundstage. He said goodbye to the director, but Derwell waved him away in distraction.

Lance stared into Brigitte's eyes, then wiggled his eyebrows in what he hoped would be an irresistible invitation. He had few lines in this scene, only some low grunting and a mumbled "Yes, my love" during the kiss.

Brigitte gazed back at him, batting her eyelashes, melting him with her deep brown irises.

"*Wolfman in Casablanca*, Scene 39, Take One."

Lance took a deep breath, so he could make the kiss last longer.

"Action!" The klieg lights came one.

In silence, he and Brigitte gawked at each other. Romantic music would be playing on the soundtrack. They leaned closer to each other. She shuddered with her barely contained emotion. After an indrawn breath, she spoke in a sultry, sexy French accent. "You are the type of man I need. You are my soul mate. Kiss me. I want you to kiss me."

He bent toward her. "Yes, my love."

His joints felt as if they had turned to ice water. His skin burned and tingled. He kissed her, pulling her close, feeling his passion rise to an uncontrollable pitch.

Brigitte jerked away. "*Ow!* Lance, you bit me!" She touched a spot of blood on her lip.

He felt his hands curl into claws, the nails turn hard and black. Hair began to sprout all over his body. He tried to stop the transformation, but he didn't know how. He stumbled backward. "Oh, God! Please no! Not again!"

"No, Lance—that's not your line!" Brigitte whispered to him.

His muscles bulged; his face stretched out into a long, sharp muzzle. His throat gurgled and growled. He looked around for something to smash. Brigitte screamed, though it wasn't in the script. Tossing her aside, Lance uprooted one of the ornamental palms and hurled the clay pot to the other side of the stage.

"Cut!" the director called. "What the hell is going on here? It's just a simple scene!"

The klieg lights dimmed again. Lance felt the werewolf within him dissolving away, leaving him sweating and shaking and standing in clothes that had torn in several embarrassing places.

"Oh, Lance, quit screwing around!" Derwell said. "Go to wardrobe and get some new clothes, for Christ's sake! Somebody, get a new plant and clean up that mess. Get First Aid to fix Brigitte's lip here. Come on, people!" Derwell shook his head. "Why did I ever turn down that job to make Army training films?"

※

Lance skipped going to wardrobe and went to Zoltan's makeup trailer instead. He didn't know how he was going discuss this with the gypsy, but if all else failed he could just knock the old man flat with a good roundhouse punch, in the style of Craig Corwyn, U-Boat Smasher.

When he pounded on the flimsy door, though, it swung open by itself. A small sign hung by a string from the doorknob. In Zoltan's scrawling handwriting, it said "FAREWELL, MY COMPANIONS. TIME TO MOVE ON. GYPSY BLOOD CALLS."

Lance stepped inside. "All right, Zoltan. I know you're in here!"

But he knew no such thing, and the cramped trailer proved to be empty indeed. Many of the bottles had been removed from the shelves, the brushes, the latex prosthetics all packed and taken. Zoltan had also carried away the old cardboard box from the corner, the one containing the jar of special makeup for Lance.

In the makeup chair, Lance found a single sheet of paper that had been left for him. He picked it up and stared down at it, moving his lips as he read.

"Mr. Lance,

"My homemade concoction may eventually wear off, as soon as you learn a little more patience. Or they may not. I cannot tell. I have always been afraid to use my special makeup, until I met you.

"Do not try to find me. I have gone with the crew of *Fraankenstein of the Farmlands* to shoot on location in Iowa. I will be gone for some time. Director Derwell asked me to leave, to save him time and money.

Worry not, though, Mr. Lance. You no longer need any makeup from me.

"I promised you would become a star. Now, every time the glow of the klieg lights strikes your face, you will transform into a werewolf. You will doubtless be in every single werewolf movie produced from now on. How can they refuse?

"P.S., You should hope that werewolves are not just a passing fad! You know how fickle audiences can be."

Lance Chandler crumpled the note, then straightened it again so he could tear it into shreds, but he didn't need any werewolf anger to snarl this time.

He stared around the empty makeup trailer, feeling his career shatter around him. There would be no more Tarzan roles, no thrilling adventures of Craig Corwyn. His hopes, his dreams were ruined, and his cry of anguish sounded like a mournful wolf's howl.

"I've been typecast!"

MEMORIAL

The roar of the ocean echoed through the empty sky, but no one was left alive to hear it. Waves, glinting from filtered light, lapped up against a long beach, leaving a deposit of deadly radiation which had made even the life-spawning sea sterile.

The sun burned down through a radioactive haze, warming nothing but the dead sands. No bird flew in the sky, no fish swam in the sea, no man walked the earth. Apart from the roar of the poisonous sea and the gentle sound of the just-as-deadly wind, the world was silent—the earth was dead.

The waves washed the shore again, taking with them a few grains of sand, exposing something to the sun's glare. More sand washed away, and the days passed.

The object became uncovered, something made of glass, clear, uncolored, but clouded slightly. Its shape was not what it had been, but was now warped slightly from exposure to the furious, raging heat of countless atomic blasts.

It had been a bottle once; and now it comprised the entire remnants of mankind. The bottle was the only representative of the human race, a memorial, a monument to the way of life which had been so suddenly destroyed.

Visitors coming and finding the earth dead would find this bottle, and from it try to reconstruct the civilization which had spawned it.

Paint on the bottle formed letters, now meaningless. The paint was blistered and burned, but the message, for all who could read it, was plain.

The words read: COKE ADDS LIFE.

BUMP IN THE NIGHT
A DAN SHAMBLE, ZOMBIE P.I. ADVENTURE

When the Boogeyman—the actual in-the-flesh Boogeyman—comes into the office and says that he's scared, you'd better pay attention. I could tell this wouldn't be a typical case for Chambeaux & Deyer Investigations.

He came through the door with a cold wind and a ripple of dread. Now, when I meet a new person, my usual response is a polite smile and a nod of greeting. This time, as soon as the Boogeyman entered, I felt my skin crawl.

He was gaunt, pale, and hairless. His eyes were sunken into shadowed sockets, his cheeks puckered against his teeth. He looked like a living manifestation of that famous Edvard Munch painting *The Scream*, or maybe a necrotic version of young Macauley Culkin's horrified gasp in *Home Alone*. He wore a trim black business suit with a narrow black tie, as if he worked for a government agency that was all letters.

"Help me, Mr. Shamble!" he said. His voice was like a hollow wind blowing through an ice cave. "You've got to help me. I'm terrified!"

For the first time in my career, both as a living detective and an undead detective, I was afraid to take the case—and I didn't even know what it was yet.

Sheyenne, my already-drop-dead-gorgeous ghost girlfriend, rose from the reception desk, and her ectoplasmic form shuddered. Her eyes went wide in instinctive surprise.

Robin, my human lawyer partner, stood at the filing cabinets reviewing notes from one of her upcoming litigations. Seeing the visitor, she reacted like someone who had stepped on a rattlesnake while simultaneously biting into too much mustard on a hamburger.

Alvina, my too-cute ten-year-old vampire half-daughter, jumped down from the work table where she'd been posting SickTok videos and Monstagram images on her social-media platforms. The kid is an indefatigable optimist, and she never fails to show her pointy baby fangs in a bright smile. She could be bright and saccharin to the point of causing low blood sugar.

Apparently, she had better defenses against the Boogeyman than I did. "I'm not afraid of anything," she said with a sniff. She came forward to face him. "Hello."

"Boo!" said the stranger.

It was like a panic alarm going off in the offices. I had to brace myself not to bolt and flee. When he saw all of us cringe, the Boogeyman raised his cadaverous hands like white surrender flags. "I'm sorry! I didn't mean to scare you. I meant Boo—that's my name. Short for Boogeyman. I was just saying hello. Wait, let me see if I can turn it down, control it."

He closed his sunken eyes and began to breathe slowly, concentrating. He inhaled through his slitted nostrils, calming himself, counting silently. My pulse wasn't racing, since I don't have a pulse, but I could feel the terror begin to subside.

Gathering our courage, Robin and I stepped forward to greet the prospective new client as Chambeaux & Deyer, shoulder to shoulder. "Professionalism beats panic every time," Robin said.

I cleared my throat. "How can we help you, Mr. Boogeyman?"

"Boo," he said, and we flinched again. "Please call me Boo. I'd like to hire your services. I'm ... afraid."

Robin gestured the Boogeyman into our conference room, and Sheyenne followed with a new client form. Alvina trotted along, as if her very cheerfulness would help us get through the meeting. Robin carried a yellow legal pad and I had my intrepid memory (although we relied on Robin's notes as a backup).

Robin got down to business. "What are you afraid of Mr ... Boo?"

"The only thing to fear is fear itself," he answered. "And that's a lot to be afraid of—a lot of fear."

After the gaunt man took a seat, Sheyenne offered him water or coffee or an energy drink, but he shook his head. "Nothing with caffeine. It makes me anxious." Boo put his bony elbows on the table and nervously straightened his tie. "I want to go straight. I don't want to scare people anymore, at least not unnecessarily. There are enough things to worry about in the world, and everybody just needs to dial it down a notch." He wiped a hand along his sunken cheek. "I might give myself an ulcer."

"Tell us more about your job," I said. "So I can get a better feel for the parameters of this case."

"My current job, the one I really love, is as an insurance salesman. Life insurance and afterlife insurance, primarily, but I also handle general casualty and property insurance. I want to give people peace of mind, let them know they'll be taken care of, even if the worst happens—and I'm very good at helping them imagine worst-case scenarios." Boo shook his head. "So many things to be afraid of—all the monsters that have returned to the world, all the people who are afraid of the monsters, and then there are lightning strikes, car accidents, falling meteors. I'm an excellent insurance salesman."

He looked at us, and suddenly the back of my mind was crawling with paranoia about all the bad things that could go wrong in everyday life.

"But I want to *ease* people's fears, not increase them," the Boogeyman insisted. "I want to go straight!" He curled his hand into a sinewy cadaverous fist. "But they won't let me out. They say fear itself is the only thing that holds us together."

Robin paused in her note taking. "Who?"

"My family!" Boo's expression fell into abject dismay, like a kid who had just been told he would never, ever, ever be able to pet a puppy again. "It's a family business."

※

We've taken on a lot of unusual clients, no questions asked—and then we start asking a lot of questions in order to round out the case. Sheyenne presented the Boogeyman with all the necessary forms to fill out, personal profile information, confidentiality releases, payment parameters, and a delineation of the services we would be expected to perform.

Robin planned to prepare preemptive restraining orders for the most pernicious members of Boo's family, while I would offer protective services, as needed. I'm a well-preserved zombie of average height; I wear a trademark fedora and a brown sport jacket with stitched-up bullet holes from one of my previous fatal cases. I'm not all that intimidating as a bodyguard. Boo could have hired contract golem security, maybe even a rock demon, but he wanted Dan Shamble, zombie P.I. I guess my reputation preceded me.

Ever since the world-shaking event known as the Big Uneasy

occurred thirteen years ago, we had all learned to be afraid of many things: monsters under the bed, hobgoblins in the closet, things that go bump in the night.

But that's just everyday life, and here in the Unnatural Quarter monsters and humans have managed to get along, mostly. Even before the Big Uneasy, back when life was supposedly "normal," people fought constantly, with a plethora of lawsuits and divorces and family feuds. That's what kept my private investigation service and Robin Deyer's legal efforts in business, except instead of representing a couple in a bitter property dispute, we'd now been hired by the Boogeyman, who wanted to extricate himself from his family's expectations.

Boo hunched over the table, reading the fine print on all the forms. He wrote in careful penmanship on every blank line, though he asked to use a felt-tip marker. "It's soft and less hazardous," he explained. "Those pointy ends on pencils or ballpoint pens could poke an eye out."

"I've always been afraid of that," I said. "And running with scissors."

Boo finished the forms, checked them over, made sure all of the I's were dotted and the T's crossed. Relieved, he looked up at me with a face that only a nightmare could love. "Now we can get down to business."

That was when the absolute fear fest began.

First it came on like a howling, yowling, grumbling, whispering, shrieking thunderstorm that rolled down the halls—and I knew that thunderstorms were definitely not supposed to be inside the halls, particularly not on the second floor.

It sounded like a train wreck of evil cackles bursting through our door. Three separate black whirlwinds, cyclones of smoke and screams, each one capped with a demonic visage of disappointment and wrath. Their horrific faces would have made the Wicked Witch of the West consider an alternate career.

Alvina shrieked in terror, and Sheyenne swelled herself up to place her ectoplasmic form protectively in front of the little vampire girl.

Gooseflesh ran all over my skin. "What are you?" I shouted. I feared I might actually wet my pants for the first time since becoming a zombie.

The three demonic spectres spoke in unison with the voice of a stern teacher assigning detention. "We are your greatest fears. We are your nightmares!"

One drifted forward, her lips stretched over broken teeth. Her eyes blazed red. "We are what our nephew *should* be doing!"

Though scared, Robin was fundamentally unflappable. She seized the half-completed restraining order and flapped it in the face of the horrific spectral women. "I'll file this if you don't leave us alone! I swear I will."

The scary manifestations were not impressed.

Then the Boogeyman came to the rescue. Boo raised himself up, and his gaunt face turned into a shrieking death's head. His neat Men In Black suit rippled out in black tatters like formal attire for the Grim Reaper. Waves and waves of irrational paranoia rippled off of him like an overworked air-conditioner unit on a hot, humid day. *"Go away, Aunties!!!"*

Though the command wasn't directed at us, I wanted nothing more than to pack up my fedora, grab Alvina, and run all the way to one coast or the other.

"You, too, Auntie Em!" Boo added to the foremost spectre. "Can't you see I'm busy here?"

The hammer of fear was like a headwind that drove the ghastly women away. They flitted backward out the door, black smoke swirling and entwining like a nightmarish locomotive in reverse. The foremost female figure swelled up in front of the Boogeyman and cackled, "That's my boy. I knew you still had it, dear." She tangled and twisted and whisked her form as she retreated, following the others down the hall.

Boo sat back down, looking rumpled. He straightened his back-to-normal business suit and shook his head. "Do you see what I mean now? They won't let me alone. I can't have a day's peace just to go to my regular office job."

"Who were they?" I asked.

Alvina added, "You called one Auntie Em?"

Boo looked at the little vampire girl. "Em," he said. "Short for Embodiment of Terror."

"I can see why you'd shorten it," I said.

"My three aunts. They want me to carry on the family traditions, but I can't," the Boogeyman said. "I just can't! Now you see why you have to help me?"

"We do." Robin looked grim and determined.

I gathered my courage and placed a firm hand on Boo's forearm. "We'll get you out of this, one way or another."

Boo stayed long enough to provide the details we needed, even the address where the three unnatural women lived. Robin walked him to the door. "It's a free country. You should choose your own career, even if striking mortal terror is the family business."

"My aunties have high standards, and unrealistic expectations," he said. Looking more relieved than when he had burst into our offices, Boo left humming "The Happy Song" under his breath....

※

The cases don't solve themselves. That's my motto.

I needed to get a clue—or several—and I began by wandering the mean streets of the Unnatural Quarter. OK, some of the streets are actually pleasant, but if Boo's aunties got their way, everyone would quiver in terror—in the Arts and Garment district, in the Old Town restaurants and galleries, in the sprawling suburbs where monsters and humans come home after a long work shift.

I tipped my fedora to a mummy matron setting up a dried flower stand. I passed a writers' discussion club at a Talbot & Knowles Blood Bar, where vampires sipped frothy drinks and debated the ideal number of adverbs per paragraph. Four deadbeat zombie teenagers were tossing dice against the brick wall of a dark alley, but they lost the energy and motivation to pick them up and look at the dots.

It was a pleasant, cloudy day with no undue gloom—just the way the Boogeyman wanted the Quarter to be. I was reluctant to get involved in family matters, but we needed to get the nightmarish aunties to back off, not just for our client's peace of mind, but for everybody.

Ahead I saw a beat cop who had waved over a long, old Lincoln sedan. With his ticket book in hand, the policeman leaned into the passenger side window as he lectured the driver, a sweet old spinster. She had hair in a bun, wire-rimmed glasses, a powdered wrinkly face, and a flowered bonnet. When the cop straightened, I recognized my best human friend, Officer Toby McGoohan.

"I can't let you off with a warning this time, ma'am," McGoo said. "Not with all the previous safety citations on your record."

"Please, officer," said the sweet old lady. "It would mean so much to me! Aren't you a good boy?"

"I'm a good *cop*," McGoo said, "and it looks like other cops have been too lenient ten times before. You need to learn how to drive better, if you're going to keep your license, ma'am."

I sauntered up, curious. "Everything all right, McGoo?"

He glanced over at me. "Hey Shamble. I'm just keeping the peace ... and keeping traffic moving."

"But I was moving!" the old lady insisted. She gripped the wheel as if it were the only thing anchoring her in place. "Ten miles an hour is still moving, and I was being cautious."

"You were moving far below the speed limit, Miss..." He looked down at the driver's license in his hand. "Miss Flora."

"Floraboding," she said.

The name was suddenly familiar to me. Floraboding, all one word, was the name of one of Boo's aunties, along with Em, for Embodiment of Terror, and Widdershins.

"There's such a thing as exercising a dangerous amount of caution," McGoo said, gesturing to the long Lincoln. "I watched you stop too long at each stop sign. You were going so slowly I caught up to you at a fast walk." McGoo tore off the ticket and handed it to her. "That's what the traffic court calls reckless safety. You make other drivers nervous, you scare pedestrians because you seem to be following them." His exasperated expression became a little more considerate. "Just be a little more considerate, ma'am. Drive faster and more recklessly from now on."

Floraboding frowned like a prune as she tucked the ticket and license back into her purse. Looking closer, I recognized parts of her frightening profile behind the sweet granny façade. "Aren't you one of Boo's aunties?" I asked.

She recoiled in alarm. "Such a good boy. Much too good!" I saw fear wash over her face. "Please don't tell him about the ticket. He can't know."

I saw my chance. "Then perhaps, ma'am, if you simply agree to—"

She pushed the button and rolled up the passenger window, cutting me off. She stomped on the accelerator, and the big Lincoln roared off leaving a rubber track on the street.

McGoo nodded. "That's more like it. People won't be so worried about her abnormal driving." He looped his thumbs into his beltloop, leaned back, and said, "Hey, Shamble, what do you call a monster made entirely out of blood?"

Thinking he had actually encountered such a creature on a case, I fell for it. "What?"

"A hemogoblin!"

I was anxious enough that even the stupid joke gave me a moment of relief.

We watched the Lincoln drive recklessly for a block, then Floraboding halted at a stop sign for so long she could have shifted the vehicle into park. Then she eased forward with immaculate caution.

McGoo shook his head. "Some people never learn."

⁂

Sometimes you need confront your fears head on. I did not know that confronting my greatest fears would entail a pleasant conversation in the sitting room with tea and cookies.

Since Boo had given us the address of his three terrifying aunts, that afternoon I dropped in for a surprise visit. I considered taking Robin with me so she could serve legal papers, but that would have made the encounter official, and I've found that an off-the-record conversation can accomplish more than getting lawyers involved—even my own firebrand lawyer partner.

I arrived at their old brick townhouse, a place with a lot of character and high rent. Potted geraniums drank up sunshine on the corners of the porch. A cross-stitched sampler hung on the door, "Home Sweet Home." I rang the doorbell, which buzzed like an electric chair.

A sweet grandmotherly old lady in a flower-print housedress came to greet me. Her gray hair was tied back with a gray ribbon, and she wore lipstick the color of rose petals. She squinted at me. "Hello, dear."

I pulled out my well-worn private investigator license and introduced myself. "Good afternoon, ma'am. I have a few questions on behalf of my client."

A second old lady bustled up to see who was at the door, then a third. I recognized Floraboding in the rear, and one of the other two reminded me of the horrifying face I had seen in our offices, Auntie Em. The third one must be Widdershins.

"We adore company, dear! We'd be happy to answer questions," said Em.

"My client is your nephew, Mr. Boogeyman."

The three old ladies lit up. "Oh, dear Boo! I wish he would come visit us."

"You visited him in our offices ... though in a slightly more menacing form."

"Only slightly?" Widdershins clucked her tongue. "I thought we were quite ghastly."

"We've had a lot of practice," said Floraboding.

Em nodded. "Only because the dear boy won't do his job."

"He has another job," I said. "One that he prefers over the family business."

Auntie Em gestured me inside. "Please, Mister ..." She took another look at my license. "Chambo."

"It's pronounced Chambeaux," I said.

Widdershins touched her ear and leaned forward. "What did he say?"

"Shamble," said Floraboding. "His name is Dan Shamble."

I followed them into the sitting room without continuing the argument.

"I'll put on some water for tea," said Widdershins.

"Good thing we have fresh-baked cookies." Em gave me a grandmotherly smile. "We bake a new batch every afternoon, just in case we have company."

The sitting room had a coffee table, sofa (with protective plastic on the cushions), and three rocking chairs, one for each of the deceptively non-terrifying old ladies. The sofa cushions crinkled when I shifted my butt. A grandfather clock ticked in the corner. The air smelled of mothballs. This was not at all the confrontational confrontation I had anticipated.

"If he's here for dear Boo, we have to be hospitable," said Widdershins.

Floraboding sighed. "I wish that dear boy would visit us himself. It's been ages, and his aunties are so lonely." She spread a doily on the coffee table.

Widdershins brought napkins and cups, and Em came in with the cookies and tea. They all sat down in their respective rocking chairs.

That's when the pleasantness ended.

"I came here in hopes of a peaceful resolution, before we file any ugly legal restraining orders," I said. "Will you please leave your poor nephew alone to live his own life?"

The three old ladies swung their sharp gazes at me like ravens that had just discovered a ripe corpse. "The boy has responsibilities," said Auntie Em. "He doesn't understand what he's doing."

"It's just a phase," said Widdershins.

Floraboding set down her teacup and leaned closer to me. "Think about it, Mr. Shamble. What would the world be like without irrational fears?"

I pursed my lips, considering. "Uh, a better world?"

Em glanced up to the window where the lacy curtains were pulled back to show a small back yard enclosed by a wooden fence. She suddenly sat up straight, and her eyebrows arched in alarm. "There's that pesky black cat again! Why does it keep hanging around here?"

I turned to see a large black cat strolling along the fence, peering into the window. It meowed, as if expecting attention.

Widdershins rose promptly from her rocking chair. "I'll take care of it." When the old lady approached the window, the black cat seemed happy to see her, but she looked flustered and embarrassed.

Auntie Widdershins transformed into a snarling, smoky, evil spirit, a black demonic form. Her eyes blazed, and her mouth dropped open to reveal sharp fangs. Noxious green fumes boiled out of her throat as she roared. "Get away!"

The cat's fur stood on end like a cartoon, and it sprang away with a yowl and vanished in a flash.

Widdershins recomposed herself into a sweet old lady, but I knew what terrors lurked inside her. She brushed down her housedress, flustered. "We mustn't let the neighbor animals get too friendly. We have a reputation to uphold, you know. It doesn't look good."

"It certainly doesn't," said Em in a stern voice.

"Absolutely not." Floraboding furrowed her brows.

I felt sorry for the cat.

Em turned back to me. "As you can see, Mr. Shamble, fear is a powerful thing. It unites people."

"We keep everyone in edge for their own good," said Widdershins, rocking in her chair. "Not just things that go bump in the night, but fears that make your skin crawl."

Em nodded. "Fear keeps everyone alert and wary, so they stay sharp."

"It's definitely not good to let people get too complacent," said Floraboding.

I looked at her, remembering McGoo's traffic ticket for dangerous caution. I wondered if the other two aunties knew how circumspect and safety conscious Floraboding was.

Widdershins got a dark gleam in her eyes, and again the three ladies rounded on me. I could feel the intense emotions boiling in the air.

"Here, let us show you," said Widdershins.

"Before you finish your tea," said Floraboding.

The three transformed into their demonic appearances, black skirling nightmares that filled the quaint sitting room. As I raised my hand trying to fend them off with a cookie, I was suddenly engulfed with pure dread.

I saw pinch-faced, shrewish Rhonda—Alvina's mother, McGoo's ex-wife, and my big-mistake brief lover—barging in to the offices and cooing over Alvina, insisting she had made a mistake and wanting her dear daughter back.

I saw sweet Alvina skipping along the sidewalk, humming to herself —and out of nowhere, a piano dropped from above and smashed on top of her.

Then I saw a nameplate on an expensive wooden desk in a fancy office lined with books, and realized one of my other greatest fears: that Robin Deyer had left us to join a large, corporate law firm.

My blood and embalming fluid turned to ice, and I shook my head to get these images away. But more came.

I saw Sheyenne glowing with romantic energy, then flitting away, leaving me behind. She had found her true soulmate in another ghost, and they wafted off together, heading toward the light. "It never would have worked out, Beaux," Sheyenne said, just before she disappeared.

And, perhaps most frightening of all, I saw McGoo standing on a stage, grinning as he held a microphone. He was pursuing a career as a standup comic.

I lurched up from the old ladies' sofa, fighting off these nightmarish visions. I looked down at a big wet stain on my crotch. In the panic, I had spilled my teacup across my lap—I swear it was just tea.

The three aunties returned to their quaint, endearing forms. They sat back in their rocking chairs in unison, lifting their teacups. "You see, everyone needs a good scare, now and then," said Auntie Em. "But our Boo could do so much better."

The other two old ladies nodded as they rocked and sipped. "It's a family tradition," said Widdershins. "Boo needs to face his responsibilities."

"I wish he'd visit," said Floraboding.

I tried to retain my dignity and ignore the wet stain on my pants as I hurried out of the townhouse. "You will hear from us," I said. These three aunties were going to be tough nuts to crack ... and they were indeed nuts.

&.

"Maybe we do need some insurance around here, Beaux," Sheyenne said. "For the office, and the business. You never know when something might go wrong."

"Something always goes wrong," I said. "It's one of the things we can count on."

I was a successful zombie private investigator, but we did not have a lot of spare operating cash. Robin was a passionate lawyer with countless cases, but she accepted too many pro-bono clients, which kept her heart full and our bank accounts empty.

"How do we afford insurance?" I asked. "We'll just live with the risk."

"We should at least get a quote," she said, making up her mind. "I'm coming along with you to see the Boogeyman."

And that was the real reason. After my horrifying tea-and-cookies encounter with the nightmarish aunties, I needed to learn more about the Boogeyman's perspective. My ghost girlfriend simply wanted to accompany me to Boo's Life and Afterlife Insurance offices, and I didn't mind at all. Whenever my beautiful ghost girlfriend is with me, my confidence increases, and I become a better detective.

Boo's Life and Afterlife Insurance offices were located in an old strip mall next to a pho restaurant, a tanning parlor, and an Egyptian-themed art gallery featuring "Canopic Jars Through the Ages."

We found the very tiny business office, just one little desk where Boo served as the main insurance salesman and policy underwriter, as well as receptionist, accountant, and coffee maker. "Gives a whole new meaning to the term 'small business,'" I said to Sheyenne as we stood in the door. Fortunately, her ectoplasmic form takes up little room, and I loomed in the doorway.

Boo sat at his desk across from a pale young human couple who looked nervous and shaky. The Boogeyman saw us and raised a finger. "I'll be with you in a moment, Mr. Chambeaux." Then he turned his full attention to the couple. "Now then, Mr. and Mrs. Vinson, have you given thought to exactly how many terrible things can go wrong every single day? In every corner of your life?

"A meteor could strike while you're out shopping for groceries." He glanced at the sweating, anxious husband. "Why, you could buy a nice bouquet for your lovely wife, and hidden in the flowers might be a … *murder hornet!*" His eyes blazed with the possibilities. "A gas main could explode beneath your house, blowing you all to smithereens. An airplane could crash into the Quarter, wiping out block after block. And you think you're safe at home? You could slip on the wet bathroom floor and fall into a full bathtub—while carrying an electrical appliance!"

"Oh," said the wife. "I hadn't thought of that."

"What if a fire demon moves into the neighboring house and he falls asleep while smoking a cigarette in bed? Or what if a child comes running toward you while holding scissors?"

"So much to worry about," muttered the man.

"And I'm just getting started." Boo calmly pulled out several thick documents. "That's why we have insurance for every imaginable scenario—and I've spent a great deal of time imaging and even creating such scenarios."

"But how much does it cost?" asked the husband.

"You only pay for what you need, Mr. Vinson." Boo's eyes grew brighter as if they had ignited from within. *"And you need everything!"*

Mrs. Vinson reached for the policies. "Where do we sign?"

Boo flipped to the last page of the thick, legal-sized documents. "If you can pay a deposit this instant, your coverage begins immediately. Otherwise…" The Boogeyman shrugged his bony shoulders beneath his black suit. "Who knows what could happen when you step out of the offices. There used to be a blacksmith shop upstairs and occasionally an anvil would fall from above."

Mrs. Vinson dug in her pocketbook. "Do you take personal checks?"

"Why, yes I do."

As the couple furiously signed every paper Boo put in front of them,

Mr. Vinson seemed in a panic. His expression fell when he glanced at me in the doorway. "Does this insurance cover zombie attacks?"

"Of course. It covers everything," said the Boogeyman. "Nothing to be afraid of."

Sheyenne and I smiled politely as the young couple fled headlong from the insurance offices.

After the clients were gone, Boo collapsed into a shuddering mass of fear. "It's hard to project professionalism when every moment you expect your life to be torn apart! Please tell me what you've learned so far, Mr. Shamble. Are the aunties going to leave me alone?"

"I've been to see them in person, but I don't think I scared them."

Boo's eyes went wide as I explained my visit to the three aunts. "You're a brave zombie."

"Either that, or reckless," I said. "Em, Floraboding, and Widdershins tried to terrify me—and they succeeded—but zombies are relentless, especially zombie detectives."

"I wish I'd gone with you, Beaux," Sheyenne said. "I could scare them right back."

"They're just lonely," Boo groaned. "And they take it out on everyone else."

"They did mention that you hadn't visited them in ages. They miss you."

"They must have terrified you greatly when you were younger." Sheyenne drifted closer, concerned. "Did they abuse you? Give you nightmares?"

"Worse," Boo said with a groan. "They cuddled me and hugged me and pinched my gaunt cheeks. They showered me with food and love and gifts—and there's only so much a person can bear! They're too sweet ... but only in private."

I recalled the ghoulish spectres that made my skin want to crawl right off my bones. "Too sweet? Not the impression they gave me."

Boo shook his head. "Oh, they wouldn't want anyone to know, because then no one would take them seriously. But when they're around their dear nephew..." He visibly shivered.

Sheyenne remained perplexed. "But if they're really just softies inside, then why do they want you back on the job to strike mortal terror into everyone?"

"They just want to retire," said the Boogeyman. "They're afraid of not being feared."

As I considered their soft spot, an idea occurred to me. "I might know a way to scare them."

Surveillance is one of the best ways to catch a bad guy in the act, or to dig up dirt on a not-so-bad guy. Or just to see what's going on.

In private investigator school, I took a full unit on Furtiveness. I learned a lot, though my grade was only mediocre because I covertly hid my work from the professor.

I couldn't stop thinking about Auntie Floraboding's odd behavior when McGoo had given her a traffic ticket for reckless carefulness. Shouldn't a manifestation of deepest fears, chaos, and mayhem be a little more *laissez faire* with safety rules? Having seen the old lady in her most terrifying incarnation, I wondered if she was covering up her real over-cautious personality?

Back at the aunties' cozy brick townhouse, I crouched in the neighboring hedges, keeping an eye out for unexpected social activities. I hid in the shadows during daylight, and I huddled in the gloom as darkness set in. It was a stakeout just like in countless movies, though without any buddy cop banter. And it was just as boring.

Finally, the front door opened, and one of the old ladies scuttled out, head down. She wore a dark shawl and a lacy hat pulled down to obscure her face. Though she had covered herself up well, I recognized Auntie Em. After what I had learned in the Furtiveness class, I immediately spotted suspicious behavior.

Em darted forward, crossed the street, then crossed the street again, clearly trying to remain unnoticed, but she didn't elude me. I followed at a safe distance. She could have traveled more swiftly if she manifested her demonic form and swooped like a howling wind through the streets. Instead, the old lady scurried along the sidewalk, moving from one seedy part of the Quarter to an even seedier part. I couldn't imagine what Auntie Em was up to. Off to provoke terror in some unsuspecting homeless camp? Or to startle bar patrons into spilling their beers? Or just to flit past children's' windows to give them quick nightmares? Maybe to hide under their bed or in the closet?

No, Em made her way to a soup kitchen—Miss Clara Baxter's Respite for Unfortunate Unnaturals. That was unexpected, and it angered me that the Boogeyman's nefarious auntie would harass these already-suffering monsters. I imagined her swooping in to antagonize them, disrupt the food servers, knock the coffee urns over, and chase the homeless trolls, vampires, and zombies back under their bridges or dilapidated crypts.

I decided to confront Em before she caused too much trouble, but before I could make my move, the old lady entered the soup kitchen, removed her lacy hat, shucked off her shawl, and donned a white apron and gloves.

Amazed and perplexed, I peered through the open door as a werewolf with a sorry case of mange shuffled past me to get a hot meal. Auntie Em stood behind the food line with other volunteers, where she ladled soup and offered plates of bread. She was serving the unfortunate unnaturals—with a smile!

I took furtive photos of her doing her part, sweet and attentive. I was so confused I tapped the bullet hole in the center of my forehead, but I found no thoughts or explanations there either.

How did this behavior fit with the manifestations of terror those three projected in public? Struggling to fit the pieces of the case together, I made my way back to the brick townhouse, wondering what nefarious, or unspeakably kind, activities the other two were up to.

It was full dark now, and I approached from the side of the building, hoping to glimpse the backyard. I heard someone make cooing noises as I crept up to the fence. A single yard light was on to illuminate the small enclosed yard, which was only big enough for a few potted plants and a small table. Auntie Widdershins was bending down, whispering and whistling. She extended a saucer of milk across the ground.

The pesky black cat stood on the rear fence, his back arched, his ebony fur full and fluffy. "Here kitty, kitty," said Widdershins.

I wondered if she was luring the poor feral animal close so she could terrify it again. But the cat jumped down, circled just out of reach, then approached the saucer, where he began lapping up the cream. "Good kitty, kitty." The old lady reached out with a gnarled hand.

I was afraid she might strangle the cat, or cause him some terrible harm ... but instead she scratched behind his ears, stroked him until he arched his back and then brushed against her leg. Even from my hiding place, I could hear him purr.

The cat swirled around, and Widdershins beamed. "Good kitty. Come back for treats whenever mommy calls you." The cat finished the cream, then bounded onto the fence and vanished off on his own nocturnal feline adventures.

Auntie Widdershins took the empty saucer and hurried back inside, thinking that no one had seen her.

I now had all the leverage necessary to get my client what he wanted.

You've seen those old "scary" movies (now viewed as either comedies or documentaries) about rotting, brain-eating zombies terrorizing a town. Sure, under the right circumstances zombies can be terrifying and intimidating—but if I meant to intimidate the Boogeyman's three horrifying aunties, I would confront them with the scariest weapon in our arsenal.

I brought our lawyer.

Now that's intimidating.

Robin Deyer has a knack for making guilty parties cringe and reconsider their bogus pleas when she walks into a courtroom. She's beautiful, professional, and holds all the power because she *knows* she's right and has the passion to prove it to everyone else.

She wore a navy-blue blazer and skirt, white blouse, and carried a briefcase, which seemed as threatening as a mugger's gun. We were going to bring down some fear onto fear itself.

Together, we stepped up to the Home Sweet Home cross-stitched sampler hanging on the door and rang the bell.

Auntie Floraboding answered, glanced at the two of us, and her grandmotherly smile expanded into a more vicious grin. "Back for more, Mr. Shamble? One good scare deserves another."

"I believe we'll be doing the scaring today, Ms. Floraboding," Robin said.

The old lady tittered and let us in. "Delightful!"

While the three aunties bustled around as hostesses, Robin and I went into the sitting room. She set her briefcase on the coffee table, snapped it open, and withdrew a manila folder. When the old ladies sat down in their rocking chairs, she flipped open the folder to reveal papers that looked legal and scary. "This is a cease-and-desist restraining order, two for the price of one. You are hereby ordered to stop harassing our client."

"We're not harassing him," said Aunt Em. "We're helping him do his job."

"The boy must learn to take responsibility," said Widdershins.

"He's our dear nephew," said Floraboding.

Robin spread the papers on the coffee table, but I knew our real weapons were still in the briefcase. "You are interfering with Mr. Boogeyman's right to the pursuit of life, afterlife, liberty, and happiness."

"You can't threaten us," snapped Floraboding. "We're the most terrifying presences in the Unnatural Quarter."

"But we wouldn't have to be, if Boo would shape up," Em muttered.

"Oh, you'll want to comply," Robin said. "Once this paperwork is filed, it will become a matter of public record ... and we'll include certain documentation that you would not want anyone else to see."

"Documentation of what?" Widdershins asked.

I took my cue and pulled out the next folder. I shared the photos of Widdershins offering a saucer of cream to the black cat, followed by a shot of the cat rubbing against her legs, and, worst of all, Widdershins grinning with love and happiness as she petted him.

"That cat!" Auntie Em said. "You were supposed to scare it away."

"I ... couldn't," Widdershins mumbled.

"You're supposed to be terrifying," Em continued. "What will people think if they see a manifestation of mortal terror coddling an alley cat?"

"Indeed, what will people think?" Robin asked, dripping with sarcasm.

It was Em's turn. I pulled out the photos of her at the soup kitchen sweetly ladling food, helping out unfortunate unnaturals.

"That's what you do with your evenings, Em?" Floraboding recoiled. "What if someone recognizes you? We'd be ruined! We're supposed to be mayhem and chaos and nightmares."

Before Em could make excuses, I displayed a copy of the traffic citation that McGoo had issued to Floraboding. "And that's a little hard to do when you're one of the safest, most cautious drivers in the entire Unnatural Quarter."

Em snatched the ticket and scanned it, then looked in horror at her sister. "You got a citation for being *too careful*?"

"And a special letter of thanks from the car insurance company," Floraboding said, casting her gaze down. "I don't like to make other drivers worry. I could get in an accident."

"None of this is an accident," I said. "It's all on purpose."

Robin had assured me that blackmail and bluffing was an accepted legal strategy. "The world will know that you're actually just softhearted, sweet little old ladies," she said. "Not frightening at all." Robin snapped shut the briefcase. "And that is just a sample of what we've uncovered. You wouldn't want us to reveal all the other deep, dark secrets we have on you."

"No," Widdershins gasped. "That will ruin our reputations!"

The three aunts sat back in their rocking chairs, looking extremely nervous.

Frowning, I whispered to Robin, "What else do we have on them?"

She lowered her voice. "There's always something. I'm just letting them play on their own fears."

I nodded. "Seems appropriate."

Em picked up the cease-and-desist restraining order. "Now, now, there's no need for you to file these papers. They haven't been signed or certified yet."

I said. "I came here the other day, hoping you would be reasonable. When that didn't work... Maybe now you three will do the right thing because you're scared."

Robin said, "This all goes away if you leave Mr. Boogeyman alone, let him live his life, and cut down on the nightmares."

The three aunts rocked silently for a few moments, hanging their heads. They glanced at one another, then in unison let out a sigh. "Very well, if that's what we have to do," said Floraboding.

"But we insist one thing in return," said Em. "Our boy Boo has to visit sometimes. He can't be a stranger. He needs to see his dear aunties."

Robin stood up, taking her briefcase and all the papers. "I think we can manage that."

The following Sunday, Sheyenne and I went out for a walk with Alvina, enjoying a pleasant few hours together. As we passed the townhouse where the three aunties lived, I was glad we didn't encounter any howling or shrieking or nightmarish activity.

The purring neighbor cat emerged from the bushes for some attention. Alvina bent under a ladder leaned against the building and petted the black cat, with one of her feet firmly placed on a crack in the sidewalk. My half-daughter is definitely fearless.

Sheyenne said, "Look, here comes Boo now. His first Sunday visit."

Striding down the sidewalk, the Boogeyman wore a clean black suit jacket and the same old thin black tie. He held a bouquet of wilted lilies in his hands. His skull-like face was pale as always, and he lowered his sunken eyes, as if nervous or guilty.

As the Boogeyman approached, the black cat hissed, arched his back, and sprang away.

Seeing us, Boo paused, drew a deep breath. "Now I have to face the music," He shuddered, looking at the Home Sweet Home sign on the townhouse door.

"It'll be a nice time," I said.

"It'll be a nightmare. Auntie Em will pinch my cheeks, and Auntie Floraboding will exclaim about how much I've grown, and Auntie Widdershins will insist that I need to eat more." His shoulders slumped, but then he raised his chin, summoning his courage. "But I can face this."

"It won't be so bad," Sheyenne said.

"Oh, it'll be bad, but I can give as good as I get." He spotted the black cat crouched by the corner of the townhouse and said, "Boo!" The cat yowled and bounded away. "I'm the Boogeyman."

He rang the bell as Sheyenne, Alvina, and I kept walking. We glanced behind us to watch the three aunties greeting Boo, hugging him, cooing over him, pinching his cheeks. They dragged him inside where he would have to endure the smothering kindnesses.

"Nothing to be afraid if," Alvina said.

I looked down at the kid. "Oh, there's plenty to be afraid of, but no need to worry about it."

The vampire girl skipped ahead, and I glanced up to make sure no pianos were falling out of the sky. I cocked my fedora and strolled along with my ghost girlfriend at my side. "Nothing to worry about," I said.

QUEST PRIZE

"Now we're in the thick of it," I said, in my best Knight in Shining Armor voice.

"Isn't that what you wanted?" asked Ruk, one of the two mercenary dragons I had hired for this quest. "To prove your bravery and win the hand of the beautiful princess?"

"The idea sounded better in the tavern," I admitted, "after a few tankards of ale."

"We still get hazard pay!" insisted Rul, the other mercenary dragon. "Increased wages as promised."

"I didn't sign up for this," said Ruk as we faced the oncoming horde of lava beasts.

"Nevertheless, it will be a battle for the ages," I said, trying to sound brave. I held up my sword and glared at the fiery things lurching toward us and the erupting volcano in the distance. "Think of what the minstrels will sing about us."

"We won't be able to hear it if we're dead," said Rul. "Besides we're too big, and most taverns won't let two full-grown dragons in."

I knew that even with my full armor, the lava beasts would cook me like a hard-boiled egg if they came too close.

I was already a well-established knight, with small holdings of my own, a trophy room in my castle with jousting-award ribbons. But I was lonely, and I decided I wanted to marry up. When the king offered the hand of beautiful Princess Lyra to the knight who proved himself worthy through great deeds, I vowed to win her hand.

But when I went to the throne room and bowed to the princess and the wise old king, I didn't think Lyra was all that beautiful, with a horse-like face, stringy hair, and a spoiled-brat sneer when she loked at me. Nevertheless, when I had gone on my sacred quest, the king blessed my sword and gave me a generous traveling stipend (I think he was eager to marry off his daughter, and I was the only brave knight who had risen to the challenge in more than a month).

PARADOX & GREENBLATT, ATTORNEYS AT LAW

You might say our little firm specializes in contradictions. In a few years Aaron Greenblatt and I are sure to be millionaire visionaries overloaded with cases, but right now our field of law is still in its infancy. We've carved out a new niche, and people are already starting to find us.

Since we can't afford a receptionist (not yet) Aaron took the call. But because he was up to his nostrils in a corporate lawsuit—a client suing Time Travel Expeditions for refusing to let him go to the late Cretaceous on a dinosaur hunt—he passed the case to me.

"Line one for you, Marty," he said as I came out of the lav, wiping my hands. "New case on the hook. Simple attempted murder, I think. Guy sounds frantic."

"They all sound frantic." I pursed my lips. "Is time travel involved?"

He nodded, and I knew there would be nothing "simple" about the case. Fortunately, temporal complications are right up our firm's alley. We're forward-thinkers, my partner and I—*and* backward-thinkers, when it's effective. That's why people call us when nobody else knows what the hell to do.

I picked up the phone and punched the solitary blinking light. "Marty Paramus here. How can I help you?"

The man talked a mile a minute in a thin, squeaky voice; even if he hadn't been panicked, it probably would have sounded unpleasant. "All I did was try to stop him from buying her some deep-fried artichoke hearts. How could that be construed as attempted murder? They can't pin anything on me, can they? Why would they think I was trying to kill anybody?"

"Maybe you'd better tell me, Mr. ... uh?"

"Hendergast. Lionel Hendergast. And I read the terms of the contract very carefully before we went back in time. It didn't say anything about deep-fried artichoke hearts."

I sighed. "What was your location, Mr. Hendergast?"

"Santa Cruz Boardwalk. The place with all the rides and the arcade games. They have concession stands and—"

"Sure, but *when* was this?"

"Umm, two days ago."

I hate having to pry all the obvious information out of a client. "Not in your time. I mean in *real* time."

"Oh, um, fifty-two years ago."

"Ah." I made a noise that hinted at a deeper understanding than I really had, yet. "One of those nostalgic life-was-better-back-then tours."

Now he sounded defensive. "Nothing illegal about them, Mr. Paramus. They're perfectly legitimate."

"So you said. But someone must think you broke the rules, or you wouldn't have been arrested. Was this person allergic to artichoke hearts or something?"

"No, not at all. And it wasn't the artichoke hearts. I was just trying to prevent him from buying them for her. I didn't want the two of them to meet."

A light bulb winked on inside my head. "Oh, one of those."

"Altering history" cases were my bread and butter.

❦

The jail's attorney-client meeting room wasn't much better than a cell. The cinderblock walls were covered with a hardened slime of seafoam-green paint. The chairs around the table creaked, and veritable stalactites of petrified chewing gum adorned the table's underside. Since prisoners weren't allowed to chew gum, their lawyers must have been responsible for this mess. Some attorneys give the whole field a bad name.

Lionel Hendergast was in his mid-twenties but looked at least a decade older than that. His too-round face, set atop a long and skinny neck, reminded me of a smiling jack-o'-lantern balanced on a stalk. His long-fingered hands fidgeted. He looked toward me as if I were a superhero swooping in to the rescue.

"I need to understand exactly what you've done, Mr. Hendergast.

Tell me the truth, and don't hold back anything. No bullshit. We have attorney-client privilege here, and I need to know what I'm working with."

"I'm innocent."

I rolled my eyes. "Listen, Mr. Hendergast—Lionel—my job is to get you off the hook for the crime of which you're accused. Let's save the declarations of innocence for the judge, okay? Now, start from the beginning."

He swallowed, took a deep breath, then said, "I took a trip back in time to the Santa Cruz Beach Boardwalk to 1973, as I said. You can get the brochure from the time travel company I used. There's nothing wrong with it, absolutely not."

"And why did you want to go to Santa Cruz?"

He shrugged unconvincingly. "The old carousel, the carnival rides, the games where you throw a ball and knock down bottles. And then there's the beach, cotton candy, churros, hot dogs, giant pretzels."

"And artichoke hearts," I prodded.

Lionel swiveled nervously in his chair, which made a protesting creak. "Deep-fried artichoke hearts are sort of a specialty there. A woman nearing the front of the line had dropped her wallet on the ground not ten feet away, but she didn't know it yet. In a few minutes, she was going to order deep-fried artichoke hearts—and when she discovered she had no money to pay, the man behind her in line would step up like a knight in shining armor, pay for her artichoke hearts, and help her search for her wallet. They'd find it, and then go out to dinner. The rest is history."

"And you seem to know the details of this history quite well. What exactly were you going to do?"

"Well, I found the woman's wallet, on purpose, so I could give it back to her. Nothing illegal in that, is there?"

I nodded, already frowning. "Thereby preventing the man behind her from doing a good deed, stopping them from going to dinner, and" —I held my hands out—"accomplishing what?"

"If they didn't meet, then they wouldn't get married. And if they didn't get married, then they wouldn't have a son who is the true spawn of all evil."

"The Damien defense doesn't hold up in court, you know. I can cite several precedents."

"But if I had succeeded, who would have known? There would've been no crime because nothing would have happened. How can they accuse me of anything?"

"Because recorded history is admissible in a court of law," I said. "So by attempting to keep these two people from meeting, you were effectively trying to commit a murder by preventing someone from being born."

"If, if, if!" Hendergast looked much more agitated now. "But I didn't do it, so how can they hold me?"

The legal system has never been good at adapting to rapid change. Law tends to be reactive instead of proactive. When new technology changes the face of the world, the last people to deal with it—right behind senior citizens and vested union workers—are judges and the law. Remember copyright suits in the early days of the internet, when the uses and abuses of intellectual property zoomed ahead of the lawmakers like an Indy 500 race car passing an Amish horse cart?

Now, in an era of time travel tourism, with the often-contradictory restrictions the companies impose upon themselves, legal problems have been springing up like wildflowers in a manure field. Aaron Greenblatt and I formed our partnership to go after these cases. We are, in effect, creating major precedents with every case we take, win or lose.

Where was a person like Lionel Hendergast to turn? Everyone is entitled to legal representation. He didn't entirely understand the charges against him, and I was fairly certain that the judge wouldn't know what to do either. Judges dislike being forced to make up their minds from scratch, instead of finding a sufficiently similar case from which they can copy what their predecessors have done.

"Do you ever sit back and play the 'What if?' game, Mr. Paramus?" Lionel asked, startling me. "If a certain event had changed, how would your life be different? If your parents hadn't gotten divorced, your dad might not have killed himself, your mom might not have married some abusive truck driver and moved off to Nevada where she won't return your calls or even give you her correct street address? That sort of thing?"

I looked at him. Now we might finally be getting somewhere. "I've seen *It's a Wonderful Life*. Four times, in fact, including the alternate-ending version. I'm very familiar with 'What if?' Who were you trying to kill and what was the result you hoped to achieve?"

"I wasn't trying to *kill* anyone," he insisted.

From the frightened little-boy expression on Lionel's round face, I could see he wasn't a violent man. He could never have taken a gun to someone or cut the brake cables on his victim's car. He wouldn't even have had the stomach to pay a professional hit man. No, he had wanted to achieve his goal in a way that would let him sleep at night.

"The man was Delano R. Franklin," he said. "You won't find a more vile and despicable man on the face of this Earth."

I didn't want to argue with my client, though I could have pointed out some pretty likely candidates for the vile-and-despicable championship. "Much as it may pain me to say this, Lionel, being unpleasant isn't against the law."

"My parents were happily married, a long time ago. My dad had a good job. He owned a furniture store. And my mom was a receptionist in a car dealership—a dealership owned by Mr. Franklin. We had a nice home in the suburbs. I was supposed to get a puppy that Christmas."

"How old were you?"

"Four."

"And you remember all these details?"

He wouldn't look at me. "Not really, but I've heard about it a thousand times. My parents couldn't stop arguing about that day my dad took time off in the afternoon. He decided to surprise my mother over at the car dealership by bringing her a dozen long-stemmed roses."

"How romantic," I said.

"At the car dealership they take a late lunch hour so they can take care of the customer rush between noon and one. When my dad couldn't find anyone at the reception counter, he went to the back room and opened the door—only to find my mom flat on the desk with her skirt hiked up to her hips, legs wrapped around Franklin's neck, and him pumping away into her."

It wasn't the first time I had heard this sort of story. "I can see how that would ruin a marriage."

"My dad went nuts. He tried to attack Franklin and as a result, ended up in jail with charges of assault. Franklin had most of our local officials in his pocket—small town. At first my mom insisted that Franklin threatened to fire her if she didn't have sex with him. In the resulting scandal, she changed her story, saying that the affair had gone on for a while, that Franklin wanted to marry her. My parents split up, but as soon as the divorce was final, the creep wanted nothing to do with her. He kicked my mom out. She had no job, and by that time my dad had lost his furniture store."

"Sounds like a mess. So what happened to little Lionel?"

"We lived in Seaside, California—that's not far from Santa Cruz and Monterey. My dad got drunk one day and drove too fast along Highway 1."

I'd been there. "Some spectacular cliffs and tight curves on that stretch of highway."

Miserably, Lionel nodded. "The road curved, and my dad went straight. Suicide was suspected, but nobody ever proved it. Then, one day my mom just packed up, dropped me off at foster care, and left. Said she hated me because I was just like my father. I lived in six different homes until I was sixteen and old enough to emancipate myself."

I tried to sound sympathetic. "Not a very happy childhood."

"Meanwhile, Delano R. Franklin did quite well with his car dealership. In fact, he opened three more. He married some bimbo, divorced her when she got wrinkles, then married another one. Never had kids, but I think his wives were young enough to be his daughters."

I wanted to cut the rant short. "All right, but what does this have to do with deep-fried artichoke hearts?"

Tears started running down his cheeks. "I remembered my mother yelling at Franklin once. He had wooed her by telling romantic stories, describing how his own parents met. The man who would be Franklin's father came to the rescue, helped find a lady's wallet at the artichoke stand, took her out to eat ... and eventually spawned this inkblot on the human race, a uniting of sperm and egg that any compassionate God would have prevented!"

I paced around the table, locking my hands behind my back. "So you figured that if you kept Franklin's biological mother and father from meeting, he would never have been born, your parents' marriage would have remained happy, and your life would have been wonderful."

"That's about it, Mr. Paramus. But Franklin had someone watching me, so I got caught."

"Watching you? How could he possibly have suspected such an absurd thing?"

"Because I, uh ..." Lionel blushed. "I told him. I couldn't help myself. I wanted the scumbag to know he was about to be removed from existence."

I groaned. In this business, the only thing worse than a hardened criminal is an unconscionably stupid client.

"You have to get me out of here, Mr. Paramus!" Given the circumstances, an unreasonable demand. "That holding cell is a nightmare. It smells. There's no privacy even for the toilet, and they took blood samples to test me for HIV and other diseases. They drew my blood! That means other people in the cell must have those terrible diseases. What if I—"

"It's just standard procedure, Lionel." I snapped my briefcase shut. "Let me work on this and see what I can come up with. I'll try to get you bail. I'll talk to Mr. Franklin and his attorney on the off chance I can get them to drop the charges."

It was certainly a long shot, but I wanted to give poor Lionel something to cling to.

I set up a meeting in the "boardroom" of the dumpy offices Aaron and I shared. I doubted I could impress Delano Franklin, but maybe I could convince him it wasn't worth the trouble to press charges. Lionel Hendergast had almost no money, and when I learned who Franklin had hired for his own counsel to go after civil damages, I knew that money—or at least showmanship—would be a primary factor in this case.

If you look in the dictionary next to the definition of the word "shyster," you'll find a picture of Kosimo Arkulian. He was overweight, with thinning steel-gray hair in a greasy comb-over that fooled nobody. He wore too many rings, too many gold chains, and a too-large gold watch, and he spoke too loudly. You've seen Arkulian on television with his boisterous ads, flashing his jewelry and his smile, treating everyone with a hangnail of a complaint as the next big millionaire in the lawsuit sweepstakes.

When Arkulian sat down beside his client, I could tell it was going to be a testosterone war between those two men. Both were accustomed to being in charge.

I gave my most pleasant smile. "Can I offer you coffee or a soda?"

"No, thank you," Franklin said.

"This isn't a social call," Arkulian answered in a brusque tone.

"There's always time for good manners." I looked at the clock on the wall. It was 1:00. "How about Scotch, then?" I had to get Franklin to take something. "Or a bourbon? I have a very good bourbon, Booker's." From my research, I knew Franklin was quite fond of both.

"If your bourbon's expensive, I'll have one of those," he said.

Arkulian shot him a glance. "I wouldn't advise it—"

"I'm not going to get sloshed," Franklin said. "Besides, I see a genuine irony in soaking this guy for a good expensive drink."

Arkulian grinned. "Then I'll have one, too."

I had been careful to wash everything in our kitchenette before the meeting started. I quickly poured three glasses of fine bourbon, neat, and handed one to Franklin and one to Arkulian. The third I placed in front of me in a comradely gesture, though I barely sipped from it. I had a feeling I'd need to keep my wits sharp.

Franklin looked like a distinguished late-middle-aged businessman gone bad. If groomed well, he could have fit comfortably into any high-society function, but he had let himself grow a beer gut. His clothes were garish, something he no doubt thought younger women found attractive. The ladies probably laughed at him until they found out how much money he had, then they played along but still laughed at him behind his back.

I tried my best gambit, pumping up the sob story, practicing how it would sound before a jury, although it was unlikely this case would ever go to trial. The law was too uncertain, the convolutions and intangibilities of time paradox too difficult for the average person to grasp.

"None of this has any bearing on what your client tried to do to my client," Arkulian said. "Sure, the poor kid had a troubled life. His mother had an affair with my client some twenty-six years ago, which led to the breakup of his parents' marriage. Boo-hoo. As if that story doesn't reflect half of the American public."

Maybe your half, I thought, but kept a tight smile on my face.

"Mr. Hendergast attempted to murder my client. It's as simple as—"

Impatient with letting his lawyer do all the talking, Franklin interrupted. "Wait a minute. This is far worse than just attempted murder." As if he needed the fortification of liquid courage to face what had almost happened, Franklin grabbed his tumbler of bourbon, and took a long drink. He set the glass down, and I could see the smear his lips had made on the edge. "If Lionel Hendergast had gunned me down in the parking lot of one of my car dealerships, he might have killed me, yes, but my legacy would have been left behind—my car dealerships, my friends ..."

"Your ex-wives," I pointed out.

"Some of them remember me fondly." He didn't even blush.

Arkulian picked up the story. "You see, what Mr. Hendergast was attempting to do would have erased my client entirely from existence. He would have obliterated the man named Delano R. Franklin from the universe, leaving no memory of him. Nothing he ever accomplished in this life would have remained. Complete annihilation. An unspeakably heinous crime! And if Mr. Hendergast had succeeded, it would have been the perfect crime, too. No one would ever have known what he did, since there would have been no evidence, no body, no victim."

I had heard my share of "perfect crime" stories, and I had to admit, this ranked right up there with the best. I didn't offer them another drink. "What exactly is it you want from my client?"

"I want him to go to jail," Franklin said. "I want him to be locked up so that I don't have to worry every morning that he's going to sneak back on another time travel expedition and try again to erase my existence."

Arkulian smiled and folded his fingers. I couldn't imagine how he could fit them together with all those rings on his knuckles. "I'm guessing the publicity on this case will give a remarkable boost to my business—and don't expect me to believe you haven't thought of the same thing, Mr. Paramus."

He was right, of course. I shrugged. "Publicity is free, after all, and TV ads are a bit out of my price range." Ambulance-chasing seemed to be paying off quite well for Arkulian. I couldn't resist taking a small jab at him. "How much *do* ten of those rings cost?"

Miffed, Arkulian stood up. "If there's nothing else, Paramus? We'll see you in court."

I let the two men show themselves out, staying behind in the boardroom. When they were gone, I took a clean handkerchief, carefully lifted the near-empty bourbon glass Franklin had used, and made sure there were sufficient saliva traces on the rim. This was all I'd need.

※

Predictably, a media frenzy surrounded the case. Arkulian held a large press conference in which he grandstanded, accusing me of leaking the story in order to get publicity. Within an hour I had a press conference of my own, accusing him of the same. Both of us received plenty of coverage, and neither of us ever admitted to making a few discreet phone calls and tipping reporters off.

Lionel put his complete trust in me, which always sparks that uncomfortable paternal feeling. But I hadn't been kidding when I told him the law is still murky in these sorts of cases. Nobody had any idea which way it would go, and even my "ace in the hole" was a long shot. I still hadn't got the lab results back.

For the preliminary hearing, we were assigned an ancient female judge, the Honorable Bernadette Maddox. I was uneasy about her age. In my experience, elderly judges don't deal well with the second- and third-order implications of rapidly changing technologies. I'd rather have had the youngest, most computer-savvy person on the bench.

I still held out some hope that Bernadette Maddox was a sweet old lady, and the sob-story aspect would work on her. Not a chance.

"Mr. Arkulian!" she roared from the bench in a battle-axe voice before he had even finished his pompous remark. "You will sit down, shut up, and let me run this show." I looked over at my rival with a twinge of sympathy. So much for the nice old lady bit. "And you will remove that disgusting cheap jewelry in my courtroom unless you have an appointment with Time Travel Expeditions to go back to the days of disco."

"Your Honor, my personal appearance has no bearing on—"

"You will remove the jewelry because it hurts my eyes. I can't even see your client through the glare from all those rings."

Cowed, Arkulian left the room. A nervous Lionel sat at the bench next to me, whispering, "Was that a good sign?"

"It wasn't so much a sign—more like a demonstration. The judge is only showing him who's boss. And let me warn you ahead of time, she's going to feel she needs to even the score and scold me as well at some point. Expect it and try not to get too upset."

"What are we going to do, Mr. Paramus?" He sounded so miserable. I felt sorry for this kid who had lost his parents, his Norman Rockwell childhood, and a lifetime of happiness, all because of Delano R. Franklin.

I had dug into Franklin's background, perhaps even more than Lionel had. There was no question in my mind that the world would be a better place if Franklin had never been born. He had left a decades-long trail of ex-wives and shady business dealings behind him. His primary legacy was a handful of auto dealerships, but since he had no heirs and couldn't keep employees around long enough to put them in positions of authority and responsibility, no one would take over the car lots upon his death, and they'd probably be liquidated. Even without Lionel's time travel help, Franklin would vanish.

Since we were the defendants, we sat back and listened as a now-unadorned Arkulian outlined the civil part of the case, explaining time travel paradoxes in painstaking detail, using examples culled not from any law library but from classic science fiction stories. He was long-winded and explained too much to the judge, treating her as if she were incapable of grasping the classic grandfather paradox.

I kept checking my watch as I mentally rehearsed my opening statement. The courier should have been here by now. I would have preferred hard facts to fast-talking, but I could proceed either way. As Arkulian rambled on and on, even Franklin looked bored.

Finally, it was my turn. I hoped the judge would stall just to give me a few more minutes, but she puckered her wrinkled lips and leaned over like a hawk from the bench. "Now then, Mr. Paramus, let's hear what you have to say. I trust you can be more succinct—or at least more interesting—than Mr. Arkulian."

I stood up and cleared my throat. Still no sign of my delivery person, and I really wanted to know which direction to go. Either my ace in the hole was a high trump or a discard. With a sigh, I reached into my briefcase and pulled out a carefully prepared document. "Your Honor, I wish I did not have to do this, but would it be possible to request a brief continuance? I have not yet received an important piece of evidence that has a strong bearing on this case."

Lionel looked over at me, surprised. "What evidence?"

"A continuance?" the judge said with a snort. "I've been sitting here all morning, Mr. Paramus! You could have said this at the very beginning. How long are you asking for?" I was about to get my scolding, and Judge Maddox was clearly primed to let loose with even more venom than she had inflicted on Arkulian.

Suddenly the large doors were flung open at the back of the courtroom. The bailiff tried to stop a man from entering, but my partner Aaron Greenblatt sidestepped him. He marched in, waving a document in his left hand. "Excuse me, your Honor. Please pardon the interruption."

I stifled a laugh. It was a real Perry Mason moment. I suspected Aaron had always wanted to do that.

My partner's face was stoic; I hated the way he covered his emotions. He could have at least grinned or frowned to give me an inkling of what he held in his hands.

Judge Maddox lifted her gavel, looking more inclined to hit Aaron in the head with it than to rap her bench.

I blurted, "Your Honor, I withdraw my request for a continuance—so long as my associate can hand me that paper." I turned, not waiting for her answer as Aaron handed the lab results to me. He finally broke into a grin as I scanned the numbers and the comparison charts.

With a huge sigh of relief, I turned back to the bench. "Your Honor, in light of recent developments I request that the attempted murder charges against my client be dropped."

Arkulian growled, "What are you playing at, Paramus?"

"I'll ask the questions here, Mr. Arkulian," the judge said, rapping her gavel for good measure. "Well then—what *are* you playing at, Mr. Paramus?"

Bernadette Maddox already knew the sordid Peyton Place story of the ruined marriage, the broken family, the miserable life Lionel Hendergast had lived because of Franklin's actions.

"Your Honor, the prosecution's client was not entirely forthcoming about how long his affair with my client's mother lasted. If I might recap: when Lionel Hendergast was four years old, his father discovered Mr. Franklin and my client's mother *in flagrante delicto*, which triggered the chain of events leading to the crime of which my client is accused."

"And?" Judge Maddox said, drawing out the word.

"In fact, the affair had gone on for at least five years previous." I fluttered the sheet of lab data. "I have here the results of DNA tests comparing the blood sample my client gave to the county jail with samples I obtained from Mr. Franklin."

I smiled sweetly at them. Franklin appeared confused. Arkulian was outraged, realizing I had probably tested the saliva left behind on his drinking glass—an old trick.

"These results prove conclusively that the father of Lionel Hendergast is not the man he always believed, but rather Mr. Delano R. Franklin."

Lionel's eyes fairly popped out of their sockets. The judge sat up, suddenly much more interested. Both Arkulian and Franklin bellowed angrily as if in competition with each other until finally Arkulian stood up in a huff, reacting in the way he had seen too many lawyers react on TV shows. "I object! This has no bearing—"

"This has total bearing," I said.

Lionel looked as if he might faint, slide off the chair, and land on the courtroom floor. I put a steadying hand on his shoulder. He looked over at the prosecutor's table, and his two words came out in a squeak. "My father?"

I forged ahead. "The prosecution has interpreted this crime entirely wrong, your Honor. My client is accused of going back in time with the intent of preventing Mr. Franklin from ever being born. But if he had done that, then Lionel Hendergast would've erased *himself* from existence as well. He would have wiped out his own father, thereby ensuring that he himself could never be born."

I smiled. The judge seemed to be considering my line of reasoning. After all, Arkulian had prepped her in excruciating detail about grandfather paradoxes and the like.

"Therefore, instead of attempted murder, my client is guilty, at best, of attempted *suicide*—for which I recommend he be remanded for therapy and treatment, not incarceration."

"This is preposterous!" Arkulian yelled. "Even if Mr. Hendergast *had* accidentally erased himself, his original intention was to do the same to my client. His own death would merely have been incidental to his stated objective. The primary target of his malicious actions was still Delano Franklin."

With a sigh of infinite patience, I looked witheringly at Arkulian, then turned back to the judge. "Again, my esteemed colleague is mistaken."

The judge was actually listening now, fascinated by the implications. I had mapped out the strategy until it made my own head spin.

"My client is accused of *attempted* murder. However, based on these lab results, such an action would be temporally impossible." I waited a beat. "If Mr. Hendergast had actually succeeded in what the prosecution alleges was his intent, then he himself would never have been born. In which case, he could never have gone back in time to prevent Mr. Franklin's parents from meeting. How can my client be charged with attempting a crime that is fundamentally impossible to commit?"

"This is outrageous! Why not debate how many angels can dance on a pinhead?" Arkulian said.

I shrugged in the prosecutor's direction. "It's a standard time travel paradox, your Honor. As Mr. Arkulian explained to the court so exhaustively."

Lionel was still staring in wonder over at the prosecutor's table. "Daddy?"

The judge rapped her gavel loudly. "I'm announcing a recess for at least two hours—so I can take some aspirin and give it time to work."

When the judge finally dismissed all charges against Lionel, I was relatively sure Arkulian wouldn't take it to appeal. The hardest part was explaining the convoluted matter to journalists afterward, so they could report it accurately; in the end, it proved too intricate for most of the wire services.

Aaron and I celebrated by going out for a fine dinner. We compared notes on cases, and he got me up to speed on his time-travel dinosaur-hunting lawsuit. I came back to the office late at night by myself—after all, that's where I kept the best bourbon—and saw the light blinking on the answering machine. Multiple messages. Four more cases waiting, none of them simple. Some actually sounded like they would be fun. Certainly precedent-setting.

Oddly, after the fallout, Lionel actually reconciled with his biological father. Months later, when I drove past one of Franklin's car dealerships, I saw a crew replacing the big sign with a new one: FRANKLIN & SON.

Funny how things turn out. Sometimes people just need a second chance, even when they aren't looking for it.

EIGHTY LETTERS, PLUS ONE

WITH SARAH A. HOYT

Letter #1

September 30, 1872
London, England

My dearest Elizabeth,
I leave this note for you, as the house was empty when I came home to pack. Doubtless you're out enjoying a quaint diversion with your women friends. As for me, I am unexpectedly off to the Suez, my dear. I've been dispatched to intercept a notorious thief who stole fifty thousand pounds from the Bank of England.

The villain Phileas Fogg is sure to leave the country and use his ill-gotten fortune to live extravagantly abroad. Detectives have been dispatched, one to each major port, and I have been chosen to keep a sharp eye on all British travelers who come through the Suez. I have a clear description of the thief, a well-dressed man with fine manners. Should I find him, I will shadow him till a warrant can be dispatched.

I'm sorry to leave you with nothing more than a note on this, our first anniversary, particularly since you never had the proper wedding you deserved. I still feel a bit of remorse over our brash elopement to Gretna Green, but you know your parents would never have consented to our love match. I still remember how haughtily your mother said that, because I need to work for a living, I should come in through the tradesman's entrance.

I trust you will keep a stiff upper lip while I'm away. The bank has offered a substantial reward to the detective who captures the thief, and I am convinced I'll get him if he comes my way. All that's needed in law enforcement these days is flair. You have to know how to nose these vermin out. And I, of course, have excellent flair. As I've told you many times, I have a veritable sixth sense for these things. Two thousand pounds will allow us to buy a better home and to hire a servant to do the house work for you. I know you expect such things out of life. It will also prove to your parents that, though you disobeyed them, you were ultimately right to choose me as your husband.

Meanwhile, I will write to you every day I possibly can. I'm sure you'll hardly notice I'm gone.

Yours, with much love,
Herbert Fix
Inspector, First grade

Letter #9

October 9
Suez, Egypt, Africa

My dear Elizabeth,

Good news! After all these days of waiting, the thief has finally come to the Suez.

Today, when the steamer *Mongolia* docked at the quay in Suez, I spotted a passenger forcing his way through the clamoring and stinking crowd of locals. You would not believe the mob of natives and black Africans that press around every passenger, offering to sell monkeys, unguents, jewelry, and the most grotesque pagan idols. One wretch even had the temerity to offer me some ground mummy which, he said, would strengthen my virile parts! I shudder to think, my dear, of you having to witness such sights.

By great luck, the fellow who came out of the *Mongolia* was in search of a government official. He nosed his way directly to me and held out a passport, for which he wished to procure a visa from the British consul. He was a wiry, dark-haired Frenchman, but he carried an Englishman's passport—his master's. Of course, I immediately glanced at the passport, and the description was exactly that of our thief! I could do no less than try to stop the man.

I told my suspicions to the consul and begged him to delay this man until I could get my arrest warrant. To my great disappointment, however, the consul said that I had no proof the traveler—Phileas Fogg—was guilty of any crime, and that without such proof he could not be detained.

I must therefore follow this rogue to his next stop, which is Bombay. I have talked to his servant, Passepartout—a good sort of fellow, but French and therefore garrulous. The man is convinced his master means to circle the globe to win a preposterous bet. Apparently, the cunning devil made a wager with the gentlemen in his club that he could go completely around the world in a mere eighty days. With my keen intellect, I realized immediately that this outrageous boast is nothing more than cover for his escape with the stolen money.

Hoping to pry more information from the talkative Frenchman, I took him on a shopping expedition to the bazaar. There, merchants offer all types of goods, including a very expensive perfume called Attar of Roses, of which a single drop can be mixed with oil or water to make many concoctions prized by the local ladies. Since you are always in my thoughts, I meant to buy you a dram of it. I also saw a fly swatter made from an elephant's tail, which I thought might amuse you. But, as I'm sure you'll understand, I had scarcely any time for frivolous purchases

Passepartout wished to obtain new shirts and other accouterments for his master. Due to the haste with which they left London, they had brought no more luggage than a carpetbag! Tell me, what man—not a thief and not in possession of fifty thousand pounds—would thus abandon his home and everything in it?

The loquacious Frenchman continually bemoaned the fact that he had left the gas burning in his room and that his master wouldn't allow him so much as a moment to run back to turn it off. This is not the natural behavior of a man who truly intends to return home.

I have applied for a warrant, which should catch up with us in Bombay. My dear Elizabeth, the reward money is as good as ours. I have not had the time to pick up any souvenirs for you just yet, but I am sure to buy you something in Bombay once the villain Fogg has been arrested.

Yours affectionately,
Herbert Fix

Letter # 20

October 20th, 1872
Bombay, British India

My dear Elizabeth,

Here I am, once more, fulfilling my promise of writing a letter a day to you. I will also post at once the letters I wrote aboard the steamer.

Unfortunately, we have made such rapid progress—Fogg bribed the owner of the liner to have the engine stoked with extraordinary zeal—that my warrant is not yet with the police here. I am more certain than ever of my quarry's guilt. What man but a fleeing criminal would throw away money in such a way?

Only those who have not had to work for their income view it as of little importance. I know you do not like it when I speak of the extravagance of the lace on your sister's gowns, but were it not for your parents' private, she would surely weigh her expense more carefully and not burden herself with so much expensive frippery.

But worry not, my dear. Soon you'll be able to afford dresses as good or better than hers. In fact, time permitting, I might pick up some fabric in Bombay, which is a city of goodly size and filled with all manner of strange things.

The streets are extraordinarily crowded with dark people attired in cotton robes. On the way to the police station, I saw a man who lay completely at ease upon a bed of sharp nails. Imagine! I also saw a man hypnotize a deadly snake by playing his flute.

I'm rather upset at not having received the warrant yet, but you may be confident in my abilities, my dear. Rest assured—Phileas Fogg, who really has no intention of going around the world, will no doubt remain several days here, which will certainly be sufficient time for me to arrest him. Meanwhile, maybe I'll find you an appropriate gift ... perhaps some silk with which the native women wrap themselves. Something called, as I understand it, a sari.

Oh, I almost forgot to acknowledge that I received your letter, which had been forwarded from Suez to the consulate at Bombay and which, vexingly, made it to town when the warrant didn't.

It is extraordinarily kind of you to say that you'd gladly forego the two thousand pounds for the sake of having me near you again. Your female emotionalism is quite charming, in its own way, but I know you are not serious. If I obeyed you, I have no doubt you'd soon resent our poverty.

And, more importantly, I cannot let the villain Fogg go unpunished.

Bear my absence with fortitude, for I'm sure the arrest warrant will come soon, and I'll return to you in glory and bearing the reward money that will start your climb back to the sphere you abandoned in order to marry me.

With my regards,
Herbert Fix

Letter # 21

October 21st, 1872

Dear Elizabeth,
The warrant is not yet here. I write in haste and frustration. It turns out that Phileas Fogg intended to leave Bombay for Calcutta via the Great Peninsular railway. I was at the point of stepping into another train carriage, when Fogg's servant Passepartout arrived breathless, hatless, barefoot, and bearing the marks of a scuffle.

Though I fear you'll reproach me for my rudeness, I confess that I eavesdropped on the conversation between him and his master. The Frenchman had lost his shoes and barely escaped after violating the sanctity of a heathen pagoda on Malabar Hill—which is forbidden to Christians (or, at any rate, to anyone wearing shoes).

I was, as I said, on the point of stepping into the train carriage when I realized that, rather than waiting for the warrant from England—which might not reach us in time—I could simply find the temple and give the heathen priests the name and destination of their transgressor. Then *they* could press charges.

You see, the British authorities are extraordinarily careful never to offend the native religions—it is part of keeping control over this great uncivilized mob—and therefore, what that fool Passepartout did was an offense before British law. I'll get a warrant for that crime, too, then meet them at Calcutta, and have both men properly arrested.

I will write to you soon and announce the date of my return home with the reward money.

Yours, in haste,
Herbert Fix

Letter #25

October 25th, 1872
Calcutta, British India

Dear Elizabeth,
At last Fogg and his servant have arrived. I was in some anxiety that something had befallen them in the jungle as they crossed the

subcontinent. I could not stop thinking of the thief and all those bank notes rotting away in the verdant wildness of India, and my reward unclaimed! I was truly in despair—but now they've arrived at last, and the magistrates had them arrested at the train. Everything was going so well.

Unfortunately, Fogg bought his way out of the situation by posting an exorbitant bail of two thousand pounds, as if it were nothing. *Two thousand pounds*—the same amount that could have made the two of us comfortable for so long, thrown out like so much rubbish!

As I've said before, money that one has not earned is easy to discard.

Sadly, it appears that the thief will escape once more, and I must continue my relentless pursuit, even if it takes me all the way around the world. He is boarding the *Rangoon*, which lays at anchor and is to depart in an hour for Hong Kong.

I have no choice but to follow, despite your half dozen letters imploring me to come home, which I recently collected from the consulate. Again, your letters have safely made the passage, while the desperately needed warrant lingers somewhere on the way. Bureaucracy can be truly exasperating.

My greatest worry now is that Fogg is flinging money about with such abandon that the reward—being a fixed percentage of the recovered money—is shrinking visibly before my eyes.

I'm sure it will still be enough to make you happy.

I shall get him in the British colony of Hong Kong. Fogg and Passepartout are now traveling with a beautiful and clearly genteel young lady they picked up somewhere in the jungles of India. I suspect an elopement, and though you might call it unworthy of me—considering that we also eloped—I should be able to arrest Fogg for *that*, too, because elopement, until sanctified by marriage, can be prosecuted as a crime. I will question Passepartout for details about this woman.

Yours,
Herbert Fix

Letter #37

November 6th, 1872
Hong Kong

Elizabeth,
We are arrived in Hong Kong after much adventure. In your letters you expressed the wish that you could join me in my pursuit. You must

realize that this traveling abroad, though exhilarating for a man, would be much too demanding for a delicate woman such as yourself. You are much happier at home.

Just before we landed we met with a hurricane, the greatest storm I've ever seen. It was as if the heavens themselves were on my side, whipping the seas and the wind into a frenzy to delay us. And while I was gripped by the most horrible nausea, I hoped we'd have to turn and run before the squall, which would slow our journey to Hong Kong. This made it more likely the warrant would arrive, and it would also disrupt whatever plans this scoundrel has for escaping the law.

Alas, the vessel braved it, and we made landfall shortly after.

Meanwhile, I learned that the relatives of the mysterious woman are not likely to chase Fogg for besmirching her honor. Auda is a mere native, despite her pale skin—an Indian princess, whom Passepartout and Fogg supposedly rescued from being burned with her husband's body, a barbarous tradition of immolation. Now she is traveling with them.

They have already reserved berths on the *Carnatic*, which was scheduled to depart tomorrow for Yokohama. But I met Passepartout on his way from the quay to his master's hotel, and he told me the *Carnatic* has unexpectedly changed its departure time to this evening instead. The Frenchman was in a great hurry to tell Fogg about it, but I waylaid the simple-minded and naïve servant and got him intoxicated in an opium den, a very common establishment in these parts.

The man will sleep for at least a day, till long after the *Carnatic* has sailed. I am sure Fogg will not leave without his man. If my plan succeeds in delaying them, I shall go to the embassy and see if there are any forwarded letters from you.

Yours,
Herbert Fix

Letter #45

November 14th, 1872
Yokohama, Japan

Elizabeth,

Once more I write in haste. Fogg, having missed the *Carnatic*, engaged a small sail boat, the *Tankedere*—and he allowed me to travel with him. He does not even suspect that I am his nemesis! And

Passepartout refuses to believe his master might be a thief. Either he is a wily accomplice, or a fool.

It is maddening to be so near him for so long and yet not to have the warrant that would stop him in his tracks. But there is nothing for it, as we're no longer in British territory. My only hope now is that he'll indeed go around the world in such a fashion hoping to confuse pursuers. I shall arrest him as soon as he lands in England again. Fogg intends to pursue travel to America aboard the *General Grant*.

I've already engaged a cabin in the *General Grant*, and I've now read the latest batch of your letters which, if you'll forgive me, are rather tiresome in your insistence that I return to you at once. I have a job to do. Despite the rate at which this scoundrel is spending the stolen money, think of the renown his capture will bring me, and how much easier it will make my rise in the world.

Only minutes ago, I saw Passepartout being dragged into the boat by Fogg. Passepartout wore a most extraordinarily fanciful oriental uniform, with wings and a false nose which would have sufficed for a family of twelve. People on deck say this is a costume worn in theater for the glory of some god or other. Foolish native habits and abominable idolatry, of course, and one wonders how even a Frenchman could bear to mix himself in it.

While I take a moment to catch my breath, let me tell you something about Yokohama. It is a city of good size, and the native quarter is lit by many-colored lanterns. There are astrologers everywhere using fine telescopes. Scientific instruments to enhance their superstition. Most ironic. For fun, I thought about having a horoscope cast for you—an unusual and exotic gift—but I had no time to delay. I must catch Fogg.

Sincerely,
Herbert Fix

Letter #64

December 3rd, 1872
San Francisco, United States of America

Elizabeth,

We are in San Francisco, the wild city of 1849, with its bandits, incendiaries, and assassins who all came here in the Gold Rush. The city looks more civilized than you'd expect, with a lofty tower in the town hall and a whole network of streets and avenues. It also has a Chinese town, that you'd swear came from China itself.

We found ourselves caught in the middle of some incomprehensible political rally—a dispute for the post of Justice of the Peace involving two men—and soon it turned into a brawl. I could not make heads nor tails of it, nor why anyone would seek to harm anyone else over such a silly squabble. I think these Americans are just hot-tempered.

In the turmoil, I actually protected Fogg from what might have been a disabling blow. Don't worry. Other than my clothes, nothing was hurt. Fogg insisted on buying me new garments, which are of a quality and cut to which even your parents could not object.

In your latest letters you reproached me for my "despicable Opium plot." I must say that you simply don't understand the business of men. Some deeds, though unpleasant, are necessary. Don't concern yourself about the matter any further.

You'll be heartened to know I'm now wholeheartedly working to speed Fogg's travel. Indeed, now that the thief is heading back to England, I am more than glad to help him. The sooner he gets there, the sooner I can arrest him. (And be back home with you, of course.)

And now we are to catch a train on the Pacific Railroad, headed for New York, from where we shall sail for London. I must rush to the train, so I don't lose sight of Fogg.

Herbert Fix

Letter #70

December 11th, 1872
New York, United States

Elizabeth,

Sorry for not writing for two days. Ran out of paper. You'd never believe what we've done in our trip across the United States. We rushed over a bridge mere moments before it collapsed, and in the process we'd gotten up such a head of steam that we didn't even stop until we'd passed the station! Then there was a herd of animals so large that they impeded the movement of the train. We had to wait until the beasts moved before the train could pass. Only imagine! The Americans call them buffalo, though Fogg said that such a classification is absurd. Not sure why.

The wonders of this continent! This world!

At one point, Fogg nearly engaged in a gunfight duel with another passenger, but they were interrupted by an attack from the savage Sioux, who kidnaped three passengers, including Passepartout—which, naturally, necessitated a rescue. Afterward, we caught an express train at

Omaha station. Fogg, apparently imagining the demons of justice after him, is not fond of sightseeing, only rushing onward and onward. All the better, for that means I'll collect my reward sooner.

Now we've reached New York at last—but alas the vessel in which we expected to cross the Atlantic sailed forty-five minutes before our arrival. Fogg will no doubt find some boat to purchase or coerce. I very much fear there's not much money left out of the fifty thousand pounds he stole, but I shall still reap fame for apprehending him. Wouldn't you like to be the wife of a hero?

Herbert Fix

Letter #80

December 21, Friday
Liverpool

Elizabeth,
We have made landfall, and I served Phileas Fogg with the warrant, but—how could misfortune befall me so? After all my labors, after pursuing him round the world, I am not to enjoy success. Despite every indication, it appears that Fogg is not the thief after all, for the man who actually stole the fifty thousand pounds was apprehended three days ago, whilst I was traveling!

Worse, that upstart Passepartout punched me when he learned my true purpose in accompanying them on their long journey. Now I am bruised and tired, humiliated, disappointed—but at least I'm home, where doubtless you'll be waiting for me.

Herbert Fix

**[On embossed letterhead identifying it as belonging to the law firm of Everingham, Entwhistle and Brown
—left on the fireplace mantel of Fix's home.]**

London
December 18th of 1872

Dear Mr. Herbert Fix,
This letter serves to notify you that your wife, the honorable Elizabeth Rose Merryweather Fix, has returned to her parents' home and is suing you for divorce on the grounds of abandonment.

Our client has further instructed us to inform you that she did not object to your poverty or even your low upbringing, but she cannot forgive your obsession with career at the expense of her peace of mind and felicity. She further instructs us to inform you that you married her under false pretenses, always having characterized your marriage as a love match, when it is clear you love nothing more than your reputation and the pursuit of your own ambitions.

Lord and Lady Merryweather advise you to pose no argument and seek no reconciliation with their daughter, as they have the means to see you dismissed from your employment.

Sincerely,
Nigel Entwhistle, Esquire

SHORT STRAWS

Yes, a dragon was terrorizing the land, so the king had offered his daughter in marriage to any brave knight who slew the foul beast. Same old story. I was new to the band of warriors, but the others had heard it all before. This time, though, the logistics caused a problem.

"We could split a *cash* reward," said Oldahn, the battle-scarred old veteran who served as our leader. "But who gets the princess?"

The four of us sat around the fire, procrastinating. Though I was still wide-eyed to be part of the group—they had needed a new cook and errand runner—I'd already noticed that the adventurers liked to talk about peril a lot more than actually doing something about it. I was their apprentice, and I wanted for us to go out and fight, a team of mercenaries, warriors—but that didn't seem to be the way of going about it.

We knew where the dragon's lair was, having investigated every foul-smelling, bone-cluttered cave in the kingdom. But we still hadn't figured out what to do with the princess, assuming we succeeded in slaying the dragon. It didn't seem a practical sort of reward.

Reegas looked up with a half-cocked grin. "We could just take turns with her!"

Oldahn sighed. "One does not treat a princess the way you treat one of your hussies, Reegas."

Reegas scowled, scratching the stubble on his chin. "She's no different from Sarna at the inn—except I'll wager Sarna's better than your rustin' princess at all the important things!"

"She is the daughter of our sovereign, Reegas. Now show some respect."

"Yeah, sure, she's sacred and pure ... Bloodrust, Oldahn, now you're sounding like *him*." Reegas shot a disgusted glance at Alsaf, the puritan.

Alsaf plainly took no offense at the insult. He rolled up the king's written decree, torn from the meeting post in the town square, and stuffed it under his belt, since he was the only one of us who could read. Alsaf methodically began polishing the end of his staff on the fabric of his black cloak. He preferred to fight with his staff and his faith in God, but he also kept a sword at hand in case both the others failed. Firelight splashed across the silver crucifix at his throat.

Reegas spat something unrecognizable into the dark forest behind him. Gray-bearded Oldahn chewed his meat slowly, swallowing even the fat and gristle without a word, mindful of worse rations he had lived through. He wore an elaborately studded leather jerkin that had protected him in scores of battles; his sword was notched, but clean and free of rust.

I sat closest to the campfire, nursing a battered pot containing the last of the stew, letting my own meat cook long enough to resemble something edible. "Uh," I said, desperately wanting to show them I could be a useful member of their band. "Why don't we just draw straws to see who goes to kill the dragon?"

Alsaf, Oldahn, and Reegas all stared as if the newcomer wasn't supposed to come up with a feasible suggestion.

"Rustin' good idea, Kendell," Reegas said. Alsaf nodded.

Oldahn looked at all three of us. "Agreed, then. Luck of the draw."

I scrabbled over to my bedding and searched through it to find suitable lots. I still preferred to sleep on a pile of straw rather than the forest floor. The straw was prickly and infested with vermin, but it reminded me of the warm bed I had left behind when running away from my home. The straw was preferable to the cold, hard dirt—at least until I got hardened to the mercenary life.

I took four straws, broke one in half so that all could see, then handed them to Oldahn. The big veteran covered them in a scarred hand to hide the short straw and motioned for me to draw first.

Tentatively, I reached out, unable to decide whether I wanted the honor of battling the dragon. Sure, being wed to a princess would be nice, but I had barely begun my sword fighting lessons, and according to stories I had heard, dragons were vicious opponents. But I wanted to be a warrior instead of a shepherd's son, and a warrior faced whatever challenges they encountered.

I snatched a straw from Oldahn's grasp and could tell from the others' expressions even before I glanced downward that I had drawn a long one.

Alsaf came forward, holding his staff in his right hand as he reached out to Oldahn's fist. He paused for a long moment, then pulled a straw forth. His black cloak blocked my view, but he turned with a strangled expression on his face, looking as if his faith had deserted him. The short straw fell to the ground as he gripped his silver crucifix. "But, my faith—I must remain chaste! I cannot marry a princess."

Reegas clapped the puritan on the back. "I'm sure you can work something out."

Alsaf was pale as he shifted his weight to rest heavily on his staff. He nodded as if trying to convince himself. "Yes, my purpose is to destroy evil in all its manifestations. A divine hand has guided my selection, and I will serve His purpose." Alsaf's eyes glinted with a fanatical fury as he strode to the edge of the camp.

"Take care, and good luck," said Oldahn.

Alsaf whirled to face the three of us, holding his staff in a battle-ready stance. "I shall be protected by my unquenchable faith. My staff will send the demon back to the fires of Hell!" He looked at the skeptical expressions on our faces, then changed the tone of his voice. "I shall return."

"Is that a promise?" Reegas asked, and for once his sarcasm was weak.

"I give you my word." The puritan turned to stride into the deep stillness of the forest night, crunching through the underbrush.

It was the only promise Alsaf ever broke.

⁂

"For our honor, we must continue." Oldahn held three straws in his hand, thrusting them forward. "Come, Reegas. Draw first."

Reegas cursed under his breath and reached out to grab a straw without even pausing for thought. A broad grin split his face. He held a long straw.

I came forward, looking intently at the two straws, two chances. One would pit me against a scaly, fire-breathing demon, and the other would give me a reprieve. Knowing that the dragon had already defeated one warrior, I decided the princess wasn't so desirable after all. Alsaf had seemed so strong, so confident, so determined. I hesitated, hoping the puritan would return at the last possible moment....

But he didn't, and I picked a straw. It was long.

Oldahn stared at the short straw remaining in his hand. Cold battle-lust boiled in his eyes. "Very well, I have a dragon to slay, a death to avenge, and a princess to win. I had thought it too late in my life to settle down in marriage—but I will adapt. My brave exploits should be sung by minstrels all across the kingdom."

"Our kingdom doesn't have any minstrels, Oldahn," I pointed out.

The old warrior sighed. "I should have volunteered to go first anyway. I am the leader of our band."

"Our band?" Reegas said, sulking in his crusty old chain mail shirt. "Rust, Oldahn—with you gone we aren't much of a band anymore."

Oldahn patted his heavy broadsword and walked stiffly across the camp. It was a beautiful day, and the sun broke through in scattered patches of green light. Oldahn looked around as if for one last time. He turned to walk away, calling back to us just before he vanished into the tangled distance, "Don't be so sure I won't be coming back."

By nightfall, we were sure.

⁂

The campfire was lonely with only Reegas and me sitting by it. Oldahn had fallen, and the fact that he was the best warrior in our group (old mercenaries are, by definition, good warriors) didn't improve our confidence. I could hardly believe the great fighter I had revered so much had been *slain*. It wasn't supposed to be this way.

I looked at Reegas, fidgeting in his battered chain mail. "Well, Reegas, do you want to wait until morning, or draw straws now?"

"Rust! Let's get it over with," he said. His eyes were bloodshot. "This better be one hell of a princess."

I picked up two straws, one long, the other short. I held them out to Reegas, and he spat into the fire before looking at me. I masked my expression with some effort. Reegas reached forward and pulled the short straw.

"Bloodrust and battlerot!" he howled, jerking at the ends of the straw as if trying to stretch it longer. He crumpled it in his grip and threw it into the fire, then sank into a squat by my cookpots. "Aww, Kendell—now I can't teach you some things! I meant to take you over to the inn one night where you would—"

I looked at him with a half-smile, raising an eyebrow. "Reegas, do you think Sarna takes no other customers besides yourself?"

Wonder and shock lit up his craggy face. "You? ... Rust!" Reegas laughed loudly, a nervous blustering laugh. He clapped me on the back with perverse pride. "I won't feel sorry for you anymore, Kendell." He drew his sword and leaped into the air, slashing at a branch overhead.

"But I'm gonna get that rustin' princess for myself. Maybe royalty knows a few tricks the common hussies don't."

He turned with a new excitement, dancing out of camp, waving farewell.

Alone by the campfire, I waited the long hours as the dusk collapsed into darkness. The forest filled with the noisy silence of a wild night. As the stars began to shine, I lay on the cold ground with my head propped against the rough bark of an old oak. I gave up sleeping on straw in fear that I would have dreams of dark scales and death.

The branches above me looked like the black framework of a broken lattice supporting the stars. The mockingly pleasant fire and the empty campsite made me feel intensely lonely; and for the first time I felt the true pain of my friends' losses. I had wanted to be one of them, and now they were all gone.

I remembered some of the stories they had told me, but I hadn't quite fit in with the rest of the band yet. I was a novice, I hadn't yet fought battles with them, hadn't helped them in any way. And now Alsaf and Oldahn were gone, and Reegas had a good chance of joining them....

Since I had talked my way into accompanying the band, nothing much had happened. Until the dragon came, that is.

Of course, if I had known my first adventure might involve a battle with a large reptilian terror, I might have put up with my dull old life a little longer. My father was a shepherd, spending so much time out with his flocks that he had begun to look like one of his sheep. Imagine watching thirty animals eat grass hour after hour! My mother was a weaver, spending every day hunched over her loom, hurling her shuttle back and forth, watching the threads line themselves up one at a time. She even walked with a jerky back and forth motion, as if bouncing to the beat of a flying shuttle.

Me, I'd just as soon be out fighting bandits, dispatching troublesome wolves, or chasing the odd sorcerer away under the grave risk of having an indelible curse hurled at me. That's excitement—but slaying a dragon is going a bit too far!

I couldn't sleep and lay waiting, listening to the night sounds. At every rustle of leaves I jumped, peering in to the shadows, hoping it might be Reegas returning, or Oldahn, or even Alsaf.

But no one came.

Finally, at dawn, I threw the last long straw on the dirt and ground it under my heel. I had only ever used my sword to cut up meat for the cook fires. I was alone. No one watched me, or pressured me, or insisted that I too go out and challenge the dragon. I could have just crept back home, helped my father tend sheep, helped my mother with her weaving. But somehow that kind of life seemed worse than facing a dragon.

I stared at the blade of my sword, thinking of my comrades. Alsaf and Oldahn and Reegas had been my friends, and I was the only one who could avenge them. Only I remained of the entire mercenary band. I had been with Oldahn long enough, heard his tales of glory, seen how the group worked together as a team. I couldn't just let the dragon have its victory.

Muttering a few curses I had picked up from Reegas, I left the dead campfire behind and set off through the forest.

The forest floor was impervious to the sunshine that dribbled through the woven leaves. A loud breeze rushed through the topmost branches but left me untouched. I knew the boulder-strewn wilderness well, and my woodlore had grown more skillful since my initiation into the band. While we had no serious adventures to occupy ourselves, there was still hunting to be done.

My anxiety tripled as I crested a final hill and started down into a rocky dell that sheltered the dragon's den, a broken shadow in the rock surrounded on all sides by shattered boulders and dead foliage. The lump in my throat felt larger than any dragon could ever be. The wind had disappeared, and even the birds were silent. A terrible stench wafted up, smelling faintly like something Reegas might have cooked.

I crept forward, drawing my sword, wondering why the ground was shaking and then I saw that it was only my knees. Panic flooded my senses—or had my senses left me? Me? Against a dragon? A big scaly thing with bad breath and an awful prejudice against armed warriors?

The boulders offered some protection as I danced from one to another, moving closer to the dragon's lair. Fumes snaked out of the cave, stinging my eyes and clogging my throat, tempting me to choke and give away my presence. I could hear sounds of muffled breathing like the belching of a blacksmith's furnace.

I slid around a slime-slick rock to the threshold of the cave. I froze, an outcry trapped in my throat as I found the shattered ends of Alsaf's staff, splintered and tossed aside among torn shreds of black fabric. I swallowed and went on.

A few steps deeper into the den I tripped on the bloody remnants of Oldahn's studded leather jerkin. His bent and blackened sword lay discarded among bloody fragments of crunched bone.

On the very boundary of where sunlight dared to go, I found Reegas's rusty chain mail, chewed to a new luster and spat out.

A scream welled up as fast as my guts did, but terror can do amazing things for self-control. If I screamed, the dragon would know I had come, the latest in a series of tender victims.

But now, upon seeing with utmost certainty the fates of my comrades, my fellow warriors, anger and lust for vengeance poured forth, almost, *almost,* overwhelming my terror. The end result was an angered persistence tempered with extreme caution.

Leg muscles tense to the point of snapping, I tiptoed into the cave where I stood silhouetted against the frightened wall of daylight. The suffocating darkness of the dragon's lair folded around me. I didn't think I would ever see the sun again.

The air was thick and damp, polluted with a sickening stench. Piles of yellowed skulls lay stacked against one wall like ivory trophies. I didn't see any of the expected mounds of gold and jewels from the dragon's hoard. Pickings must have been slim in the kingdom.

I went ahead until the patch of sunlight seemed beyond running distance. My jerkin felt clammy, sticking to my cold sweat. I found it hard to breathe. I had gone in too far. My sword felt like a heavy, ineffective toy in my hand.

I could sense the lurking presence of the dragon, watching me from the shadows. I could hear its breathing like the wind of an angry storm but could not pinpoint its location. I turned in slow circles, losing all orientation in the dimness. I thought I saw two lamplike eyes, but the stench filled my nostrils, my throat. It gagged me, forcing me to gasp for air, but that only made me gulp down more of the smell. I sneezed.

—and the dragon attacked!

Suddenly I found myself confronted with a battering-ram of fury, blackish green scales draped over a bloated mass of flesh lurching forward. Acid saliva drooled off fangs like spears, spattering in sizzling pools on the floor.

I struck blindly at the eyes, the rending claws, the reptilian armor. The monster let out a hideous cry, seething forward, fat and sluggish, to corner me against a lichen-covered wall. My stomach turned to ice, and I knew how Alsaf, Oldahn, and Reegas must have felt as they faced their death—

Let me digress a moment.

Dragons are not exactly the best-fed of all creatures living in the wild. Despite their size and power, and the riches they hoard (but who can eat gold?), these creatures find very little to devour, especially in a relatively small kingdom like our own, where most people live protected within the city walls. Barely once a week does a typical dragon manage to steal a squalling baby from its crib or strike down an old crone gathering herbs in the woods. Rarer still does a dragon come across a flaxen-haired virgin (a favorite) wandering through the forest.

Hard times had come upon this particular dragon. Only impending starvation had driven it to increase its attacks on the peasantry, forcing the king to offer his daughter as a reward to rid the land of the beast. The future must have looked bleak for the dragon.

But then, unexpectedly, a feast beyond its wildest dreams! This dragon had greedily devoured three full-grown warriors in half as many days, swallowing whole the bodies of Alsaf, Oldahn, and Reegas.

And so, when the dragon lunged at me in the cave, it was so *bloated* and overstuffed that it could barely drag its bulk forward, like a snake which has gorged itself on a whole rabbit. Its bleary, yellow eyes blinked sleepily, and it seemed to have lost heart in battling warriors. But it snarled forward out of old habit, barely able to stagger toward me....

I won't, by any stretch of the imagination, claim that killing the brute was easy. The scales were tougher than any chain mail I could imagine, and the dragon didn't particularly want its head cut off—but I was bent on avenging my friends and winning myself a princess. If I could just accomplish this one thing, I could call myself a warrior. I would never have to prove myself again.

Alsaf, Oldahn, and Reegas had already done much of the work for me, dealing vicious blows to the reptilian hide. But I still can't begin to express my exhaustion when the dragon's head finally rolled among the cracked bones in its lair. I slumped to the floor of the cave, panting, without the energy to drag myself back out to fresh air.

After I had rested a long time, I stood up stiffly and looked down at the dead monster, sighing. I had won myself a princess. I had avenged my comrades.

But perhaps the best reward was that I could now call myself a real warrior, a dragon-slayer. I imagined I could think of a few ways to make the story more impressive by the time I actually met my bride-to-be.

The monster's head was heavy, and it was a long walk to the castle.

THE SACRIFICE

The foul-smelling mist exhaled from the cave opening, a swirl of brimstone and smoke. A soft reptilian growl echoed, low and steady. The dragon was still sleeping, but when he awakened, he would be hungry.

The young woman, the virgin sacrifice, struggled against the ropes that bound her to the stake. Her wrists were already raw, but she couldn't get away. She waited for the monster to emerge, to devour her.

The charred bones strewn about the lair—crushed skulls, cracked femurs drained of marrow, curved rib cages—gave evidence of previous meals that had not satisfied the beast.

She tried to be strong, straining and grasping against the bonds, but she didn't dare twist too hard, because that might make her wrists bleed, and blood would certainly draw the dragon. A tear stole aimlessly down her cheek, but she forced herself not to whimper. The fear, too, would bring him out.

Months ago, the dragon had awakened from its ancient slumber and terrorized the countryside. With broad razor wings, it swooped down on the shepherds' flocks, roasting sheep and leaving charred fields. It attacked the villages next, setting thatched roofs on fire, burning cottages to the ground, feasting on any victims it could seize.

When the priests consulted their holy texts, they knew there could be only one solution to appease the dragon: a virgin sacrifice, a pure young woman offered to keep the beast at bay. And the townspeople, her own people, had turned on her. They chose her because she was the least important, an orphan with no one to speak on her behalf. Though she was pretty, kind, and well loved, she had no dowry and was not likely to find a husband anyway. She had no say in the matter.

Now she was tied to the stake before the lair, waiting, doomed, sure the dragon would soon emerge, a nightmare of scales and fangs and deadly fire. And it would see her there, a sacrifice.

But all she could think of was the brave knight and his kisses, his reassurances ... how he had held her the night before. It was their secret. None of the villagers suspected.

But she wondered if the dragon would know ...

TECHNOMAGIC

"Any sufficiently advanced technology is indistinguishable from magic."

—Arthur C. Clarke

"Twenty-seven years for a rescue ship? You've got to be kidding! What am I supposed to do on this planet in the meantime? How am I—"

—Taurindo Alpha Prime, last transmission from scout vessel before crashing in the Nevada desert (loosely translated)

The first garish posters had said *The Great Taurindo!*—some over-enthusiastic publicist's idea, not mine—but my fame grew so rapidly that within a few years the marquees in the Las Vegas amphitheaters shouted my name in letters even taller than I was. (And I am slightly greater in height than the average Earthling, though I look just like one of them.)

The evening's crowd was sprawled out at various tables, more than could comfortably fit in the room, thanks to the outrageous ticket prices people were willing to pay to see me perform. The rich ones sat in the best seats, drinking expensive cocktails, while busloads of budget tour groups crammed together at the long tables, jabbering their schemes for how to win at the nickel slots.

Everyone fell silent as the show began. I cracked my knuckles in the shadows at the edge of the stage, waiting, making sure my smile looked right. Many species in the Galaxy believe the flashing of one's teeth to be a threatening gesture, but on Earth it's considered friendly. Just another of the odd details about them.

The master of ceremonies announced me as the "World's! Greatest! Magician!" Sometimes I'm called a magician, other times an "illusionist"—neither of which is truly accurate, since what I do is not magic nor illusion, but the real thing ... courtesy of my planet's highly advanced technology. None of the spectators knew that, though.

The broad stage reminded me of when I had taken my oral exam before the xeno-sociology degree committee back on the homeworld. I strode out and took my bow as I introduced the evening's first spectacle.

"Remember the old saw about the woman being cut in half in a box?" I said. The audience chuckles. No one from my planet would have understood the reference, but this was a hoary old trick performed *ad nauseam* by Earth magicians. Simple enough to master, but I had added a new twist. "Tonight I'll show you a *new saw*, a very large saw in fact." I smiled again.

The lights flashed. Hot white beams reflected from the highly polished, stainless-steel teeth of the giant chainsaw blade that would slice me in two before their very eyes.

The audience loved the show so far—my lovely assistants were wearing even skimpier outfits than usual.

"I won't hide in a box, I won't use mirrors or distractions. I will lie on this table in plain sight, and this chainsaw will cut me in half—*as you watch!* You'll see it all, every second of it."

The music built. The lights dimmed.

I stepped back into the artificially deep shadows at the back of the stage, and then I sent my perfect clone forward out into the brilliant light. He was an identical match for my body, cell for cell, although his brain was completely blank. It was all the vapid simulacrum could do to stagger across the stage and lie down on the table under the motionless chainsaw.

The beautiful assistants strapped him down, and he didn't resist, instinctively smiling out at the audience like an idiot. All clones smile. It's a secret they seem to share in their brainlessness.

The eyes of all the men in the audience were trying to catch a glimpse of just a bit more through my assistants' scanty uniforms and paid little attention to the mechanics of the actual trick. Others were trying to figure out what the gimmick was—while some few, the blessed ones, remained happy enough just to be entertained.

The music swelled loud and dramatic. The chainsaw blade spun up with a loud roar that built to a threatening whine, like a dentist's drill for King Kong.

The lighting technicians slipped a thick red gel over the spotlights, bathing the stage in an ominous crimson glow, as the deadly blade began to descend, rattling as the chain teeth whipped around and around in a circle. The clone lay twitching on the table, bound by the restraints and staring with uncomprehending eyes up at the sharp spinning blade about to rip him to shreds.

That's show biz, as they say.

Timing was everything now, and I had to depend on my crew. They knew what they were supposed to do.

The chainsaw slammed down, ripping through the clone's ribcage and sparking on the steel tabletop. Blood flew in a bright arc—one of the more picturesque ones, I thought. The clone let out a shriek of instinctive pain that was abruptly cut off ... then all the lights went out for an instant to be replaced by only a single faint spotlight on the retracting chainsaw blade still slowly spinning, dripping blood.

The audience swelled with thin screams. I wondered how many of them would faint this time, though I had done this trick many times and they must have *known* there would be no accident. Not this time. Not any time.

I could have kept the lights up, of course, since this was all real. I could have shown the audience the gory, anatomically correct mess on the table. But that would have gone beyond the bounds of good clean entertainment. Instead, the glimpse of the bloodied saw and the clone's genuine scream was all they needed to know.

As the lights dropped to black, the automatic nanocritters—microscopic destructive robots—began the busy-work of taking my clone apart cell by cell, dissolving him into a simple protein mass in the space of less than a minute. And when the entire body was denatured, the liquid obediently seeped into drains in the table (placed there ostensibly for spilled blood). I would use the protein mass to grow a clone for another performance.

The lights came up again with enough flash and dazzle to temporarily blind the audience, and there I stood in the middle of the stage, intact and smiling, taking my bow to thunderous applause—as always.

৯

Outside the bright lights of the casino, I melted into the crowd, where I could study the way humans interact. I've never gotten tired of it, even after so many years.

On the sidewalk at a street corner, where impatient pedestrians waited for DON'T WALK to change to WALK, I saw an aspiring magician walking among the people, pestering them, showing off to the best of his ability. Doing card tricks, pulling colored scarves from his sleeves—amateurish stuff, but I stopped in mid-stride with a warm glow of nostalgia. Perhaps he hoped for some sort of special attention as he stood overshadowed by the huge marquee for *The Great Taurindo!*

I watched him for a while. This struggling magician with stars in his eyes and the reckless hope for fame reminded me of one of the first Earthlings I had ever met....

Just before my burned-out scout ship crashed out on this planet's desert wastelands, I was able to salvage only a few things from the hulk. After transmitting my distress call and pinpointing my position for the eventual rescue ship, I hurried away from the ship as the self-destruct nanocritters began to turn the hull and engines to indefinable dust.

Swallowing hard, I hiked across the rocky scrub in the general direction of the large city I had spotted just before impact.

Because of my profession studying alien cultures, I had been through the "first contact" routine numerous times before, and this one went off without a hitch. But as I ambled through the streets of Las Vegas, trying to fit in while staring wide-eyed around me, I came upon a street magician. He had a battered cardboard box open on the sidewalk, in which had been scattered bits of paper and round metal (obviously the monetary currency in use).

The magician extended a deck of playing cards to passers-by, asking them to select a card, whose identity he would then guess. In another trick he hid a bright red ball under one of three bowls, rapidly shuffled them around, then asked someone to find it—and invariably they guessed wrong.

At first, I suspected these humans had telepathic powers, but as I watched I soon realized this was not the case. The magician was merely fooling his audience with sleight of hand. And people were tossing him money for it.

I watched him for some time, but since I had no local currency to give for the performance, I wandered away.

I began to think that I could do such stunts, only better—given my superior technology. Among the few items I had snagged from the ship before its quiet self-destruct was the wonderful Central Autonomic Molecular Device—a complex whirlwind computer, synthesizer, and nanotechnology processor. I called it the "gizmo," ignoring the pretentious technical terminology that I didn't understand anyway. The machine was far beyond my level of education and training—I was a xeno-sociologist and observer, not an

TECHNOMAGIC • 83

engineer. The palm-sized gizmo *worked*, and that was all I needed to know during my exile here.

I was stuck on Earth for twenty-seven years, and I would have to make something of myself in the meantime. And magic fascinated these people.

As I assimilated into this culture, I came upon an interesting observation called Clarke's Law. It said that "Any sufficiently advanced technology is indistinguishable from magic." The postulate had been derived by a visionary who also developed the concept for this planet's geosynchronous communication satellites, had popularized the idea for the space elevator as an alternative to expendable launch vehicles, and had also written the story for an amusing film called *2001: A Space Odyssey*, which I enjoyed very much. (I wonder if Mr. Clarke's awe of alien intelligences might have been so great if he'd had the pleasure of meeting the bovine slugs of Merricus or endured the screeching carrion ballets of Vulpine Five, however.)

Clarke's postulate about technology and magic gave me an idea. With the gizmo to serve me, I simply had to learn what sort of magic the Earthlings wanted to see and how to make a good show out of it.

Showmanship proved to be the hardest part. Simply displaying an endless string of miracles would not be enough. (Besides, Central Authority back home would have been very annoyed if I accidentally started a new religion on Earth.)

I watched Earth's best performers, astonishing magicians and illusionists, trying to learn the secret to a good show. At times I was confounded, wondering if these showmen somehow had access to contraband extraterrestrial technology themselves. It didn't matter—I knew my gizmo was superior to anything they might have. I could do better.

It took me a long time to understand their attitude toward entertainment—but once I did, it became a key to grasping the human psyche. While Earthlings are endlessly curious and easily perplexed, these people honestly didn't want to know *how* a magic trick was performed. They might claim so, and half mean it, but they would rather be intrigued and amazed. They'd be outraged if every magician went on their endless talk shows and explained all the secrets.

That would squash the thrill for them, the *magic*.

❧

One of my simplest tricks (and therefore one of my favorites) was transporting myself instantaneously from one part of the arena to another. It was a trivial teleportation gimmick—but with the appropriate buildup, the music, the lights, the smoke and mirrors, the gorgeous assistants, and pounding drums, it became an amazing feat. Other Earth magicians had done similar acts, some with people, some with animals—but no one did it with my method (so far as I know).

After selecting a volunteer from the audience—a fidgety young man with too-short pants and a sweat-stained polyester shirt—I climbed into a vertical metal box at the back of my stage, holding the lid open. An identical box stood at the far end of the seats, a good distance away, containing my unwitting volunteer. The young man stood inside the box as if it were a coffin, looking out and wanting to shrink away from the sudden attention.

The assistants sealed the door of his box. The young man's eyes were bugging out and his throat bobbed as he gulped.

Waving from the stage, I closed the door on my box, activating the instantaneous teleportation circuit in the gizmo strapped to my waist.

Less than a second later, I emerged intact in the opposite booth, while assistants opened the box on the stage, allowing the wide-eyed volunteer to stumble out, gawking in amazement and completely at a loss as to how he had traveled a hundred meters in an instant. He rubbed his still-tingling skin and blinked into the bright lights and the applause. He grinned like a clone.

༺༻

My promoters and agents (*these* people are true aliens, even among Earthlings) kept insisting that I do bigger and more daring stunts—and I obliged, attempting to surpass even the greatest illusions ever performed by master magicians. Though some of the spectacles required more power, my precious gizmo had a century-and-a-half useful lifespan, according to its warranty. I trusted the engineers from my planet. They knew what they were doing.

Most outrageous trick: I made the Empire State Building vanish at midnight, right under floodlights and helicopters and in front of the slack-jawed faces of the gathered crowd.

In the blind instant when the spotlights shut off, I touched the gizmo at my waist to *disintegrate* the entire skyscraper, all 102 stories (plus television tower). When the lights came back up again, only shaven foundations remained of one of the tallest buildings on this planet. A few disconcerting sparks flickered up from severed electrical cables, nothing more.

I sincerely hoped the publicists had evacuated the building as they'd promised.

Once the cheers and applause began to subside, we dropped the lights again and I re-integrated the building, according to its molecular pattern stored in the gizmo's computer. Simple enough, when you think about it, given a little bit of engineering know-how ... or at least a machine that can do it all for you.

❦

Then I made my big mistake.

It was a trick I had done dozens of times, and it had never proved difficult before. Overconfident, I let my guard down, forgetting how truly alien these Earthlings are, how they panic when there isn't the least bit of danger. I "screwed up," to use their own quaint phrase.

For the finale of my act I had taken to *flying*—my trademark performance, as it were. I strapped an auxiliary anti-gravity pack to my chest just below the gizmo itself, using it to levitate and flit about the stage.

As always, it gave the Earthlings an added thrill to see a randomly chosen audience member fly along with me. (Showmanship, showmanship!) This evening I had picked out a pretty young blonde with a good figure, gleaming smile, and giggly personality—audiences responded best to sexy volunteers, though the anti-grav belt could have lifted even one of the hefty matriarchs who sat sipping wine coolers and killing time before they got back to the slot machines.

"Are you ready to fly?" I asked the young lady, raising my rich voice for the audience. Her eyes were as large as those of the mantis people that had nearly devoured me on Karnak Delta. Her name was Tiffany, naturally.

I held her trembling hand as the assistants came out with hoops, swooping them around me to prove that I had no wires attached to my body, no flying harness (just the gizmo and a small anti-grav generator). Tiffany saw the tests and she saw my face and then looked around. Standing right beside me, she knew better than anyone else that this was no trick.

I held her snugly around the waist like Superman and Lois Lane, and we lifted off, drifting above the stage. I should have noticed her growing uneasiness. We were skewered by the blazing spotlights that tracked our every movement, drifting back and forth. Tiffany was stunned—but her amazement lasted only a moment.

When I soared out over the audience and the tables, alas, it proved too much for her. She became hysterical to get down, struggling in my grasp so that I had to clutch her just to keep her from plummeting to the stage.

"Stop it!" I whispered, but she didn't hear me. The audience was too busy shouting their *ooohs!* and *aaaahs!* I whisked us back over the stage. The flying routine was the climactic end to my show, and I wanted to milk it for as long as possible—but I couldn't swoop around and do my typical stunts with a writhing, panic-stricken human in my arms!

Tiffany clutched my shirt, her long fingernails scratching my chest, grabbing for anything to hold on to. Her hands snatched the thin strap that bound the gizmo to my waist. The strap snapped.

The gizmo fell thirty feet down to the hard stage.

I heard a *clunk*, then a broken *tinkle*. The audience muttered, wondering if they had caught me at something. The spotlights weren't on the stage floor where my woefully damaged device lay, so I covered the gaffe quickly by shouting, "Tiffany, calm down! I think your teeth just fell out."

This brought a chuckle as I lowered us to the far end of the stage with the last trickle of reserve power in the anti-grav belt. I felt sick inside, but "the show must go on," so I took my bows and said my goodnights, letting Tiffany return to her giggling friends. She would probably tell them how much fun it had been.

When the lights went down, I dashed across the stage to retrieve the debris and hurried back to my dressing room, where I refused all visitors for the rest of the night....

I stared down in dismay at the broken innards of the gizmo, the convoluted circuits, the delicately imprinted control paths and microchips far beyond any technology Earth has ever created. The warranty wouldn't do me any good now.

As I said before, I am a xeno-sociologist, not an engineer. I stared down at my ruined miracle-working machine and thought again of Clarke's Law. The electronic paths and schematics meant absolutely nothing to me. The high-tech gizmo might as well have been magic.

I knew this would be my last night of performing. Without the gizmo the Great Taurindo was nothing, unless I learned how to do magic the hard way....

So the years passed. I had amassed a considerable fortune during my years as a star, and I was able to continue living comfortably, though I never set foot on the stage again. I became something of a legend, the reclusive master illusionist who had suddenly quit performing and would tell no one why. I gave no interviews. Numerous books were written about me and my reasons, offering wild speculations, though none so preposterous as the truth.

In the privacy of my home, I continued to practice a few tricks for my own entertainment. I became quite proficient, actually, but nothing good enough to meet the expectations of those who had seen me perform before.

When at last the twenty-seven years had passed, and I received the signal from the rescue ship, I felt an overwhelming joy ... as well as a not-inconsiderable sadness at leaving this interesting backwater planet.

I rushed into the desert to the pickup point, abandoning my home and all my possessions at the darkest hour of night—my sudden disappearance would only increase the mystique about me—and ran to meet the ship.

The pilot and crew were in a great hurry. A Cultural Inspector from Central Authority hustled me off to my seat in the passenger compartment, and we roared back out through Earth's atmosphere. Finally, when we had reached our hypercruise speed, the Cultural Inspector came to debrief me—and I had been waiting for her.

"So, Taurindo Alpha Prime," she said, "you have spent many years on this planet. Tell me what you have learned of their culture."

I smiled. "I can do better than that—I can show you."

From a pocket in my jumpsuit I withdrew a standard deck, shuffled with a dazzling flourish and a snapping blur of sound, then fanned and extended them toward her.

"Pick a card," I said, "any card."

AGE RINGS

Out in front of Grandma's farmhouse, the long-handled axe rested on the stump, its blade firmly embedded in the wood. The stump was wider than Aaron's arms could encompass, but he was only eight. A grownup might be able to reach all the way around.

It was an ancient box elder tree, much like the others in the yard, with drooping branches and knobby bark. This one, though, had been cut down when their own father had been a boy on the farm. The wide stump had served for decades as a chopping block, all of the wood split and stacked up against the farmhouse wall.

His twelve-year-old brother Nate stood looking down at the wide trunk, the weathered gray wood, the numerous scars and notches from the axe. They were both bored, and Nate liked to explain things. Aaron was a captive audience.

"How old do you think this tree was when Grandpa cut it down?" Nate asked.

"I don't know," Aaron said. "A hundred years?"

"There's a way to tell," Nate said, bending down. "Look at the stump. You can count the age rings. All of those circles. Each one marks a year."

"Really?" Aaron bent down, saw the concentric rings tightly packed at the center from when the tree had just been a sapling, then spreading outward all the way to the last shreds of bark. "One ... two ..."

"The thick rings are from a good year, when the tree grew a lot, and the thin rings are from bad years. Each one leaves a mark, and you can just count."

Aaron studied the lines, fascinated by this clear method. So many of them! "This tree was really old." He eventually lost count and gave up.

"Nate," he asked, "how old do you think *Grandma* is?"

His brother considered. "I don't know. Let's go find out." He yanked the axe out of the chopping block and headed for the house.

LETTER OF RESIGNATION

Dear Mr. Escher,

I quit. I just can't take it anymore.

—Your housecleaner

RUDE AWAKENING

I was resting in peace and surrounded by warm red dreams when the lid of my coffin flew open. A madman brandished a pointed wooden stake and a heavy mallet. When I saw the murderous gleam in his eyes, I knew he was trying to kill me.

"Foul demon!" he shrieked with such passion that spittle flew from his lips.

His challenge gave me a fraction of a second, and I snatched a handful of the native soil in the bottom of my coffin and hurled it into the killer's face. The spray of dirt caught him in the eyes, and he lurched backward.

I flung myself out of the coffin on its raised pedestal, careful not to snag my cape. I may be undead, but my heart was pounding. Who was this man? What did he have against me?

No time to think; just react.

As soon as I touched the flagstones of my castle's main vaulted chamber, I sprang to my feet and bounded away from the coffin. My attacker was already rubbing the soil from his eyes, still clutching his mallet and stake. I knew that wouldn't stop him for long.

I felt a chill as I saw several lengths of chain he had curled next to my coffin. My blood ran even colder than usual. He could have chained me up inside, imprisoned me forever.

What a jerk!

As I stumbled away, I felt sluggish, lethargic after being awakened from a deep sleep, made even worse by the fact that I'd fed well the night before. I felt bloated, not as fast as I should be. Damn it!

It had been such a good and satisfying dinner. I had sampled the rich blood of a tavern wench, who unwisely went out after dark to get washing water from the well. I also sipped from a stable boy and a traveling tinker. It was like a sampler platter, and I didn't drain so much that anyone would complain. I knew that my three beautiful vampire brides had also shown restraint, though they were a bit rash by choosing to slip in and feed upon the women in the local nunnery. It had been a fine night, a full moon, a lingering mist on the ground.

And now this nightmare.

"I will send you back to hell, foul bloodsucking monster!" the madman howled. I heard him gathering his implements of death, coming relentlessly after me.

My thoughts spun with panic and confusion. Who was this man? Why was he trying to kill me? How had he found me?

He had broken into my castle in broad daylight, my most vulnerable time. I could never escape outside or I'd be roasted by the purifying rays of the sun. Long black velvet curtains covered the castle windows, blocking the bright sunlight, but I could see the fiery golden lines. It must be noon.

I had only one choice—hide in the lower levels, the dungeons and the catacombs. I ran across the torch-lit chamber to the arched entrances leading into the deeper dungeons. I could escape there. I entered a shadowy catacomb and the shadows deepened, but my night vision intensified.

But when I reached the first of the descending passages, I came to an abrupt halt. My stomach churned, nauseated. The attacker had spread garlic across the threshold—a dozen bulbs blocking my way with a smelly impenetrable barrier!

I spun, raced to another passage, and again I came upon garlic. Then I noticed to my horror that he had draped strands of poisonous bulbs around the windows and the other deep passageways. This killer had left nothing to chance. He meant to stalk me, toy with me. I was trapped —in my own castle!

With a loud whistling sound, a wooden crossbow bolt struck the stone wall next to me and clattered to the floor. He was trying to shoot me through the heart! I swirled my cape to distract his aim, ducked, and bolted away from the garlic, so dizzy I could barely see.

"Today you will die, Count Ordoff!" He fired several more crossbow bolts in rapid succession. Two pierced my cape and one grazed my side. I felt a flash of pain before I rapidly healed, but I didn't waste breath returning his challenge. I needed all my faculties to think of a way I could escape. How was I going to get out of this alive?

Why was he trying to kill me? Think! Think!

But I recalled how many of my closest vampire friends had disappeared over the years. There had been dark and frightening rumors about a serial killer on the loose, an insane stalker who tracked down our safest daytime resting places, who broke into our homes to slaughter us while we slept. So far, he had eluded justice.

Now he was after me.

My castle should have been a fortress, a safe place I could go to ground, have quiet time with my three lovely vampire brides. I had let my guard down. I had been deceived by my pursuit of happiness, my pleasant unlife, my fine home, my fortune.

My brides are exciting women; Ashley, Tiffany, and Sienna—each one carefully chosen. We'd been together for half a century, but it still felt like a honeymoon. We could play card games. Tiffany liked to dabble with watercolors. I toyed with writing my memoirs.

And this monster had shattered our peace! But together, we could fight him off. I had to get to them.

Another chill made my cold skin crawl: my brides had their own darkened chamber with three separate coffins draped with frilly lace—especially Sienna's. She was the youngest, just a teenager when I'd turned her, and she still liked girlish decorations.

Were they all right? What if the stalker had gone to them first? I hurried.

As another crossbow bolt ricocheted against the stone walls, I reached the bedchamber of my three brides. I saw the sickening sight—their coffins were open, and empty. Ashley's had been toppled off its pedestal, as if she had fought back. A stake inside Sienna's coffin protruded from a pile of ashes in the vague outline of a female form surrounded by diaphanous fabric. I recognized one of my favorite negligées.

"No!" I howled.

On the floor another mound of ashes filled the bright red nightgown that Tiffany liked to wear. I clutched at the garment, lifted it up. Ashes trickled onto the flagstones. I wailed again. He had slain my beloved wives, one by one. The bastard!

Anger welled up inside me. Now I didn't want to just survive. I wanted to kill this awful man who had brought such tragedy to my peaceful home. Curling my lips back to show my fangs, I rose up, cast Tiffany's red nightgown aside, and turned to find the hunter standing there, grinning. He was a cruel-looking man with a thin face, a goatee, deep-set eyes, and a crooked nose.

"Aha, I have you!" He splashed an open vial of liquid at me, and I barely dodged in time. Holy water! Several droplets smoked and sizzled on my hand, seeping through the sleeve and burning my arm.

But I didn't care. I looked at Ashley's toppled coffin. "You killed them!"

"And this time they'll stay dead," he said with a laugh. "Next, I'll kill you!"

Using my vampire strength, I hurled Sienna's coffin at him, knocking the serial killer backward. I bolted past, running back into the main chamber where a curving stone staircase led to the upper gallery from which hung my favorite tapestries and the black velvet curtains that masked the windows. My coffin was still down in the main chamber, its lid open ... the place where I had been so peacefully sleeping not long before. It had been quite a rude awakening.

The stalker raced after me, discarding his crossbow with a clatter because he had spent all his bolts. He still brandished his mallet and his stake, though—and no doubt he carried an arsenal of other sadistic weapons.

I bounded up the stairs because it seemed the most likely escape, though it was not a tactically wise thing to do. The madman panted but kept up with me.

"There are many ways to kill a vampire," he said, as if trying to frighten me. "A wooden stake through the heart, that's my preference. I like to watch a vampire writhe and scream as he turns to dust. But there is also exposure to sunlight, to cremate you under the harsh light of day. I could drown you in running water, but your castle is so old, it doesn't have running water. Or, there's my favorite—cutting off a vampire's head and stuffing his mouth with garlic. That's always amusing."

I kept running, up and up, not deigning to respond. My initial conclusion was reaffirmed. This was an evil, insane man.

"Or, in a pinch," he said, "I could just wrap chains around your coffin and trap you inside for all eternity. One of those alternatives is going to work today."

I reached the top of the landing in the gallery only to find that he had placed more garlic up there, blocking my way. I couldn't go any farther —I was trapped at the top of the staircase. I faced him ascending the steps, and the hated garlic cutting me off from the other direction ... and the long drop-off to the flagstones of the main gallery below. I had no place to go. He was closing in.

Pulling out his stake and mallet, he advanced toward me, sure that I couldn't escape. Instead, I fell backward off the bannister and into open air.

Unlike what you've read in stories, vampires can't actually transform into bats. I fell with my cape flapping around me, and I crashed onto the hard flagstones. That really hurt.

From high above, the stalker glared down at me before his gaze flashed to the black velvet curtains. With an evil leer he leaped outward and grabbed the velvet, using his own weight to dislodge the curtain rods, tearing the fabric as he fell away from the castle windows. Blazing streams of golden sunlight poured in, and I scrambled out of the way, blinded. The air itself turned into an unbearable oven.

I crawled out of the direct beam, but I could still feel my clothes and my skin smoking. My coffin sat open on its pedestal in the middle of the room. I wasn't thinking straight, but I knew it was shelter, the only protection I could see. Trying to avoid the direct sun, I staggered around the edge of the room, looking for a way to the coffin.

But by the time I reached it, the killer had gotten there first. He stood in front of the open lid holding up a heavy wooden crucifix like a shield. Blocking my way.

After all my years of being an undead, though, I was for the most part an agnostic, and such symbols didn't have the effect on me as they once did. The fact that I was blinded by sunlight and could barely see the crucifix made it possible for me to resist.

I knew what I had to do. With this serial killer on the loose, I would never be safe in my castle again, even if I found a hiding place. I had to get rid of this bloodthirsty man who had murdered my three brides and likely dozens of my vampire friends over the years. No one would be safe until this man was destroyed.

I bent low and charged forward fast enough that the sunlight wouldn't sear me too much. The killer looked startled as I struck him in the center of the chest with my lowered head, driving him backward. He squawked and flailed, dropped his wooden crucifix. Out of his pockets the wooden stake and a heavy mallet also clattered on the floor. I didn't care about those.

I knocked him backward into the coffin. He fell, sputtering, startled, and I slammed the lid down, trapping him inside. The ambient sunlight scorched my skin, but I endured the pain. I had to stop this madman before he struck again.

I could hear him pounding, struggling. He tried to push up the coffin lid, but he couldn't fight against my strength. I could only endure the sunlight for a few more seconds, but I had to make sure. I seized the lengths of chain he had left on the floor. The killer had intended to trap me, but instead I wrapped the chains around the coffin, one loop, then another, and I secured it.

The killer struggled inside the coffin—*my* coffin. He pounded and shouted, but his muffled voice sounded as if he had a lump of dirt in his mouth. Maybe he did. But he was secure for now, trapped and out of the way.

The sunlight was too bright, and I had to get out of there. I staggered away from the main gallery and into the blessed shadows. Thankfully, he hadn't put garlic on my secret, hidden passageways, and I made my way toward a small secondary crypt where I always kept a spare guest coffin, just in case a friend stayed over for the day.

I could rest and recuperate there in healing darkness. After my terrifying ordeal, I would be safe at last, and I could recover from my terror ... and deal with my grief over the loss of my loved ones.

Come nighttime, though, when I was strong again, I intended to go back to the chained coffin and deal with this stalker. Poetic justice. I was sure a stake through the heart, or the decapitation with a seasoning of garlic—would be just as effective on a human monster.

And then we could all sleep easy.

THE FATE WORSE THAN DEATH

(WITH GUY ANTHONY DE MARCO)

Lying in the dark in a perfectly restful daytime nap, feeling sated with fresh warm blood (Type O Negative, his favorite), Vlad sensed the intruding presence even before the silent alarm triggered his vibrating watch. The watch buzzed against the mahogany wall of his cozy coffin, warning him.

Always interruptions! Someone was trying to break into his fortress, probably up to no good. "Rest in peace" was harder to achieve than he had ever imagined.

Vlad was a light sleeper, had been for centuries, and even modern sleeping aids like Ambien or Lunesta didn't help. But even with his powers, it was good to remain alert. Careless vampires didn't stay immortal for very long.

He hit the snooze button on the annoying vibrating watch and sighed, not willing to crawl out of the snug coffin just yet. After all, why did he have all those defenses? The intruder should be taken care of without him needing to lift a sharp fingernail.

Vlad couldn't remember the last time someone had bothered to track him down with evil intent, so he doubted this would be a vampire hunter. It was broad daylight, but his mansion was quiet, apparently unoccupied; it was probably a common burglar trying to score some quality electronics. People didn't realize most burglaries happened during the day. And burglars didn't realize how much trouble they would be getting into if they tried to steal from Vladimir Dracul! Especially if they woke him up during daylight hours.

Eight hundred and eighty-two years of existing among those who feared his presence had jaded him. The burglar would be inept, with no idea of the disaster he was about to face. Vlad sighed again and stretched as far as the confines of the coffin would allow. *Too bad,* he thought, *I actually feel depressed that there's nobody left with the guile and fortitude to challenge me.*

He wriggled to a more comfortable position and began to doze. The electric blanket kept him toasty, even though his blood remained cold. The blanket reminded him of his childhood, and he stifled an urge to suck his thumb, remembering the embarrassing previous time, when he'd painfully impaled his thumb on a sharp tooth.

Just as he was drifting off, the alarm watch buzzed again—more urgently this time, to inform him that the intruder had eluded the expensive paramilitary guards and breached the second perimeter of his fortress. Vlad woke further. That was interesting, but the paramilitary guards were flash and dazzle, rather than substance. The intruder was in for an even bigger surprise.

He smiled as he imagined the look of fear and despair that would spread over the hapless thief as he came face-to-face with one of Vlad's *true* guardians. Still feeling sleepy, he settled deeper into his comfortable memory foam. He listened carefully, sure he would hear the sounds of rending and feeding any moment, accompanied by a few delightful screams.

The thought of so much blood and raw meat made him contemplate breakfast after sunset. He didn't always drink blood; that was just a special treat, and—with his vampire metabolism—could actually be fattening. Pork chops, he decided ... yes, he would have pork chops. Maybe with some applesauce and a nice baked potato. He felt blessed that he never needed to worry about high cholesterol. *Blessed!* The thought made him chuckle, which sounded especially loud inside the coffin.

Minutes went by, and he heard no sounds of a struggle, no shouts or growls, no wails of despair. Vlad frowned severely enough that the tips of his fangs protruded from his lips. How had the intruder gotten past his hellhounds? The creatures of the night that prowled his middle sanctum were hungry, fast, and angry at being locked indoors. The three monstrous beasts were the second, third, and fifth most dangerous beings within a mile in any direction (the fourth being the bloodthirsty and sadistic mafioso who lived three estates to the north). Humming the *Jeopardy!* theme song, he cocked his ear to catch any hint of noise from outside his coffin.

Then the lid began to creak open, slowly, tentatively. Startled, Vlad jumped and whacked his head—fine mahogany was definitely a hard wood. Calming himself, he lay back and settled, trying to appear dead and harmless, while he kept his eyes open a slit. The groaning hinges of the lid droned on with painful slowness, and Vlad had to stifle an urge to shout, "Get on with it!" or push the cover open himself.

"Good afternoon, sir," said a lone figure looming over the coffin. "Sorry to interrupt your nap, but we have important business, you and I."

Giving up his slumbering ruse, the vampire sat up to look at his guest while rubbing the small knot growing on his forehead from where he had hit the coffin lid. The intruder was a thick-bodied nerd type with round glasses and a faded Jethro Tull T-shirt. He held a black Evangelion anime backpack in his left hand and wore a black leather belt full of pouches emblazoned with yellow Batman logos.

So, Vlad thought, not the typical burglar—or vampire hunter.

"Good afternoon to you," said the vampire in a thick Transylvanian accent. He had lost his accent over the centuries, but sometimes it seemed appropriate. "Why, may I inquire, are you in my bedchambers at this ungodly hour?"

Usually, when an intruder broke into his fortress, subdued his defenses, and pulled open his coffin, the routine involved sharp sticks and mallets.

The pudgy young man shifted nervously, swung his backpack to one side, and backed away to let the vampire swing his legs out of the coffin. Vlad knew he was intimidating as he stood up to his full six-foot-eight height. He slapped dust from his black tuxedo jacket while observing the intruder.

From behind his round glasses, the man's eyes went wide. "Gosh, you're bigger than I thought you would be." He blinked a few times and then remembered the rest of his manners. "My name is Marvin. Marvin Drake. I'm a computer forensics and security expert. Glad to finally meet you, sir. It was quite difficult to track you down."

Vlad gave a slight bow to his guest. "Then you must know full well who I am. I will, of course, have to deal with you in the usual manner, but your methods intrigue me. I need some answers." He extended a hand, curled the fingers. "I can glamor you into revealing—"

"Oh, that won't be necessary, sir. I came here to talk." Marvin pulled out a gallon baggie filled with a mushed-up yellowish goop. He opened the top to release a pungent smell. "And I did not come unarmed."

Laughing, Vladimir dipped his index finger into the mixture, swirled it around, and pulled out a taste of the garlic and onion. He popped it into his mouth. "*Mmm*, tasty, although it does need some cilantro and a dash of salt. Did you bring any chips?"

Normally, when he demonstrated that he was impervious to the usual defenses against vampires, his adversaries would react with intense fear, but Marvin Drake smiled with delight, showing off crooked, unbrushed teeth. It reminded Vlad of Renfield. Ah, Renfield ... The poor man spent years in rehab trying to kick his habit of eating flies.

"Good, sir. Just checking. How about this?" He yanked out a gold cross from his utility belt and pressed it close to Vlad's face.

Moving faster than humanly possible, since he was no longer human, he snatched the cross out of Marvin's hand and inspected it with a practiced eye, turning it over in his hand. "Gold-plated. I really have to start spreading rumors that only solid gold or silver crucifixes work. At least they're worth something." He tossed the cross back, and Marvin juggled to catch it.

The young man's spreading grin made the vampire pause. There was something wrong with the situation, or with this oddball young man, but Vlad couldn't put a cold finger on what it was. He glanced around at all of the meticulous cobwebs strung along the walls and ceiling—just props, but much easier to maintain than real cobwebs; the ornate candelabras, the suit of armor, the medieval weapons on the wall, all to make his current dank castle feel just like home.

The intruder cast a glance to the heavy, black velvet curtains that hung over the black-painted windows. "Should I even bother opening the curtains to let in the sunlight? I don't suppose that would make you catch fire and explode?"

"No, but the bright light might give me a headache at this hour, and you've been annoying enough already. What is it you want?"

Marvin seemed satisfied to have the preliminaries dispensed with. "May we sit, sir? I really need to have a talk with you." He indicated a small café-style table a few feet away, where Vlad had his coffee after waking up.

The vampire apprehensively took a seat opposite the strange visitor, who was not at all the typical vampire killer. "You're not going to lunge at me with a wooden stake, are you?"

"Would that kill you?"

"No, but it would ruin my favorite ruffled silk shirt, and then I'd have to get truly medieval on you."

"Thanks for the warning, sir. I don't think we have to bother. I have a business proposition for you." Marvin looked puppy-dog hopeful.

"I need answers first." Vlad leaned over. "I want to know how you found me, and how you got in here. Obviously, I have flaws in my security."

Marvin leaned back in his filigree metal chair, adjusted his Jethro

Tull shirt. "As I said, I'm a computer forensics and security specialist. I've been tracking you for years. With all of your quirks, Mr. Dracul, you leave a fairly large data footprint for anyone who knows where to look. Pretty easy, if you know how to do forensic research." He rummaged in the backpack and removed his smartphone.

"For instance, your method of obtaining real estate through a particular set of shell corporations let me keep up with your movements. You typically stay at one location for three to six years before moving on. You tend to stay in Victorian or castle-type estates, which limits your pool of available homes. You prefer colder climates, probably because it resembles the Carpathian Mountains."

"That, and I don't want to get moldy," Vlad said, but he was impressed with what the intruder said. His summation was quite accurate. The centuries had made him complacent, and he forgot that technological advances allowed people to process huge amounts of data in near-real-time. "Very clever, Marvin. That explains how you located me. But what about my paramilitary guards? My mercenaries?"

"I was able to track down their personal cell phone numbers and sent them all a YouTube video of a kitten playing with a crocodile. They were so entranced, I walked right past them." He smiled. "You really should watch the clip. It's very funny."

"Seen it already." Vlad frowned. "But my true supernatural guardians are relentless in their pursuit of intruders. How did you get past the hellhounds?"

"Easier than expected," said Marvin. "They're just giant dogs with a bigger appetite. I tossed them each some pork chops laced with LSD and a large ball of peanut butter." He grinned. "Right now, their mouths are stuck shut, and they're watching pink Hello Kittys ride purple unicorns."

"Where did you get the pork chops?"

"From your freezer, sir. They looked fresh."

So much for his planned breakfast.

"And how did you know beforehand that all of the traditional vampire-repelling techniques wouldn't work?"

Eager, Marvin pressed his chest against the metal tabletop, and Vlad could physically feel the pounding of his guest's youthful Mountain Dew-fueled heart. "I did my homework, sir. Two years ago, when I was bored, I did an analysis of all of the classic books in the public domain. Starting with Bram Stoker, I found that many of the great writers of the last century had some subtle literary commonalities that were statistically improbable. I created a surgically precise literary model that uses a simulated aggregate English professor modeled after personality profiles from more than a thousand arrogant college literary department heads. According to my deep analysis, all of those literary works over the centuries appeared to be written by the same person. I assumed that you were the person who wrote Dracula to feed people the wrong methods to defeat you. But you were writing long before that. You created all those books, didn't you?"

Vlad was embarrassed. "I'm impressed that you could figure it out. The creative writing bug bit me a lot harder than the ancient vampire who turned me. I've been ... dabbling for a while, yes. But I gave up on critique groups back in the eighteenth century."

Maybe this young man would take a look at his poems. No, those were too personal....

Marvin enthusiastically bounced on his chair, his greasy brown hair flapping up and down. "Imagine my surprise when I discovered that my favorite classic stories and novels were actually ghostwritten by an immortal vampire under numerous pen names! Now I know how you can afford all those castles and mansions with all those royalties!"

"All my big sellers are in the public domain," Vlad pointed out.

But Marvin was too excited to hear. "All the top writers in the history of literature were really one ... *ummm*, person. Speculative fiction, romance, erotica, historicals, *New York Times* bestsellers, award winners, and all of them are on my bookshelves."

Vlad felt uncomfortable and exposed. It was hard enough to keep his secret as a vampire, but maintaining a host of pen names was even more of a challenge. He would probably have to kill this intrepid man anyway.

"What's to keep me from reaching across this table and draining you dry?" He felt his senses go alert, his claws itching to tear flesh and spill blood, his fangs ready to plunge into a pudgy throat ... forget the pork chops.

"Nice gambit, but I was the school chess champion from 2006 to 2009. I took precautions. You don't dare harm me."

"And I was the national chess champion in 1782. I played against George Washington, a fellow vampire. He lost a bet and forfeited his fangs, which is why he used wooden teeth." Vlad sneered. "Let me guess, you told a friend where you were going, and they'll call the authorities if you go missing."

Marvin squirmed in his chair, glancing at a large black spider that sat on the table, unmoving. "No, I did something more ... drastic. I have an automated post that will go out on Facebook, Twitter, Pinterest, Tumblr, Reddit, Google+, and every other social media website— including the undead ones like Myspace. The post gives explicit directions on how to find you and where you are now." He nudged the smartphone on the table in front of him. Pointing to a toothy icon on his screen, he said, "Heck, there's even an app for that."

Vlad waved his hand in dismissal, though he was uneasy. "That would only bring a convenient meal for me. I should thank you for arranging breakfast in bed, or casket, as the case may be."

It was Marvin's turn to lean across the small table. "Oh, it's far, far worse than that, sir." He looked into the vampire's red-rimmed eyes and whispered, "Unless you do as I demand, the post will tell everyone that you *sparkle when you sleep!*"

If it was possible for Vlad to look paler than his normal self, he hit a new level of waxy pallor. "You wouldn't dare!"

Marvin flipped the spider over on the table. It had a stamp that said *made in China*. The spider web was nothing but fake Halloween-store cotton strands. Looking around, Marvin indicated all of the faux spooky objects in the coffin chamber. "For you, it's all about appearances, Mr. Dracul. I know that about you, and that's why the sparkly vampire defense is my endgame."

Vladimir sat stiffly in his chair, breathing heavily at the thought of being chased by every pre-pubescent young lady and their mothers, no matter where he hid. "What ... what do you want from me? You wish me to turn you into an immortal vampire?"

"No, nothing like that." Marvin bent over, reached into his backpack, and produced an enormous stack of dog-eared papers. "Your words inspired me to become a writer. I want you to be my literary mentor." He slid the manuscript across the table. It was titled *The Ears of Argon*, Volume 1 of the "Body Parts of Argon Saga."

Vlad was appalled. "Read amateur manuscripts? I'd rather die—and I have done that already."

"More than that, sir. Let me cowrite a short story with you for my favorite humorous speculative fiction anthology series." Marvin's voice had an edge. "Either you can help me make my *prose* sparkle, or ..."

The vampire shuddered uncontrollably. "You're insane!" He saw with dismay that the manuscript was marked as Part One of Volume 1. The title was in all caps, Old English letters. Marvin's backpack had even larger stacks of paper inside.

Marvin leaned back, looking at him eagerly. "Go on, start reading. I'll sit here quietly, I promise. I just want to watch your reactions."

Vlad picked up the first page, dreading that even an immortal lifespan would not be long enough ... but he would do anything —*anything*—to stop that message from going out.

TIME ZONE

I had just gotten home from work, ready to start dinner for myself, when the phone rang. It wasn't even 5:30 yet, but the dinner hour is exactly when phone solicitors like to prey on customers. I answered with a "Hello" that was more like a sigh.

"Ronnie! Are you all right? We're so worried!" Not a salesman, then —my parents, back in Wisconsin.

I had moved to California only a month ago, and my parents seemed as lonely as I was. They often called just to hear my voice.

Right after college I had taken a job for a large company in the San Francisco area. I was a young man living on my own for the first time, far from home. My fiancée would follow me in six months, but for now I was solo, except for babysitting her dog, a fat and snorting pug named Beau that she loved for reasons more unfathomable than the reasons why she loved me. Beau greeted me now with far more exuberance than I wanted, demanding attention while I concentrated on the phone.

"Of course, I'm all right. I just walked in the door from work. Did you forget about the time change again? I'm not usually home this early." My parents lived in rural Wisconsin, had never traveled farther than the adjacent states, and certainly never left the country. Their business was local, never had to worry about calling New York or Los Angeles. "You're two hours earlier, remember?"

"No, the earthquake!" my mom said. "It's been on the news non-stop."

My dad broke in, talking on the extension. "A major quake. San

Francisco is leveled. We couldn't get through—the phone lines have been jammed for more than an hour, but we tried and tried."

I looked around my intact townhouse. "Everything's normal. No earthquake."

Beau snorted and farted, wagged his tail so forcefully that his entire body wobbled. I bent over to pat him on the head, hard.

"We're watching the report on Fox right now," my dad said. "Total devastation. We thought you were hurt. We couldn't get through."

I thought about fake news. My parents have often been duped. "No quake, honest. Not even a little devastation."

My mom was crying. My dad was tense. "I'm reading the crawl right now! Magnitude 6.0 earthquake hit the East Bay at 5:35 pm."

I looked at the clock on the wall. "It's not even 5:35 yet. You're forgetting the time change again. You're two hours ahead."

At my feet, Beau whined and then began barking, much more agitated than his usual excitement about my lukewarm affections. Then he began to howl.

"I'm so glad." Mom's voice still sounded strangled with disbelief. "I don't know how to explain it."

I tried to shush the dog, but Beau was going crazy.

"Nothing to worry about, Mom." I wondered what other crackpot conspiracy theory would set them off next.

The clock hit 5:35.

The ground started to shake beneath my feet.

DARK CARBUNCLE
(WITH JANIS IAN)

A graveyard. Night. Lurid branches scrabble across the blood-red moon. Silence, whispers, then a hush of anticipation. Fifteen boom boxes encircle a grave. Giant woofers (removed just that morning from an unsuspecting car) sit with bass ends flat against the massive gravestone.

Here at peace at last lies Thor
Troubled by the Dark no more

The four aging fans in attendance for the midnight show—the ritual —had polished their studs, mangled their hair, added dye where needed and bleach where not. They wore their finest black leather, but left the jackets open to expose too-small T-shirts from concerts past, fabric memories that paid homage to their hero's mind-blowing shows, when he'd been alive. *Thor.* The writer of the greatest song in the history of mankind.

"Man, we really should have put a line from 'Dark Carbuncle' on his tombstone instead," Conk said. "I mean, so everybody could see his genius for all eternity." His given name was William, and he went by the handle of "William the Conqueror" from some impressive historical guy, though most of his friends didn't get it. They thought "Conk" just meant he liked to bash things.

"Anybody can hear his *genius* just by playing the song, shithead," said Kutfist, ending with the sharp sneer he'd practiced all week. "Trust me, we didn't want to deal with the rights issues."

"Yeah, but dude, 'Dark Carbuncle' is an awesome song, right?" said Dredd, and though he'd said it many times before, nobody disagreed. Especially not on this night of nights.

The lone girl in the group, swaying to the music of a silent song, twisted a lock of hair around her finger. "Kinda creepy, ya think?" Despite the spider web tattooed on her chin, Longshanks was always the first to back away from anything remotely disturbing. "I mean, we're *raising him from the dead....*" Her voice trailed off.

"God, lighten up, 'Shanks. You've been this way since grade school. What can he do to us? He'll be in our power." Sneering, Kutfist turned toward the others with a shrug. Women. Jeez.

"Yeah, and 'Dark Carbuncle' is such an awesome song ..." Dredd's usual sentence trailed off as a cloud covered the moon.

"It has to be tonight, on the anniversary," said Conk with finality as he connected the last of the speakers. The Wikipedia entry had been very specific on that point.

Kutfist scanned the graveyard in disappointment. "I can't believe we're the only ones here. Elvis gets *tons* of fans on his Death Day every year!"

"Elvis fans don't know that 'Dark Carbuncle' is an awesome song," Dredd assured him. "Or they'd be here."

Longshanks tugged harder on her hair. "And what's he gonna look like with a fractured skull, Kut? I mean, part of his head might be gone. Ecchhh."

Kutfist pushed his trifocals further up his nose. "Shut up, 'Shanks. The man was a *god*. That last show we saw was *unbelievably amazing*. He'd never have killed himself, never. We can finally find out the truth now, so just stop worrying and shut up."

Nodding, Conk stood up. Brushing leaves off his hands, he pulled a few folded sheets from the back pocket of his jeans and handed them each a paper with the lyric printed backwards phonetically. That was the worrisome part. They knew the lyrics forward well enough to sing them the required seven times, but the backwards part made Conk nervous. "We've gotta get it right, or we'll end up raising Frank Sinatra or something. Seriously, you can't be too careful with the Dark Side. Don't screw it up."

With tears in his eyes and excitement in his heart, he reached down to the nearest boom box and pushed PLAY.

Thor opened what was left of his eyes and knew he wasn't in the Ritz. It had been a long time since he'd stayed in high-class hotels on tour, and now suddenly he experienced a flashback rush of the last images he remembered.

A motel room, after the show, his ears still ringing from feedback and amps turned up to eleven. Used to be his ears would ring from the screaming fans ... used to be all-night parties, used to be groupies and sex—but the groupies were not as attractive now, and Viagra could only do so much. Ditto the gigs, no more backstage excitement when Mick visited, no more telling the roadie to bring the chick from row five back to the luxe hotel. Now, a gig was just a gig, something to get through until he figured out what to do with the rest of his life.

He hadn't slept a full night in months—years—and now somebody was playing that damned song so loud it echoed right through the walls of this fleabag purgatory of a room. Where the hell was this?

Thorton Velbiss—Thorny to his friends (not many of those), Thor to his fans (not many of those either)—was not having a good day. First, that pounding bass drum was unacceptable. The only noise he wanted to hear with this kind of hangover was the sound of vodka over ice. Second, his fucking hit record from two decades ago was playing, with the bass booming so wide he could swear the damned thing was sitting on his face. The only time Thor would tolerate listening to "Dark Carbuncle" was on stage, during a show, when he lip-synched his way through it for an audience of haphazardly fat metalheads bent on reliving their youth.

I was ferocious back then, ya know? Really fero. And taller, I think. Maybe just skinny. Now I have to wear a corset. Still, I had a hell of a good run. Just one hit, but it kept me in chicks and booze....

Fuck, no, it's a horrible song. Piece of shit me and Dirk the Drummer whipped up one night while we were wanking off. Farthest wank got to title the song. He won.

I hate that fucking song.

'Sides, I can't hit that high note, never could. Brought a ringer into the studio, never thought it'd be a hit. We had great shit on the album, great shit ... and all anybody ever wants to hear is "Dark dark dark. Dark dark dark. Dark dark dark, I'm a da-da-da-da-carbuncle."

Makes you want to puke.

Gotta lip-synch it now anyway, can't even hit the low notes. At least I remember the words. Stupid effing words—even I don't know what they mean. Last time I saw the big El, Scotty Moore had to hand him the lyrics to "Love Me Tender." Speaking of hand ... Hand me that vodka, wouldya?

He'd forgotten there wasn't anybody here. What the hell, he'd serve himself.

He'd been an altar boy in his youth, a good little Catholic, though that was part of his own secret past. The headbangers would never understand it. He hadn't prayed in ... what? Thirty years? Not since he'd picked up a Les Paul, plugged it in, and let wail.

Now, as he felt around for the bottle, trying to shake the cobwebs out of his head, he wondered who'd have the nerve to play that scrotum of a song right on top of his room. *Boom boom boom.* Trying to shut out the sound, he drifted back to the last gig.

It was like reliving a nightmare over and over again, singing that song every night. His agent said this tour could maybe revive his career (but then, he always said that)—opening for some fifteen-year-old one-hit wonder. At least if there was any justice in the world, it *should* have been one hit, but the kid was coming off his fourth top ten record. Turned out he was a metal fan, though, and loved "Dark Carbuncle" (and wasn't *that* embarrassing) and demanded Thor as his opener (though what his Top 40 demographic would make of it, only God knew).

Thor had checked into the motel under a fake name, just in case anybody noticed. Grabbed a quick nap (not that the fans needed to know about that either!), packed his crotch, hit the lobby. Out by the kid's tour bus, a few rabid Thor fans began jumping up and down, one paunchy guy with dreadlocks yelling "Dude! Dude! 'Dark Carbuncle' is an awesome song!" Thor stopped to see if they wanted autographs and noticed two wore pizza delivery uniforms.

"How should I make this out?" he asked a girl with a weird chin tattoo. Glancing at her nametag, he hazarded a guess. "To Tiffany?"

The girl went beet red. "Uh, no, *Longshanks*—just make it to Longshanks."

He smiled inwardly, but outwardly gave her the long, slow, *I could change your life, babe!* look. She brightened and giggled at her friends. At least he'd made *somebody's* day.

On to the show, which sucked. Of course. How the hell can anyone play music at two in the afternoon, under a wide-open sky, looking out at a bunch of hayseeds whose big weekend excitement was probably going to be the pig race? Real waste of Oreos, that one. He sped through the set, not even bothering with the pyro at the end, sneering when people applauded the opening chords of "Carbuncle." Idiots.

I used to dream about being a Beatle, you know? Back in the day, I played the Garden. Twice. Well, only once as the lead act, but still. Alice Cooper, Ozzie, Rob Zombie, they had nothing on me. Eating a live bat, hell—I used to shove worms up my nose, just to line the coke! Now look at me ... playing some friggin' rodeo for a hundred bucks. Pathetic, that's what it is.

Why couldn't I have died young, in a private plane crash? At least that would be a respectable ending.

Afterward, back at the motel—still daylight out!—he drank most of the quart of Stoli that Mr. Four-Hit-Wonderkid had nervously presented him at sound check. Scratching at his empty stomach, Thor decided to surf the vending machines for dinner. Peanut butter cups and a vodka chaser, the perfect road meal.

He barely registered the Muzak droning through the elevator speakers, until he caught himself humming along. Son of a bitch! Bland whiter-than-white harmonies accompanied by easy-listening strings. *Dark dark dark. Dark dark dark. I'm a da-da-da-da-carbuncle, hiding in the dark.* Unbelievable. His song. That frigging publisher had sold him out, turned him into effing elevator music, music for supermarkets and dentist's chairs. Fucking asshole. And his agent was probably in on it, too. Scum, they were all scum.

He'd show them. If he couldn't die young, at least he could die tragic. "Dark Carbuncle" as elevator music—the last straw of all last straws.

Thor stormed back to his room and grabbed the .38 he always carried. Flopping backwards on the bed, he spun the cylinder—five bullets, one empty chamber. Go out like a man, yeah, playing Russian Roulette. They'd all be sorry then, even those stupid pizza-parlor rejects. Barrel to the head, *click click* and it's over. Jimi, Kurt, make way for the next dead rock legend.

Thor raised the gun. Winced at the cold feel of metal against skin. Paused. Squeezed.

Click.

Click? A barrel loaded with Super-X 500 hollow points, and all it can do is go *click?* Unbe-fucking-lievable.

He tried again.

Click.

Hell, how could you *lose* at Russian Roulette? He hurled the gun across the room, where it skittered to a halt on the bathroom floor. Throwing his legs over the bed, Thor grabbed the vodka, took a long slow drag, and made his way to the bathroom, where he somehow managed to drop the bottle on his toe. Yelling out loud, he jumped—and landed barefooted on the gun, which spun crazily against the tiles while he fell backward.

Sickening crack of his head against the tub. He lay on the cold, hard floor, feeling his life ebb away. Frigging humiliating way to die ... for both a former choirboy and a former rock star.

On the other hand, maybe God wouldn't consider this a suicide. Good news. His last thought was that he'd finally be able to get some effing sleep. Safe in the arms of the afterlife.

Until some fuckheads called him back for an encore....

※

Graveyard, night, big speakers booming, a familiar chorus sung again and again with enthusiasm, if not harmony.

> *Mmm, I ain't no spoonful*
> *Baby I'm a mouth-full*
> *and I'm gonna tumble,*
> *rumble crumble tumble*
> *your Dark Carbuncle*
> *Dark Carbuncle*

Conk, Kutfist, Longshanks, and Dredd sang the beloved words seven times seven (almost as many times as in the actual song), and three times more backward, until they were hoarse with it. Conk finally signaled the end of the ritual by switching off the boom boxes. They reeled in the sudden hush, breathing heavily.

"How long is it supposed to take?" Longshanks whispered.

"Give him a few minutes." Conk tried not to sound uncertain. The Wikipedia entry had been unclear on that point. "He's coming all the way back from the dead."

Kutfist sneered. "He never started the concerts on time either."

"Yeah, I loved waiting for 'Dark Carbuncle.' What an awesome song," said Dredd. No one disagreed.

Suddenly, the earth began to tremble, and something stirred beneath the leaves. The ostentatious tombstone they'd banded together and paid for all those years ago pulled loose and tumbled backwards, leaving a gaping hole.

Five grime-encrusted fingers pushed through the soil, followed by a hand, then another, clawing at the dirt in slow motion. Finally, a body heaved itself out of the grave. Covered in dirt, putrid clothes, and rotting skin, Thor raised himself up and tried to wipe the crust from his eyes.

The four fans cheered, whistled, and applauded as he swayed. "Omigod, it's him, it's really him!" Conk dropped the papers and stared. What a Wiki entry *this* would make!

Longshanks was jumping up and down. "He looks just like he did on the *Avenger's Revenge* tour!"

"He's staggering like he did on that tour, too," Kutfist said, without the sneer this time. He looked nervously around. "C'mon, gotta get him to the van."

The undead rock star lurched and shambled, looking disoriented but not entirely out of character. "Come on, Thor!" Longshanks pleaded. She lifted up her T-shirt to flash her breasts; Thor had never noticed her when she'd done it at concerts, but this time he shuffled toward her, making moaning, sucking sounds from deep in his throat.

"Hurry up, get him into the van!" Conk said in an urgent whisper. "Before some other fans show up. He's ours!"

"Wait! We can't leave the speakers—I borrowed them from my uncle's catering company," Kutfist said. "He's got a Bar Mitzvah tomorrow, he'll kill me!" Fortunately, since Thor was having a hard time orienting himself toward a vertical life, they had plenty of time to retrieve the gear and pack it into the pizza van they'd "borrowed" from work.

Conk started the engine while Kutfist and Dredd turned in their seats to stare at Thor, who was crammed into the third-row seat with Longshanks. "Now he's with his true fans!" She sniffed, then frowned. "Is he supposed to smell this bad?"

"I think that's just an old pizza I forgot to deliver last week," Conk said.

As the van careened out of the cemetery, Dredd leaned over the seat and said earnestly, "Dude, 'Dark Carbuncle' is an awesome song!" He extended his hand, then thought better of it and withdrew.

They jabbered excitedly as they headed off to Conk's garage. "I'm gonna have him teach me guitar. We could do some killer riffs together!"

"I want him to sign some autographs—impress my girlfriend for sure," Kutfist said. "Hmm, maybe even sell them online."

Longshanks tentatively nudged one of the scraps dangling off Thor's ruined face. "Hey, we could sell pieces of his skin. Talk about a real collector's item!"

Kutfist returned to the sneer. "What are you thinking? Anybody who'd buy Thor's skin could clone him—then we won't have the only one."

Longshanks dropped her gaze. "Well, we'd still have the original. A clone is no better than ... a cover band."

"How about we just sell locks of hair?" Conk suggested. He didn't want them to argue during this ultimate moment of fannish glory.

As the van pulled up to the two-car garage, the undead legend seemed to be getting his bearings, croaking slightly more comprehensible words. "What ... happened? Where am I?"

"You're with us—your real fans!"

Parking in the dark garage, they opened the doors and helped Thor out of the van. Conk hit the button and closed the garage door, then triumphantly switched on the lights to reveal the setup waiting for them in the other parking space—a small stage, microphone, boom box, and guitar.

Herding Thor forward, Kutfist shouted, "We brought you back from the grave for this, dude!"

Thor automatically stepped onto the stage and into the light, then stared at them in confusion. Longshanks sprang onto the stage beside him and shoved the guitar into his hands. "Omigod, Thor—now you can sing 'Dark Carbuncle' for us, night after night after night!"

Thorton Velbiss fell to his knees and screamed.

※

Surely this was Hell. Surely.

When he'd emerged from the darkness, he'd wondered what the fuck was going on. Why was he covered in dirt? Some super-extravagant part of the stage show he couldn't recall?

Then he remembered, and now he knew exactly what had happened. This was truly eternal punishment. Every bit of his Catholic upbringing rose in his throat—the priests' lectures, the nuns' scoldings, the fear of damnation. It was too much for any man, let alone a dead one.

Rotting ligaments snapped as he dropped to his knees and began to cry. For the first time in years he prayed, and for the first time in his life he really meant it. He confessed, he repented, he begged forgiveness. He reminded God of his years as an altar boy, how he'd been in the soprano choir until his voice had changed. He also pointed out that, technically —though God seemed to have overlooked the detail—he hadn't committed suicide and didn't deserve damnation. It was merely an unfortunate accident.

"Just please get me out of here! I want to go to Heaven. I'll do whatever you say, you won't regret it! Please!" He put more soul into the request than he'd ever spent on one of his stage performances, but even Thor was surprised when the cluttered garage and tiny group of fans swirled away into mist.

※

The new place was bright and shining, filled with sunlight and rainbows. He saw smiling beings in white robes with wings gathered on a nearby cloud, and an impressive, bearded man on a gleaming golden throne in front of him.

Holy shit, exactly the pictures the priests had painted, down to the last cliché! Choking back tears, Thor knelt before Him.

"Welcome Thorton Velbiss, my wayward son." The Almighty smiled with a warmth that made Thor tremble. "I am so glad you are finally among us. We have prepared a heavenly reception for you."

Thor could only stammer, "Thank you, thank you, Lord!" He didn't know what else to say. Everything was so ... clean. So ... cheerful.

"Rise, my son. Rise, and greet your Father."

Thor rose and moved toward the throne.

"Later, there will be manna, and angel food cake," God promised, patting him on the shoulder. "But first, I have a small request."

God seemed almost shy as he said it, and Thor thought *I could really like this guy*. "Anything, Your Omnipotence. *Um*, Your Magnificence. Anything you want, just name it!"

Taking him by both shoulders, the Lord turned him toward the nearby cloud, where the choir of angels suddenly pulled back their wings, revealing the electric guitars they wore. One sat behind a drum kit.

Snapping His fingers, God materialized a 1959 custom Les Paul and held it out to Thor. "Play 'Dark Carbuncle' for us, my son. I have always loved that song."

Thor fell to his knees, screaming.

TEA TIME BEFORE PERSEUS

The lonely Medusa sat inside her ever-growing statue garden. She waited for more company to arrive, hoping that today there might be a chance for some conversation.

SANTA CLAUS IS COMING TO GET YOU

'Twas the night before the night before Christmas, and all through the house little sounds were stirring ... creeping, whispers of noise, echoes of things better left unseen in the darkness, even around the holiday season.

Jeff stared up at the bottom of his little brother's bunk. Ever since Stevie had gotten rid of the night light, he always feared that the upper bunk would fall on top of him and squish him flat.

A strong gust of wind rattled the windowpane. Wet snow brushing against it sounded like the hiss of a deadly snake, but he could hear that his brother was not asleep. "Stevie? I thought of something about Christmas."

"What?" The voice was muffled by Stevie's ratty blue blanket.

"Well, Santa keeps a list of who's naughty and nice, right? So, what does he do to the kids who've been naughty?" He didn't know why he asked Stevie. Stevie wouldn't know.

"They don't get any presents I guess.... Do you really think Mom and Dad are that mad at us?"

Jeff sucked in a breath. "We were playing with matches, Stevie! We could have burned the house down—you heard them say that. Imagine if we burned the house down ... Besides, it doesn't matter if Mom and Dad are angry. What'll Santa think?"

Jeff swallowed. He had to get the ideas out of his head. "I gotta tell you this, Stevie, because it's important. Something a kid told me at school.

"He said that it isn't Santa who puts presents out when you're good.

It's just your Mom and Dad. They wait until you go to sleep, and then they sneak out some presents. It's all pretend."

"Oh, come on!"

"Think about it. Your parents are the ones who know what you really want." He pushed on in a whisper. "What if Santa only comes when you're bad?"

"But we said we were sorry! And ... and it wasn't my idea—it was yours. And nothing got hurt."

Jeff closed his eyes so he wouldn't see the bottom of the upper bunk. "I think Santa looks for naughty little boys and girls. That's why he comes around on Christmas Eve.

"He sneaks down the chimney, and he carries an empty sack with him. And when he knows he's in a house where there's a naughty kid, he goes into their bedroom and grabs them, and stuffs them in the sack! Then he pushes them up the chimney and throws the bag in the back of his sleigh with all the other naughty little boys and girls. And then he takes them back up north where it's always cold and where the wind always blows—and there's nothing to eat."

Jeff's eyes sparkled from hot tears. He thought he heard Stevie shivering above him.

"What kind of food do you think Santa gets up there at the North Pole? How does Santa stay so fat? I bet all year long he keeps the naughty kids he's taken the Christmas before and he eats them! He keeps them locked up in icicle cages ... and on special days like on his birthday or on Thanksgiving, he takes an extra fat kid and he roasts him over a fire! That's what happens to bad kids on Christmas Eve."

Jeff heard a muffled sob in the upper bunk. He saw the support slats vibrate. "No, it's not true. We weren't that bad. I'm sorry. We won't do it again."

Jeff closed his eyes. "You better watch out, Stevie, you better not cry. 'Cause Santa Claus is coming to get you!"

He heard Stevie sucking on the corner of his blanket to keep from crying. "We can hide."

Jeff shook his head in despair. "No. He sees you when you're sleeping, and he knows when you're awake. We can't escape from him!"

"How about if we lock the bedroom door?"

"That won't stop Santa Claus! You know how big he is from eating all those little kids. And he's probably got some of his evil little elves to help him."

He listened to Stevie crying in the sheets. He listened to the wind. "We're gonna have to trick him. We have to get Santa before he gets us!"

SANTA CLAUS IS COMING TO GET YOU

☙

On Christmas Eve, Dad turned on the Christmas tree lights and hung out the empty stockings by the fireplace. He grinned at the boys who stared red-eyed in fear.

"You guys look like you're so excited you haven't been able to sleep. Better go on to bed—it's Christmas tomorrow, and you've got a long night ahead of you." He smiled at them. "Don't forget to put out milk and cookies for Santa."

Mom scowled at them. "You boys know how naughty you were. I wouldn't expect too many presents from Santa this year."

Jeff felt his heart stop. He swallowed and tried to keep anything from showing on his face. Stevie shivered.

"Oh, come on, Janet. It's Christmas Eve," Dad said.

Jeff and Stevie slowly brought out the glass of milk and a plate with four Oreo cookies they had made up earlier. Stevie was so scared he almost dropped the glass.

They had poured strychnine pellets into the milk and put rat poison in the frosting of the Oreos.

"Go on boys, good night. And don't get up too early tomorrow," Dad said.

The two boys marched off to their room, heads down. Visions of Santa's blood danced in their heads.

☙

Jeff lay awake for hours, sweating and shivering. He and Stevie didn't need to say anything to each other. After Mom and Dad went to bed, the boys listened for any sound from the roof, from the chimney.

He pictured Santa Claus heaving himself out from the fireplace, pushing aside the grate and stepping out into the living room. His eyes were red and wild, his fingers long claws, his beard tangled and stained with the meal he'd had before setting out in his sleigh—perhaps the last two children from the year before, now scrawny and starved. He would have snapped them up like crackers.

And now Santa was hungry for more, a new batch to restock his freezer that was as big as the whole North Pole.

Santa would take a crinkled piece of paper out of his pocket to look at it, and yes, there under the "Naughty" column, would be the names of Jeff and Stevie in all capital letters. He'd wipe the list on his blood-red coat.

His black belt was shiny and wicked looking, with the silver buckle and its pointed corners razor-sharp to slash the throats of children. And over his shoulder hung a brown burlap sack stained with rusty splotches.

Then Santa would go to their bedroom. Jeff and Stevie could struggle against him, they could throw their blankets on him, hit him with their pillows and their toys—but Santa Claus was stronger than that. He would reach up first to snatch Stevie from the top bunk and stuff him in the sack.

And then Santa would lunge forward with fingers grayish blue from frostbite. He'd wrap his hand around Jeff's throat and draw him toward the sack....

Then Santa would haul them up through the chimney to the roof. Maybe he would toss one of them toward the waiting reindeer who snorted and stomped their hooves on the ice-covered shingles. And the reindeer, playing all their reindeer games, would toss the boy from sharp antler to sharp antler.

All the while, Santa stood leaning back, glaring, and belching forth his maniacal "Ho! Ho! Ho!"

❧

Jeff didn't know when his terror dissolved into fitful nightmares, but he found himself awake and alive the next morning.

"Stevie!" he whispered. He was afraid to look in the pale light of dawn, half expecting to find blood running down the wall from the upper bunk. "Stevie, wake up!"

Jeff heard a sharp indrawn breath. "Jeff! Santa didn't get us."

They both started laughing. "Come on, let's go see."

They tumbled out of bed, then spent ten minutes dismantling the barricade of toys and small furniture they had placed in front of the door. The house remained still and quiet around them. Nothing was stirring, not even a mouse.

Jeff glanced at the dining room table as they crept into the living room. The cookies were gone. The milk glass had been drained dry.

Jeff looked for a contorted red-suited form lying in the corner—but he saw nothing. The Christmas tree lights blinked on and off; Mom and Dad had left them on all night.

Stevie crept to the Christmas tree and looked. His face turned white as he pulled out several new gift-wrapped boxes. All marked "FROM SANTA."

"Oh, Jeff! Oh, Jeff—you were wrong! What if we killed Santa!"

They both gawked at the presents.

"Jeff, Santa took the poison!"

Jeff swallowed and stood up. Tears filled his eyes. "We have to be brave, Stevie." He nodded. "We better go tell Mom and Dad." He shuddered, then screwed up his courage.

"Let's go wake them up."

COLD DEAD TURKEY
A DAN SHAMBLE, ZOMBIE P.I. ADVENTURE

When an Aztec mummy stopped me on the streets of the Unnatural Quarter, I knew it had to be an important problem. "Excuse me, are you Dan Shamble? Zombie P.I.?"

"*Chambeaux*," I corrected automatically, because so many people—both naturals and unnaturals—make the mistake. "But yes, that's me—of Chambeaux & Deyer Investigations."

The day was bright and sunny, and we had paused under a street light where two precariously balanced werewolves were stringing holiday lights. One mockingly dangled a fistful of mistletoe over the other, demanding a kiss. The second werewolf said, "Not with your ugly furry muzzle!"

Across the street, a skeleton lounged with a saxophone against another lamppost, ready to play a mournful holiday tune, but it was all for show because the skeleton wasn't a very effective sax player, due to his lack of lungs. Skeleton musicians usually stick to playing the piano.

The Aztec mummy was withered and shriveled. The remnants of his raisin-like eyes were set deeply into hollows in his face. He hobbled along, his back bent, his knees of the extra-knobby variety. His clothes were gaudy and colorful, the finest Aztec chic. He extended a gnarled hand, and I shook it, careful not to break any bones. Mummies can be so brittle, and most refuse to be rehydrated as a matter of pride.

"How can I help you, Mr.—?"

The mummy cleared his throat, and a small moth fluttered out. "Kashewpetl." I realized it was his Aztec name rather than a head cold. "And I need you to track down my turkey. A special *wish turkey*." He leaned forward, and his intent raisin eyes transfixed me. "I need to have it by Christmas."

"That's the day after tomorrow," I said.

"I know! We better hurry."

We walked past an auto repair shop where two vampires were placing a large inflatable snowman in front of a sign that said: "Special Holiday Blowout Tire Sale!"

"I'm happy to hear your case, Mr. Kashewpetl." It would certainly be better than my early morning duties.

I had just finished delivering a little holiday cheer—serving divorce papers to a recently separated reptile-demon couple. Due to financial circumstances, they were forced to cohabitate their single-family lair apartment, and the male reptile demon had hired Chambeaux & Deyer to take care of the paperwork. Robin had filed the correct forms, and I had to present the papers to the soon-to-be-ex-wife-demon. A formality, but it wasn't one of my happiest duties.

The female reptile demon answered the door and took one look at my gray skin, my Fedora tilted down so that it mostly covered the bullet hole in my forehead. I tried to smile, but she curled back scaly lips to expose needle-like teeth. "What do you want? We're not buying." Her forked tongue flicked in and out.

"I assure you there's absolutely no charge," I said. "Mrs. Algotha? Frieda Algotha?"

A big, lumbering, scaly male demon lurked in the hall. "Who is it?"

"Some zombie selling subscriptions."

"Not selling." I handed her the paperwork. "Just serving."

That was when she really went into a hissy fit, snapping and snarling, and her husband—our client—snarled just as loudly back at her. Their scaly tails lashed, smashing into the wall, cracking the plaster, knocking down knickknacks. Then the demons began blaming each other, and Frieda Algotha stormed off to lock herself in a room. "My mother always told me I should have married Bill!"

I stood there awkwardly, wanting very much to be in some different kind of hell. The big, ferocious crocodile guy sulked in the foyer. "I had to do it, Mr. Chambeaux," he said, as if I were his bartender. He wore a big frown on jaws that looked powerful enough to snap a Volkswagen in two. "Christmas is always rough on cold-blooded creatures. This one's going to be worse than usual." He closed the door on me.

Give me a good murder (or re-murder) case, a missing creatures problem, a stolen items recovery any day. I hated divorce cases. I hoped the Aztec mummy had something a lot more interesting for me....

"Would you like to meet me back at our offices? I can set up an appointment." Sheyenne, my beautiful ghost girlfriend, is our office manager and organizes all of our paperwork. My human lawyer partner, Robin Deyer, has a caseload as large as mine.

When all the bizarre supernatural creatures returned to the world more than a decade ago during the unexpected cosmic event of the Big Uneasy, there had been quite an uproar until all the monsters settled into a semblance of normal life in the Unnatural Quarter. Everybody—naturals and unnaturals—just wanted to get through the days, and nights, as best they could, and even the unnaturals experienced as many everyday problems as regular people did. From our main offices, Robin took care of their legal needs, and I was handy whenever somebody needed a detective. A zombie detective.

"I would rather talk to you right now," the mummy rasped. "Time is of the essence." He indicated a sign in a clothing shop with giant painted letters touting: "Christmas Countdown! The End of the Sale Is Near!" He set off. "Let's walk."

Because his back was hunched, and his legs so bent, he moved with an exaggerated oscillating gait. "Are you sure?" I nodded to his stiff joints.

"It's just the way I was made. Aztec mummies are bound up and preserved in a sitting position. Unlike those uppity Egyptian mummies, we're *naturally* dried, not wrapped up in linens, and we're buried in a cloth sack instead of stuffy sarcophagi and fancy tombs. Who needs a pyramid, anyway? And nobody scooped *my* brain out through my nose. It's still perfectly intact, thank you."

I could see I had struck a nerve, so I changed the subject. "Tell me about your turkey."

We passed a group of banshee Christmas carolers who sang their hearts out, and all the nearby plate glass windows trembled in fear.

"Right, let me explain. I needed the wish turkey to get my favorite sled back," said Kashewpetl, an explanation that did not serve the purpose of explaining anything.

"Your favorite missing sled?" I asked.

"My precious toy from when I was a boy. Ah, the good times I had, the perfect sled, constructed with the best jungle materials—the finest sled in the whole Yucatan! My cousins and I would climb the slopes of Popocatepetl, one of the largest volcanoes in Central America—seventeen thousand feet high! Great powder on the snow slopes, at least when Popocatepetl wasn't erupting lava."

The mummy let out a desiccated sigh. "Those were the best days of my life, innocent times, perfect days when my parents and I would go see the ritual temple sacrifice, when we kids would run through the jungle and play Dodge the Jaguar ... when I had my first love—a girlfriend so special that I still remember her even a thousand years later."

Another long sigh. This time, two moths came out of his lungs. "Sweet, beautiful Suzitoq. We used to sled together. I'd put her in front of me, and we'd slide down the treacherous ice slopes. When we got to the bottom, I would steal a kiss. Good times!" Then he grew much more somber. "Then she went sledding with one of my rivals, Burtputl, but he used a far inferior sled and it broke. Suzitoq tumbled over a cliff." He hung his shriveled head. "I never forgave Burtputl."

We passed a small stand where a saggy-faced ghoul was selling gray snow cones. I asked the mummy if he wanted one—he was my client, after all—but he shook his head and continued his story.

"Suzitoq is long dead now, but I kept that sled for the rest of my life as a reminder of those golden days. I never married, became a bitter old man—I admit it. I saved enough money so that I could be thoroughly mummified. But after I died, Burtputl stole my sled, and it's been lost all these centuries. He probably wrecked it." Kashewpetl snorted. "I'd do anything to have it back. That's why I need your help, Mr. Chambeaux."

"What does that have to do with a missing turkey?"

"Not just any turkey," said Kashewpetl. "A *wish* turkey."

That must be a key part to the case. "So what's a wish turkey?"

"A special turkey that I raised from a chick. The Chosen One. I tattooed arcane symbols on its hide, tied special amulets to its feet to infuse the bird with the most potent Aztec magic. I pampered it, fattened it, even brought beautiful lady turkeys to his cage. It was necessary to give my wish turkey the most hedonistic lifestyle a turkey could want, considering what was to happen to him."

I bought one of the brown snow cones from the ghoul vendor. I would rather have had a beer at the Goblin Tavern after work—and I intended to do so anyway—but for now I sucked on the dirty ice of the cone. "And what was going to happen to him?"

"Ritual sacrifice," said Kashewpetl.

Of course.

"The holiday season holds a very special magic, a secret and fuzzy kind of Christmas magic. After I sacrificed my wish turkey, I could cook him up and extract the sacred wishbone. Then, if I cracked the wishbone, I could wish for *anything I wanted*." His shrunken raisin eyes blazed brighter. "I could have what I desired most in the whole world. I could wish for my sled back."

I wondered why he wouldn't simply wish for Suzitoq back, but I doubted the Aztec mummy had thought this through. So, I asked the more compelling question. "What on earth does an Aztec ritual sacrifice have to do with the magic of *Christmas*? The two aren't the least bit connected, on either a cultural or a religious basis."

Kashewpetl raised his arms so quickly I was afraid his elbow joints would snap. "One mustn't question! One mustn't doubt. One mustn't think too hard about it, or the magic fades away. And the magic of the wish turkey wishbone is powerful indeed. Don't diminish it, Mr. Chambeaux."

I slurped on my brown snow cone, spit out a bit of gravel, and metaphorically zipped my lips shut. "It's none of my business, and not part of the case. So tell me what happened. Your turkey's gone missing?"

"Yes, he got out of his cage somehow. I never imagined he could figure it out—turkeys aren't the brightest animals in the menagerie, you know. But I need him back in the next day or two, when the magic is strongest. He's out there somewhere, probably lost and alone and hungry."

"Did your wish turkey suspect what you were going to do to it? Did he know he was about to be sacrificed?" It would have given it the motive to flee.

Kashewpetl gave me a strange look. "There are times when he can't even find his water dish right there in his own cage."

"I see. Well, if you come by the offices later on—" We stepped across the street to get to the other side—I wondered if that was what turkeys did too, and for the same reason. I wasn't watching, and suddenly a delivery truck barreled toward us. The truck driver honked his horn and swerved to avoid hitting us. I leaped to one side as I grabbed the mummy, since his hobbling gait was insufficient for leaping away from large careening vehicles.

The driver was a zombie wearing a trucker's cap and work overalls. "Watch where you're going, idiots!" He screeched to a halt, then leaned out the driver's side window, ready to yell something else, then his face changed. "Dan? Dan Chambeaux? Man, I'm sorry about that."

I recognized Steve Halsted, my "dirt buddy," a zombie who had risen from the grave the same night I did. Recently, Steve had been running deliveries around the Quarter and he sometimes served as a long-haul trucker. "What's your hurry, Steve? Driving that fast, you're going to hit somebody who isn't already dead."

He looked flustered. "Sorry, I'm carrying a load of fresh ripe toadstools, and I've got to deliver them before the spores go bad. On my way!" He peeled off in the truck.

Kashewpetl said, "I'll head back home to keep searching. Here's where you can find me." He wrote his address on a scrap of torn bandage that looked as if it had been ripped from an old Egyptian mummy, maybe out of spite.

"I have to get back to the office, then I'll go file a police report," I said. "We'll find your turkey, Mr. Kashewpetl, and we'll find him before Christmas, I promise."

"Thanks. It just wouldn't be a holiday season without a ritual sacrifice."

※

Sitting at her desk in the Chambeaux & Deyer offices, Sheyenne was positively glowing when she saw me. Ghosts tend to do that. I gave her an air kiss, because that's all we could do—our lips passed right through, but I felt an ectoplasmic thrill regardless. Since I was a zombie, it had been a long time since my heart went pitter-pat, but at least Sheyenne made it go *thud* a little faster.

"Papers served on the Algothas," I said. "Not much Ho-Ho-Ho going on in that house today."

"Sorry, Beaux. Not everybody can have a perfect relationship like us."

"We don't exactly have a perfect relationship, Spooky, considering we can't even touch, or hold hands, or kiss, or do the stuff that happens after the ellipsis dots when the door closes at the end of an old romance novel."

"Being intangible does have its drawbacks," she admitted. She straightened the papers using her poltergeist power and stuffed them in a file. I told Sheyenne about Kashewpetl, and she filled out the paperwork for the intake of the new client, then scolded me for not discussing the appropriate fees. The mummy had looked so intense and distraught that I hadn't had the heart, but I understood it was necessary.

Without Sheyenne keeping us on the commercial straight-and-narrow, Robin would be a sucker for sob stories and do every case as pro bono. She's a bleeding-heart, which is why all the monsters in the Quarter come to her when they have a meaningful case. As a zombie, I was just as relentless as a detective, though a bit colder. Working together, we get the job done, solve the cases, and keep our customers satisfied.

"Robin's with a new client," Sheyenne said, "if you want to meet her."

We run a tight office and know each other's cases, even when my detective work and Robin's legal work don't overlap. I knocked politely before opening her office door; inside, she sat at her desk, facing the new client. Robin's a beautiful young African-American woman from an upper middle-class family. She went to college, got her law degree, but instead of choosing to work for some wealthy corporation, she wanted to help the downtrodden, and there were very few who were more downtrodden than the unnaturals after the turmoil of the Big Uneasy. Here in the Quarter, it seemed that something truly unusual came up every day.

Such as the client sitting across from her right now.

I had never seen a Medusa with flowers in her hair before. The gorgon sat in a chair wearing a hippie peasant dress covered with frilly appliques. She smelled of patchouli mixed with dry reptile. Her hair, which was a nest of serpents, swirled and writhed. I cringed, knowing that Medusas have a penchant for turning people to stone much like their unrelated but just as petrifying counterparts, cockatrices and basilisks.

This Medusa, though, was an obvious peacenik, with a peace symbol pendant hanging down from her scabrous neck. Each one of the serpents was blindfolded with a little yellow ribbon tied around its head. The fanged mouths each bit down over a rosebud, neutralizing the fangs.

I smiled and stepped in. Did I mention that we see these sort of cases every day?

"Hello, Dan!" Robin sat forward in her chair, looking thoroughly unpetrified. On the desk sat a yellow legal pad and an animated pencil that was automatically scribbling notes. The pad and pencil set had been a gift last Christmas, when we'd helped the actual Santa Claus recover his stolen Naughty-and-Nice list. "Meet Saffron, my new client."

The gorgon turned to me, and all of the blindfolded and flower-filled snakes also swiveled in my direction, as if looking for a target. When Saffron smiled, she showed multiple fangs. "Pleased to meet you, Mr. Chambeaux."

I had taken off my Fedora and hung up my sport jacket, and I was ready to help. "Need any zombie detective work?"

"Ms. Saffron is seeking legal advice on some rather pressing but esoteric issues," Robin explained.

The Medusa sounded sweet and somewhat vapid. "What do you think, Mr. Chambeaux? Wouldn't you like world peace, an end to conflict and strife, no more hunger or disease, every single person living a happy life, no more prejudice?"

"I suppose that would be nice." I didn't think she was actually looking for an insightful answer. "Sounds like a pretty long Christmas list."

"All good citizens should wish for those things, and if we pull together, if every one of us helped the poor and the needy, if we just stopped hating one another, the world would be a better place."

"I can't argue with that. But, uh, was there a legal question involved?"

"That's what we're trying to determine," Robin said.

Saffron put her elbows on Robin's desk, and her snakes drifted around as if they were all stoned. "Now, I know that stealing is wrong, but what if you steal with the best of intentions?"

Robin frowned. "The law is the law. You can't just steal things."

"But what if a loved one was dying of a disease and some evil corporation was keeping the cure locked away? Wouldn't I be justified in stealing it, not just for my loved one but for curing the world?"

"I doubt any jury would convict you," Robin said, "but it's still against the law to steal private property."

"And what if a large army had the actual secret to ending wars forever so that no one else has to die in combat, but they keep it locked up because war is big business? Wouldn't I be justified in stealing that secret, giving it to the world, and bringing peace?"

"Your justifications sound convincing," Robin repeated, "but you might still go to jail."

"You don't mess with big business or the military industrial complex," I warned.

When the Medusa sighed, all of her snakes went limp with disappointment. "At least I'd go to prison with a clean conscience." Saffron still wasn't ready to let the problem go, though. "But what if—"

I backed out of the office, knowing that she might ask the perennial question about dancing angels and pinheads. "This one's above my pay grade, but Robin can solve it if anyone can."

I was glad I only had to find a lost turkey.

*

At the UQPD precinct station, I met Officer Toby McGoohan adjusting his cap as he was leaving the station to go on his afternoon rounds. He stopped and saw me, and a grin broadened on his freckled face. "Hey, Shamble. Maybe you can help me with a question."

I knew I was in for trouble. "What, McGoo?"

"If the Zombie Apocalypse happens in Vegas, would it stay in Vegas?"

Yeah, I'd shambled right into that one. McGoo is my BHF, my Best Human Friend. Through bad life choices and just plain dogged persistence, we had both reached for big dreams and successful careers—and we both ended up here, just trying to get by. He'd been on the beat for years; we helped each other on cases; we had always hung out together when I was a living human detective, and we still hung out even after I'd been murdered. It took him awhile to get used to his undead pal, but friendships last longer than rigor mortis.

"Enough jokes, time to get down to business. I need your help, McGoo."

"You need a lot of help," he wisecracked. "Official business? Or something we can talk about over beers tonight?"

"Official police business. I need to file a missing turkey report."

McGoo took it in stride. As I said, unusual cases crop up in the Quarter every day. He led me back to his cubicle and rummaged in his desk drawer. "I think we have a form for that."

It turned out, to my surprise, that half a dozen missing turkeys had been reported in the last week, all across the Quarter. "Is that unusual?" I asked.

He shrugged. "It's the holiday season, and everyone wants a turkey dinner."

"But most grocery store chains have ridiculously cheap sales on holiday turkeys. Why risk jail time instead of just buying one of the five-dollar specials?"

McGoo's eyes narrowed. "Don't try to talk logic when it comes to turkey thieves. They're the worst—take it from me."

McGoo had a small cluttered desk in the main pool, but he rarely spent any time there because he's the sort of cop who likes to be walking his beat, seeing problems with his own eyes—and picking up fodder for more bad jokes. He handed me the sheet. "You're perfectly capable of filling out a missing-turkey form on your own."

"Thanks for the vote of confidence," I said while he amused himself by playing a game of Cockroach Crush on his phone. Sadly, I couldn't actually finish the form. I knew some of the answers: name of owner, date the bird went missing. Under distinguishing marks I wrote down "Aztec ceremonial tattoos marked on hide, charm bangles tied onto feet." But as to the details of the night on which it had gone missing, or even what names the turkey responded to, I was at a loss. I would have to go back to the Aztec mummy to get the final details.

"Get started with this, McGoo." I slid the incomplete form over to him. "I'll come back with more information later today. I've got to see a mummy about a turkey."

Even from halfway down the suburban street it was plain which house belonged to Kashewpetl. It was a modest rambler, but the garage was a ziggurat, a stair-stepped pyramid with a small sacrificial altar on top where the mummy intended to sacrifice his wish turkey on Christmas Eve. Right now the platform had a bird feeder and a wind vane. The mailbox was adorned with Aztec symbols.

Kashewpetl's neighbor, though, was obviously an *Egyptian* mummy, his house built in the shape of a pyramid, the sides sloped to a perfect triangular apex, only two stories high. Considering the slope of the angled ceilings, I doubted that the upstairs or attic would have much usable space.

Not content with pink lawn flamingoes, the Egyptian mummy neighbor had a sphinx in the front yard (though only a small decorative model) and a statue of Anubis. I saw the Egyptian mummy out in the yard holding a garden hose, watering a hedge between his and the Aztec mummy's property.

Being neighborly as he saw me shamble along, he raised a bandaged hand, but when I turned toward the Aztec mummy's door, he looked away in a huff. There seemed to be no love lost between the neighbors.

I knocked on Kashewpetl's door and entered. The Aztec mummy had been sitting in a recliner chair that perfectly accommodated his bent-over posture. "I need a few more details for the missing turkey report, and I'd also like to have a look at the cage, see if we can figure out how it got loose."

Kashewpetl used the remote to switch off the TV. He was obviously a single man who lived alone, someone who dwelled in the past—more than a thousand years of it. On the wall hung the large ornate disk of an Aztec calendar with the words "Today's Date Is ..." The calendar was one of the extended post-2012 holocaust editions with extra dates added. A sticky note marked with festive holly leaves and berries marked *Christmas Day!!!* only two days hence.

Kashewpetl shuffled to the back room. "I gave the turkey his very own bedroom—the master bedroom in fact, nicer than mine."

In the hallway hung two framed pictures, one of an Egyptian pyramid and the other showing a bandaged mummy—both obscured by the circle/slash of the universal No symbol. I frowned at the anti-Egyptian sentiment. "I take it you're not on the best of terms with the pyramid next door?"

The Aztec mummy's face was too desiccated to feature a genuine frown. "We don't see eye socket to eye socket—mainly because he's full of himself and still living in another age. He's uppity, gets his bandages cleaned at a high-priced rewrapping and styling salon, then makes insulting comments that Aztec mummies aren't real mummies, that we're just pretenders, naturally desiccated, with no embalming process." He looked at me. "That's enough reason to hate your neighbor, isn't it?"

"I suppose so," I said. I take a lot of pride in that, keeping my body in shape—which includes regular touch-ups at the embalming parlor—so I don't rot and fall apart like too many of my less-conscientious zombie comrades.

"And his girlfriend is even worse, a total dingbat," Kashewpetl continued. "His name is Eff-Tup. I did some digging in the city records, found out that he wasn't even nobility back in Egypt! That he went through the whole expensive mummification process due to a paperwork error. Eff-Tup was just a traveling papyrus salesman, and now he thinks he owns the Nile." He snorted, making a hollow whistle through his empty nasal cavities. "Once I get my wish turkey back and I have my favorite sled, I'm not going to let him use it. Ever."

I didn't think there were many toboggan hills in the Quarter, but I let the mummy have his dreams.

Inside the turkey's master bedroom, the walls had been strung with Christmas decorations, tinsel, glittering ornaments, a small set of speakers with an MP3 player and Christmas carols playing on a constant loop.

"What are all the festive decorations for?" I asked.

"To celebrate the season, let him feel the holiday cheer. I figured if the turkey was marked for death, I should at least keep him happy. After all, he's granting me my wish to get my favorite present back."

"Do you think the wish turkey felt that he was fulfilling a destiny? That he had a well accomplished life?"

The Aztec mummy's stiff neck tilted forward at an odd angle. "Mr. Chambeaux, no matter what the circumstances, there's really not much more that a standard turkey can hope for."

The cage had a simple hook-and-eye latch that had been popped open to leave the door wide. Inside was a water dish, a food dish, and an expansive bed stuffed with goose down (*Would that bother a turkey?* I wondered.); a postage-stamp-sized picture of Kashewpetl hung on the cage wall. Gold chains and colorful ribbons dangled from the bars for decoration, and a plum-sized, mirrored disco ball hung from the roof. Decadent and hedonistic indeed, if you were a turkey.

I looked at the simple hook and eye, flipping it back and forth with my clumsy fingers. A turkey could easily have knocked it loose. "Are you certain he didn't get out by himself?"

Kashewpetl rolled his tiny shriveled eyes. "Turkeys can drown in a rainstorm because they aren't smart enough to close their beaks when they look up into the pouring rain."

"Just checking all the bases." I raised the other obvious possibility. "Do you think someone stole it?"

"Kidnapped my turkey? Why would anyone do that?"

Sometimes the client doesn't see what's right in front of him. "You said it's a *wish* turkey. Maybe somebody else wanted the wishbone."

He looked horrified. "Oh no! Mr. Chambeaux, we've got to find my turkey before Christmas! If we don't, everyone's holiday will be ruined."

Not the turkey's, I thought.

⁂

Back at the Chambeaux & Deyer offices, late at night before midnight on Christmas Eve, Robin worked through dinner on the convoluted new legal case of the Medusa with a conscience. I needed to call McGoo (for the fifth time) to find out if he had any leads on my lost turkey—or on any of the lost turkeys, because what happened to one gobbler might have happened to another.

We gathered in the conference room to discuss the day's work, partly to exchange information and leads, partly as a support group. "My new client is an Aztec mummy," I said. "He's lost some kind of magical turkey that he thinks will be able to restore a long-lost sled he had as a child. He wants to give it to himself as a Christmas present."

"A sled?" Sheyenne asked. "Can't he just buy a new one? For a lot less than what he'd be paying in our fees."

"Nostalgia," I said, as if that explained everything. "That's reason enough for Kashewpetl."

Robin said, "Bless you."

"So, did you resolve the moral dilemma with the hippie gorgon?" I asked.

Robin sighed. "Saffron has a deep abiding sense of right and wrong, but she has no clue about the law. She thinks that if she steals something for altruistic reasons, then it's not stealing. I tried to explain, but she keeps wanting me to find a loophole."

"Did she tell you what she stole?" Sheyenne asked.

"Some kind of magical talisman that makes wishes come true," Robin was obviously skeptical. "Chalk it up to fairy dust and the like. I believe Saffron is the type to plan her grocery shopping trips according to her horoscope."

"Hmm, a talisman that makes wishes come true? Sounds like my client's missing wish turkey."

"A wish turkey, did you say?" Robin looked at me. "She did mention something about a wishbone. She and her boyfriend acquired it, but I think he's just doing it to keep her happy. He's an Egyptian mummy named Eff-Tup."

I sat up straight. I couldn't believe the solution was right there. "They took that wish turkey out of the cage in Kashewpetl's house, right next door. We should make a pyramid call to Eff-Tup and Saffron, so I can retrieve my client's stolen property!"

Robin looked horrified. "But you can't use the information from *my client* against them! It's a conflict of interest for me. Not ethical."

"But we're doing it for the right reasons," I said. "Saffron would certainly understand that." Suddenly it all became clear to me: The Medusa wanted world peace, an end to war, the cures for all sickness, an end to poverty. That was how she intended to use the wish turkey. Kashewpetl just wanted an old sled back, a trivial and selfish wish. There shouldn't be any contest as to which one had the better *reason* for sacrificing the magical turkey.

But from our experience in dealing with Satanic contracts and practical jokester genies, wishes had a way of coming true—but in unexpected and often disastrous ways. I realized to my horror that one way to end all poverty, sickness, and war, and to bring about world peace, would be to simply wipe out all life on Earth.

Not exactly a solution I would like to have. I wondered how powerful that wish turkey really was, and I decided that wasn't a risk I wanted to take.

"It's not a conflict of interest," I said to Robin. "Stealing is stealing, whether or not Saffron's wish sounds better than my client's."

Robin hung her head. "You're right, Dan. And the law is the law. We'd better bring in the police, though. We'll get the turkey back, hold it in custodial care, then let the courts decide."

"That'll take until well past Christmas," Sheyenne said.

"There's always next Christmas," I suggested. I called McGoo, so we could plan our late-night raid. Just how he wanted to spend Christmas Eve.

❦

Because McGoo had the uniform and the badge, he was the one who stepped up to the door of the Egyptian pyramid house. He pounded hard, knocking the festive wreath askew. It was long after midnight, but even the traffic on the main residential street was high, apparently for pre-Christmas Eve parties.

McGoo pounded again. "Mr. Eff-Tup, Saffron the Medusa—open up, this is the police. We have a warrant to search for stolen magical poultry."

Robin accompanied us, in case she needed to provide legal protection for her gorgon client. Sheyenne's spectral form drifted by my side, snuggling up even though we couldn't feel each other. Sometimes solving cases was the only kind of date we got to have.

The door opened, to reveal the white-wrapped Egyptian mummy. "We don't want any, it's late. You should be—" He looked at Officer McGoohan with his badge and Robin with the search warrant. The Medusa came to the door smiling airily; now she had mistletoe entwined among the rosebud-stuffed serpents on her head. They seemed drugged; maybe too much eggnog.

"Good to see you again, Miss Deyer! Honey, invite them in for some cookies." She seemed oblivious to why the guests might be there.

The mummy tried to slam the door on us, but McGoo stuck his shoe in the way, then forced his way in. He propped the door wide open.

I said, "We have reason to believe that you might be harboring a kidnapped wish turkey."

"No wish turkeys here," said Eff-Tup.

"What about other turkeys?" McGoo asked. "Several have gone missing."

The mummy shrugged. "It's that time of the season."

From the back of the pyramid we heard the sounds of rattling cages, squawking noises. Ducking under the extremely angled walls, we barged through the kitchen door to see a pyramid-shaped utility shed. Through mesh windows we heard more noises from inside, birds and other creatures.

"I need my lawyer," the mummy cried.

"Go ahead and call him. I have a warrant."

Behind the first storage unit was a tiny, stuffy corral that held a hobbled unicorn, filthy and skeletal, its mane and tail drooping and tangled. The creature's eyes were forlorn and sad, with less than ten feet of space to plod back and forth. The corral was filled with bright purple lumps of unicorn manure, each one sprouting pink flowers. When the unicorn snorted miserably, small rainbows came out of its nose.

"This is disgusting!" McGoo said.

"We kept it for its own good," said Saffron. "We were going to make the world full of magic and light."

Hearing the commotion from next door, Kashewpetl stormed over in his lurching stiff-jointed gait and shouted through the wide-open front door. "What's going on here?"

"In the back, Mr. Kashewpetl," I called. "I think we found your wish turkey."

Sheyenne went to comfort the poor unicorn and untie it.

Eff-Tup stood in front of the pyramidal storage unit, barring our way. "You'll never break the lock!" he insisted. It was secured with a simple hook-and-eye clasp. Did no one understand security these days?

McGoo easily flipped the hook.

Behind us, the Aztec mummy barged and took one look at the pyramid utility shed, furious. "Right here? My own neighbors? After I wish for my special sled, I'll never let you use it!"

"We're going to wish for world peace instead," said Saffron, "as soon as we get around to sacrificing the turkey."

McGoo swung open the flimsy door to reveal a shed of horrors—and not nice ones. We saw cages and cages of rescued, and then imprisoned, magical creatures. A trio of magic flower fairies huddled in gloom, looking brown and neglected, as if they hadn't been watered or fertilized in days. A multicolored feathered serpent was all scales and bones. Even a sullen, small lawn gnome hunched down in a cage much too small for it, so that its perky pointed cap was crumpled under the wire-mesh enclosure. "Help us," he moaned.

"Ugh," McGoo said, glowering at the Egyptian mummy and the Medusa. "There's nothing worse than incompetent do-gooders."

"We meant well!" Saffron said.

Then I spotted the turkey sporting Aztec ceremonial tattoos and golden bangles around its feet. "Here, Mr. Kashewpetl!"

The Aztec mummy stormed forward as best he could with his petrified joints. "That's my turkey! It's *my* wish! *I* get to sacrifice it! I want my sled!"

"That turkey's just a pawn," Robin said to me.

Even in this less-than-ostentatious cage, the turkey seemed fat and happy, without a care in the world. Kashewpetl flung the wire door wide, kicked the cage, rattled it. "Get out of there! Let's go home—up to the altar. It's Christmas Eve!"

The turkey squawked and fluttered out of the cage, its body so huge it could barely step forward, but it waddled out as if it were some sort of feathered Aztec god.

"You will not take our wonderful creatures!" And suddenly the peacenik Medusa seemed as fierce as one might expect a gorgon to be. Her eyes blazed bright, and her serpent hair writhed and flashed. But the snakes were all blindfolded and they couldn't get their fangs free of the rosebuds.

Eff-Tup threw himself on Kashewpetl, and the two mummies

wrestled, in a rather stiff and slow-motion fashion. They fell against the cages, knocking the groaning lawn gnome off to the side.

"Careful! You'll break something!" shouted Kashewpetl.

"I intend to!" Eff-Tup said.

I found an empty plastic grocery bag hanging on a hook next to an unused unicorn pooper-scooper. I dumped the bag and yanked it over the Medusa's head, just in case those snakes figured a way out. McGoo easily pulled the mummies apart without tearing too many bandages.

During the tussle, though, the wish turkey flapped its wings, gobbled—and then bolted. It was too fat to run quickly, but we were preoccupied and didn't notice until it had already waddled through the pyramid house and sprinted out the open front door.

"Get the turkey!" I said, and suddenly we were all running.

All the pell-mell pursuers only made the turkey bolt faster. Gobbling, it ran into the busy street.

"Catch it!" Kashewpetl wailed so loudly that four moths came out of his lungs. "My sled!"

Saffron finally tore the plastic bag from her head. "World peace!" she cried.

The turkey waddled at full speed out into the street, and the gold bangles on its feet tripped it up—right as a delivery truck cruised by, well above the speed limit. The turkey looked up, caught the headlights. We all shouted in unison.

The truck honked its horn ... then rolled right over the turkey. With a loud squawk and a spray of feathers, it turned into flattened roadkill, all its bones smashed flat—including, no doubt, the wishbone.

The delivery truck screeched to a halt, and the zombie driver swung out, indignant. We all rushed to the scene, crowding around the truck. I recognized the driver. "Steve!"

He pulled down his cap and looked at me, deeply upset. "Now that's a fine Christmas Eve present! I wish you all would look both ways before crossing the street!"

Suddenly, the smashed wish turkey glowed, and as Robin, Sheyenne, and I stood together with McGoo, the two mummies, and Saffron the Medusa, we all felt the irresistible compulsion to look to our right, then to our left, assuring ourselves it was safe to enter the street.

Kashewpetl wailed. "That was *my* wish!"

Steve came up to me. "Sorry I snapped at you, dirt-buddy. I know I was going too fast, especially in a residential area."

"What are you doing out here?" I asked.

"Residential delivery—and sweet overtime. Plenty of necromancers have moved out to the suburbs, thanks to the high rent in the Quarter."

He turned to look at the flattened mass of meat and feathers and bones. "Great, I gotta hose that off tonight. I hope that wasn't someone's Christmas turkey dinner."

"No, it wasn't," I said.

The Aztec mummy hunched over the flattened bird, trying to extricate the wishbone, which had already been broken into multiple pieces. "I wish I could have it back. I wish I could have my wish! I wish I could have my sled!"

The Medusa plucked another piece of the wishbone. "I wish I could cure all roadkill turkeys."

But the wish turkey had already exhausted its power, and none of their wishes came true.

McGoo stepped to Eff-Tup, Kashewpetl, and Saffron. He looked angrier than I'd ever seen him. "I'm calling this in. I've only got one set of handcuffs, so don't make me decide how to use them. Right now, you're going to help us catalogue and free all of those magical creatures from those cages."

"That unicorn really needs to be taken care of," said Sheyenne.

Robin had already made a call. "The UQ Unhumane Society's on the way. They'll be taking charge of these creatures until we can assess them for care or treatment. I'm sure that gnome is going to press charges, and I'm here to help expedite that."

I placed a commiserating arm around the hunched shoulders of the Aztec mummy. "I did find your missing turkey, Mr. Kashewpetl. I'm sorry it didn't turn out the way we would have liked."

"There's always next Christmas," he said. "I've waited this long. Someday I'll get my sled back. I'll raise another wish turkey. And next Christmas Eve …"

"If you have a wish turkey that grants whatever you want, why don't you just ask for Suzitoq back?" I asked.

He looked startled. "Good idea! I'll raise two wish turkeys, sacrifice them both, snap their wishbones so that I can have Suzitoq back—and our sled."

"Sounds like a plan," I said.

Sheyenne drifted close to me. "I wish we could just have Christmas together, Beaux. You and me."

"In that case, Spooky," I said, "you don't need a magic turkey. I promise I'll make your wish come true."

LOINCLOTH
(WITH REBECCA MOESTA)

All alone in the props warehouse on the back lot of Duro Studios, he made his case to Shirley in his mind, rehashing the argument they had had the night before. This time, though, he was bold and articulate, and he easily convinced her.

Walter Groves opened another one of the big crates and tore out the packing straw mixed with Styrofoam peanuts. "Not exciting enough for you, am I? You don't feel fireworks? I'm too sedate—not a man's man? Think about it, Shirley. Women say they want nice guys, the shy and sensitive type, men who are sweet and remember birthdays and anniversaries. Isn't that what you told me you needed—someone just like me? You've always despised hypocrites. But what do you do? You fall for a bad boy, someone with tattoos and a heavy smoking habit, someone who can't keep a job for more than a month, someone like that last jerk you dated, who treated you rough and left you out in the cold.

"But I loved you. I treated you with respect, drove you to visit your grandmother in the hospital, and fixed your computer when the hard drive crashed. I got out of bed when you called at three in the morning and came to your apartment just to hold you because you had a nightmare and couldn't sleep. I gave you flowers, dinners by candlelight, and love notes—not to mention the best six months of my life. 'Someday, you'll regret it. Maybe not today. Maybe not tomorrow, but soon'"—he pictured himself as Bogart in *Casablanca*—"'you'll realize what you threw away. But I won't be waiting. I'm a good man, and I deserve a wonderful woman who values me for who I am, who appreciates my dedication, and wants a nice, normal life. Go ahead.

Have your shallow, exciting fling with Mr. James Dean in *Rebel Without a Cause*. I'll find someone sincere who wants Jimmy Stewart in *It's a Wonderful Life*."

Scattering straw and packing material, he pulled a long plastic elephant tusk out of the prop box. The faux ivory was sharp at one end and painted with "native symbols." He glanced at the label on the box: Jungo's Revenge. After marking the name of the film on his clipboard, he listed the stored items beneath the title. He sighed.

If only he could have come up with just the right answers last night, maybe Shirley wouldn't have dumped him. If only he could have been tough like Mel Gibson in *Braveheart*, confident like Clark Gable in *Gone with the Wind*, or romantic like Dermot Mulroney in *The Wedding Date*. Instead he had squirmed, speechless with shock, his lower lip trembling as if he were Stan Laurel caught in an embarrassing failure. Walter had made no heartfelt appeals or snappy comebacks; those were as much fiction as a script for any Duro Studios production.

Shirley had grabbed her stuff—along with some of his, though he hadn't had the presence of mind to mention it—and stormed out of the apartment.

Sharon Stone in *Basic Instinct*. That's who she reminded him of.

The large, black walkie-talkie at his hip crackled, and even through the static of the poor-quality unit, he heard the lovely musical speech of Desiree Drea. Her voice never failed to make his heart skip a beat, then go back and skip it all over again. "Walter? Mr. Carmichael wants to know how you're coming with the props. He needs me to type up the inventory."

"I ... um ... I—" He looked down at the box, searching for words, and seized upon the letters stenciled to the crate. "I'm just now up to *Jungo's Revenge*. I've finished about half of the work."

As Desiree responded, he could hear the producer's voice bellowing in the background. "Jungo! It's all worthless crap. Trash it."

The secretary softened the message as she relayed it. "Mr. Carmichael suggests that it's of no value, so please put it in the dumpster."

"And tell him he damn well better stay until he finishes," the voice in the background growled. "We need that building tomorrow to start shooting *Horror in the Prop Warehouse*."

"Tell him I'll do what needs to be done," Walter said, then clicked off the walkie-talkie, though he would gladly have chatted with Desiree for hours. He didn't have anything better to do that evening than work, anyway. He was very conscientious and would finish the job.

Chris Carmichael—producer of low-budget knock-off movies. The

Jungo ape-man series, a bad Tarzan knock-off, had skated just a little too close to Tarzan's copyright line. The threatened legal action had caused the films to flop, even though they were direct to video. Walter had seen one of them and thought that the movies were bad enough to have flopped all on their own, without any legal difficulties to help them along. If anything, the publicity had boosted the sales.

He pulled out the other plastic elephant tusk, then some ugly looking tribal masks, three rubber cobras, and a giant plastic insect as big as his palm that was labeled "Deadly Tsetse Fly." Walter shook his head. He had to agree about the worthlessness of these props. There wouldn't be any collector interested in even giving them shelf space. If there had been enough fans to generate a few collectors, the Jungo franchise might never have disappeared.

Near the bottom of the crate he found a rattle, a shrunken head, and another tribal mask, but these props were far superior to the others. They looked handmade, with real wood and bone. The shrunken head had an odd leathery feel that made him wonder if it was real. He shuddered as he took it out of the crate.

It seemed unlikely that Chris Carmichael, a tightwad with utter contempt for his audiences as well as his employees, would spend money on the genuine articles to use as props. Maybe a prop master had purchased them online or found them in a junk bin somewhere. Beneath the last of the witch doctor items, at the very bottom of the crate, he found a scrap of cloth that made him smile as he pulled it out and brushed off the bits of straw that clung to it.

A leopard-skin loincloth, the only garment Jungo the Ape Man had ever worn in the films—all the better to show off his well-developed physique, of course. Walter tried to remember. According to the story, Jungo had killed a leopard with his bare hands when he was only five years old and had made the loincloth out of its pelt. Apparently, the loincloth had grown along with the boy. Maybe the leopard had been part Spandex.... Jungo was probably the type of man Shirley would have fallen for—wild, tanned, brawny, and barely capable of stringing together three-word sentences. Walter groaned at the thought.

Now Desiree was another story entirely. Even on the big studio lot, they often crossed paths. He saw her in the commissary at lunch almost daily—because he timed his lunch hour to match hers. She was strikingly beautiful with her reddish-gold hair, her large blue eyes, her delicate chin, and when she smiled directly at him, as she had done three times now, it made him feel as if someone in the special effects shop had created the most spectacular sunrise ever.

But Walter still hadn't gotten up the nerve to ask if he could sit and eat with her. He was a nobody who did odd jobs around the lot for the various producers. Some of them were nice, and some of them were ... like Chris Carmichael. The man was Dabney Coleman in *9 to 5*, or Bill Murray before his transformation in *Scrooged*. Carmichael had put in a requisition and Walter had pulled the card: One man needed to clear prop warehouse. It was really a job for four men and four days, but Carmichael always slashed his budgets to leave more money in his own expense account. Carmichael didn't even know who Walter Groves was.

But Desiree did. That was all that mattered.

He gazed at the leopard-skin loincloth, hearing Shirley's words ring in his head. "You aren't a man's man. You don't let yourself go wild." He sniffed, trying to picture himself in the role she seemed to want him to play. What if Desiree felt the same way? What if all women thought they wanted a nice man but were only attracted to bad boys?

He picked up the witch doctor's rattle and gave it a playful shake, then put it down by the mask and the shrunken head. Even though she had hurt him, he wasn't the type either to put a curse on Shirley, or to transform himself for her into a muscular hunk of beefcake like Jungo. He would have needed an awfully large special effects budget to pull that off. Walter held up the leopard-skin loincloth to his waist and considered the fashion statement it would make. It looked ridiculous—even more so in contrast with his work pants and his conservative windowpane plaid shirt.

"If I wore this, what would Desiree think?" Would it convince her that he was a wild man, or would she just think him pale-skinned and scrawny? All alone in the prop warehouse, he had no particular need to hurry up. Carmichael, who never noticed anyone's hard work, had already said that the props were junk.

Before he could change his mind and think sensibly, Walter unbuttoned his shirt and peeled it off. Taking a deep breath, he slipped off his shoes and trousers and tied on the loincloth. He surveyed the effect, looking critically at his skinny chest, thin arms, white skin, and the leopard-skin loincloth. He cast a skeptical glance at the witch doctor mask. "Exactly how did I expect this to bring out the wild man in me?"

Then something happened.

His heart began to pound like drumbeats in his ears. His skin grew hot and his blood hotter. He felt dizzy and then very, *very* sure of himself. The worries and confusion of his life seemed to float away like soap bubbles on the wind. His attention focused down to a single pinprick. Everything was so clear, so simple. He had worried too much, *thought* too much, suppressed all of his natural desires. He drew a deep breath, kept inhaling until his chest swelled. Then on impulse, he pounded on his proudly expanded chest. It felt good and right.

He didn't have to worry about the prop inventory or about Shirley. She had made a bad choice, and she was gone. He no longer needed to think of her. Outside the sun was bright. He was a man, and Desiree was a woman. Everything else was extraneous, a distraction. He was a hunter and he knew his quarry. A real man relied on his instincts to tell him what to do.

He let out a warbling call, broadcasting a defiant challenge to anyone who might get in his way. Barefoot, he sprinted like a cheetah out of the prop warehouse and onto the lot. He had seen where Desiree worked. He knew where to find Chris Carmichael's trailer. His vision tunneled down to that one focus.

He streaked past the people working on various films. Someone made a catcall, but most of the crews ignored him. Employees at Duro Studios were accustomed to seeing axe murderers, Martians, barbarians, and monsters of all kinds.

Chris Carmichael's headquarters were in a dingy, gray-walled trailer on the far end of the east lot. The success of a producer's films earned him clout in the studios, and Carmichael's track record had earned him this unobtrusive trailer and one secretary.

Desiree.

Walter yanked open the door and leaped in. He hadn't decided what to say or do next, but an ape-man took matters one step at a time. He reacted to situations, without planning in excruciating detail beforehand. Instead of startling Desiree at her keyboard and the producer on the phone, he blundered into a shocking scene that would have made his hackles rise if he'd had any. Carmichael stood with both hands planted on his desk, crouched like a predator ready to spring. Desiree shielded herself on the other side of the desk, trying to keep it, with its empty coffee mugs, framed pictures, and jumbled stacks of scripts, between herself and Carmichael.

He leered at her, moved to the left, and she shifted to the right. She was flushed and nervous. "Please, Mr. Carmichael. I'm not that kind of girl."

"Of course, you are," he said. "If you didn't want to break into pictures, why would you work in a place like this? I can make you an extra in my next feature, *Horror in the Prop Warehouse*. Ten-seconds screen time minimum, but there's a price. You have to give me something." Now he circled to the right and she moved left.

"Please, don't do this. I don't want to file a complaint, but I'll call security if I have to."

"You do that, and you'll never work in this town again."

Before she could reply, Walter let out a bestial roar. He wasn't sure exactly what happened. Seeing red, he acted on instinct, and charged forward. He grabbed the producer by the back of his clean white collar, yanked him away from the desk, and spun him around. As he spluttered, Walter the ape-man landed a powerful roundhouse punch on Carmichael's chin and knocked him backward into the chair he reserved for visiting actors.

Startled, Desiree gasped, but Walter was already on the move. He bounded over the desk, slipped an arm around her waist, and crashed through the screen of the trailer's open window, carrying his woman with him. The rest was a blur.

When he could think straight again—after the witch doctor's spell, or whatever it was wore off—he found himself on the rooftop of one of the backlot sets, sitting next to Desiree, his lips pressed against hers. With a start, he drew back. Her hair was rumpled, her cheeks flushed, and she wore an expression of surprise and amusement. "That was a bit unorthodox, Walter," she said, "but you were amazing. You saved me when I needed it most."

"What have I done?" Walter glanced down at the loincloth, flexed his sore knuckles, and knew with absolute certainty that he would soon die from embarrassment. He was sitting half-naked on a roof at work and had just made a complete fool of himself in front of a woman he had a genuine crush on. "I'm sorry. I'm sorry!" He scuttled backward, stood to look for a ladder or stairs, and quickly found an exit. "I didn't mean to hurt you. Mr. Carmichael's going to get me fired, for sure."

"Who, Chris? He has no clue who you are," she said. "Anyway, I'm going to hand in my own resignation. I've had enough of that man."

"I ... I need to put something decent on. I can't understand what got into me." He felt his cheeks burning. His legs wobbled, and his knees threatened to knock together. Some ape-man!

Before Desiree could say anything more, he bolted, cringing at the thought that someone else might see him this way—that Desiree *had* seen him. He was sure Jungo never had days like this.

❧

By the time he got home, Walter was consumed with guilt. He felt flustered, exposed, and too embarrassed for words. He couldn't believe what he had done, prancing around the lot in nothing more than a loincloth, crashing into the producer's trailer offices. He had punched out Chris Carmichael! Then, after jumping through a window with

Desiree, he had somehow whisked her off to a rooftop and *kissed her*! He was the very definition of the word "mortified." To make matters worse, Walter had gotten dressed again, called in a friend to finish clearing out the warehouse, then slunk off the lot, taking Jungo's loincloth with him. He could justify this, since Carmichael had made it clear that the props could be thrown into a dumpster.

He sat miserably in his empty apartment—without Shirley—and wondered how he could possibly make it up to Desiree. He didn't much care about Chris Carmichael. The man was a cad, but Walter himself had stolen a kiss from Desiree, practically ravished her! Considering the power the loincloth had worked on him, he could easily have gotten carried away. In the process of saving Desiree, he had proved that he was no better than that jerk of a producer.

And Walter had just left her stranded there, on the roof of the movie set. No, no, that wasn't Walter Groves. That wasn't who he really was. Though he wanted nothing more than to crawl under a rock, he knew what he had to do for the sake of honor. He had to go find Desiree and beg her forgiveness.

For a long time, he stood in the shower under a pounding stream of hot water, rehearsing what to say until he knew he couldn't put it off any longer. Every moment he avoided her was another moment she could think terrible things about him. He dried his hair, dabbed on some aftershave, and put on his best dress slacks, a clean shirt, and a striped blue necktie. This was going to be a formal apology, and he wanted to look his best. Pulling on his nicest, though rarely worn, sport jacket, he rolled up Jungo's loincloth and stuffed it into the pocket. Though it didn't make any sense, he would try to tell Desiree what had happened, explain how the magic had changed him somehow into a wild man, someone he wouldn't normally be.

After dialing information, then searching on the Internet, he tracked down a local street address for D. Drea. He knew it had to be her. Gathering his resolve, he marched out to go face her. He didn't need the crutch of a loincloth or some imaginary witch doctor's spells to give him courage to do the right thing. He would do this himself.

On the way to her apartment, he didn't let himself think, forcing himself onward before the shame could make him turn back. He had to be like Michael Douglas in *Romancing the Stone*, not Rick Moranis in *Little Shop of Horrors*. Nothing should disrupt the apology. Leaving his cell phone in the car, he walked to the door of her apartment, raised his hand to knock, then hesitated. He wasn't thinking clearly. He really should have brought flowers and a card. Why not go to a store now, buy them, and then come back?

He heard shouts coming from the other side of the door, followed by a scream—Desiree's scream!

He froze in terror. What should he do? Desiree was in trouble. Maybe he should run back outside, get his cell phone and call 911. He could bring the police here, or better yet, pound on her neighbors' doors and find someone who was big and strong. She screamed again, and Walter knew there could be only one solution. He tried the knob, found the door unlocked, and barged in. He found Chris Carmichael already there, reeking of cheap cologne and bourbon.

"Leave me alone," Desiree said. She held a lamp in one hand, brandishing it like a club.

Carmichael let out an evil chuckle. "Now that you no longer work for me, we can have any sort of relationship I want. There are no ethical problems."

She raised the lamp higher. Walter stepped forward, outraged but quailing at the idea of a fight. When Desiree saw him, her eyes lit up.

Carmichael turned.

Walter blurted, "Hey, What-what's going on here?" He wished he could hide or, at the very least, run back out of the apartment and return to do a second take of the scene. He needed to be a tough guy, like Dirty Harry in *Sudden Impact*—"Go ahead, make my day"—and the best he could come up with was a Don Knotts-worthy "Hey, what's going on here?" He groaned.

Carmichael recognized him, and his eyes grew stormy. Ignoring Desiree for the moment, the larger man lurched toward Walter, grabbed him by the shirt, yanked his tie, and drew Walter closer to him. "You're that little freak that sucker-punched me in my office, aren't you? Where's the spotted underwear?"

"I-I-I don't need it."

"You'll need an ambulance is what you'll need."

Indiana Jones would have done something different. He would have punched the villain, starting an all-out brawl, but as Carmichael lifted him and twisted his tie, he could only make a small *meep* sound.

"You put him down," Desiree cried, and Walter's heart lurched. She was actually defending him!

Carmichael laughed again. "You can't even save yourself. How do you expect to help this mouse?" He pushed Walter up against the wall, clenched his fist, and drew back his arm, as if cocking a shotgun.

Walter was sure his head would go straight through the drywall. "Wait. Wait, please." He swallowed and drew a deep breath. "If you're going to do this, let me face it like a man. I ... I'd like to use the restroom, please."

Carmichael blinked, then gave him a knowing smile. "Oh, afraid you're going to wet yourself, eh?" He let Walter slump to the floor. "Sure. Why not? Desiree and I were just enjoying an intimate conversation. We can wait."

He glared at her and she sat down on the sofa, not sure what to do. Walter scurried into the bathroom and closed the door, his mind spinning. Maybe Desiree kept a gun in the bathroom, perhaps taped behind the toilet tank, like in *The Godfather*. But he found nothing there and a quick search of the drawers and the medicine cabinet revealed no other weapons he could use to save the day.

He stuck his hands in his jacket pockets and his fingers brushed a patch of sleek fur. The loincloth. It was his only chance.

Walter burst out of the bathroom wearing nothing but the scrap of leopard-skin. Barefoot and bare-chested, his mind filled with the thoughts of a hunter. Testosterone and adrenaline pumped through his veins and he let out a wild yell, pounding on his chest. His hair was a mess, his eyes on fire. Seeing his enemy, the producer, he lunged toward him like a hungry lion attacking a springbok. Walter felt total confidence and did not hesitate.

Chris Carmichael, who used his position of perceived power to intimidate people, faltered. When he saw Walter leap toward him, he suddenly reconsidered what he'd been about to do.

Walter let out another roar. His lungs seemed to have twice their normal capacity. "*My* woman!"

Carmichael had probably never been challenged before. A producer, even a bad producer of second-rate movies, could boss people around in Hollywood. But Walter the ape-man, wearing nothing but his loincloth in Desiree's apartment, had no doubt that he himself was king of the jungle. Carmichael turned, took several steps in retreat, then paused. Through his hunter-focused gaze, Walter watched his prey, preparing to throw himself on the man if he made a move in the wrong direction.

Desiree decided for both men, though. As Carmichael started to turn back, she lifted her lamp, and smashed it on his head. He crumpled to the carpet like King Kong falling off the Empire State Building. The rush in Walter's mind drained away, and he found himself standing naked in Desiree's apartment, except for the ape-man's loincloth. He shivered, and goose bumps appeared on his arms. "What did I do this time?" he said, looking down at the producer with dismay.

But Desiree was close to him. Very close and very beautiful. "You protected me, Walter. You saved me." She slid her arms around his waist and gave him a hug. "You're my hero."

It was not the magic of the loincloth that made his heart start pounding again. "You-you don't mind?" he asked in surprise.

"I'll show you how much I mind in just a minute." She stepped away and looked down at the unconscious Carmichael. "But first, help me take out the garbage. We'll put him in the hall and call the police." Walter and Desiree rolled the man like a skid row drunk into the apartment hallway.

Desiree closed the door, locked it, and turned to face him. Suddenly he felt as if he were the prey and she the hungry lioness.

He gulped. "I'm really a nice guy most of the time. But I can be bad, if I need to be."

"Walter, I *like* that you're a nice guy. It's the first thing I noticed about you, even from a distance. You may not have known I was watching, but I've seen you hold doors for other people, help them carry things when their arms were full, loan them lunch money, listen to what they say. Most of the time, that's exactly what women want. It's what *I* want. But women are ... complex creatures. So once in a while we also like a bit of a wild man. You seem like the best of both worlds to me."

"You may never be safe," he pointed out. "What if Mr. Carmichael comes back? I don't think he'll leave you alone."

With a lovely smile she led him to the couch and sat him down. "In that case, maybe you'll just have to stay here to protect me."

There was a stirring in the loincloth, and he felt very self-conscious. "Maybe I should get dressed in real clothes."

"No, Walter. You stay just the way you are." Desiree leaned over to kiss him.

GRUMPY OLD MONSTERS

THE ORIGINAL COMIC SCRIPTS
(WITH REBECCA MOESTA)

Our concept here is to tell a story that's bright and open and fun. The pages aren't too crowded and not overly packed with dialog balloons. Much of the story, and the humor, is visual. The key will be the artist's designs for the individual monsters themselves. If we do this right, the story will immediately translate into animation. *Grumpy Old Monsters* should be enjoyed by all ages, fun for younger readers yet with enough sassy satire that adults will think it's a hoot. Think *Toy Story* or *Monsters, Inc.*

ISSUE #1

PAGE 1

PANEL 1

Big panel, most of the page (or both panels could be worked together into a full-page, if the perspective is right). This is an establishing shot of the old monsters' home, looking something like Norman Bates's house, or the Munsters' haunted mansion. The grounds are well kept, but there are bars on the windows, an ambulance and a hearse parked together in the drive.

On the front porch in a rocking chair sits the dilapidated MUMMY, watching the grass grow. He is small in this panel, but we'll see plenty more of him in the next pages.

PANEL 2

A weathered, rickety sign hanging on a post. The words read:

Rest In Peace
A Retirement Care Facility for Mature Monsters with Special Needs

PAGE 2

PANEL 1

The Mummy sits in his rocking chair on the porch. His bandages are yellowed, frayed, starting to unravel. Parts of his skeletal body can be seen through openings. Some of the bandages have been retied in clumsy bows or knots. His teeth are gnarled, with plenty of gaps. His gaze looks out from dark sockets, but with one hand he holds a drooping bandage out of his eyes. (Throughout, as a gag, loose bandages can be dropping in front of his eyes and he struggles to see.)

CAPTION

By the grace of Ra, how did I ever end up here?

CAPTION

I have watched armies of slaves erect great pyramids, towering obelisks, and mysterious sphinxes.

PANEL 2

In the front lawn of the Rest In Peace home, a punk gardener kid with his baseball cap turned backwards whistles obliviously as he pushes a lawnmower

CAPTION

In this days, people worked a lot harder. They took pride in their jobs....

PANEL 3

Inside the front door, a plump and cow-faced nurse in starched uniform sits at the reception desk, very slowly typing forms on an old manual typewriter.

CAPTION

This place...I swear, it saps the life out of you.

SFX(TYPING)

Plunk Clink

PANEL 4

With the nurse in the background, we see a rotting shambling zombie from Night of the Living Dead, in a tattered nursing home robe. The funny part is that he's plodding forward using an old-folks' aluminum walker with rubber pads, heading toward the rec hall.

LOUDSPEAKER

The funeral flower arranging class is about to being in the rec call! Don't be late!

SFX(WALKER)

Plud

PAGE 3

PANEL 1

The Mummy in profile, closeup, as he stares out at the grounds, reminiscing.

CAPTION

Oh, I had my glory days, though....

PANEL 2

Flashback. Egyptian priests in a temple next to a sacrificial fire, raising a curved golden dagger. Ankhs and other magical items lie around. Against the wall is propped a golden sarcophagus.

CAPTION

Back when my bandages were fresh, and the curse itself was new and full of possibilities.

PANEL 3

The sarcophagus opens, and the walking mummy emerges (looking a lot newer, with fine bandages all neatly tied). His arm is stiffly outstretched, like Karloff.

CAPTION

There was a time when even queen Nefertiti would have found me dashing....

PANEL 4

Mummy shambles down a hall, chasing hapless victims (possibly turn-of-the-century British types).

CAPTION

I felt needed, *useful*. I had a job to do, and I sure enjoyed it.

PANEL 5

Classic movie shot of a beautiful and utterly helpless woman holding her hands up to her face and shrieking in utter terror.

CAPTION

Yep, I was quite the wild one....

PANEL 6

Mummy from the front, extreme closeup. Maybe just the lower half of his face, so we can see his rotted smile through his bandages.

CAPTION

...Back in the day.

PAGE 4

PANEL 1

Closeup of the Mummy's bandaged foot at the base of the rocking chair. A curious, sweet-looking field mouse is sniffing at the bandages, as if it's looking for cheese.

PANEL 2

Closeup of the Mummy's eyes, one of them half covered by the drooping bandage. His eyes are wide with sudden alarm.

PANEL 3

The Mummy begins frantically patting his loose bandages on his chest and ribcage like a man who's suddenly got poison ivy.

MUMMY

What—? I am the great *Pu-Ho-Tep*!

PANEL 4

With bandaged fingers, the Mummy peels apart several of the large windings on his chest so he can get a better look.

MUMMY

In the name of Ra, I will not tolerate—

PANEL 5

The Mummy peers into the vacant dark hole there and his shoulders sag as he finally gives up.

MUMMY

Curses! Another mouse nest...

PAGE 5

PANEL 1

Bold and cute, the field mouse scampers up the Mummy's leg.

PANEL 2

The mouse climbs into the gap in his chest bandages the Mummy has peeled apart.

SFX(MOUSE)

Eeep!

PANEL 3

The Mummy looks down at his chest, maybe we see the mouse's vanishing tail. He grumbles, disgusted with what he has seen.

MUMMY

Hrrrrrmmm

PANEL 4

The Mummy goes back to sitting alone and staring at the grounds.

MUMMY

No respect... absolutely no respect!

GRUMPY OLD MONSTERS • 161

PAGE 6

PANEL 1

Sitting at a table by himself in the retirement home's dining room, DRACULA looks at a bowl of jiggly red molded goop in front of him. He is old, gaunt, but still dapper, like Fred Astaire if he was a hundred years old. He's dressed in his usual fancy tuxedo, vest, and cape, but we can't see his fangs.

DRACULA

Ahh, look vat's on today's menu. *Bluuch!*

PANEL 2

Closeup of a spoon filled with thick gelatinous blood jello. Dracula is holding the spoon, turning it sideways, and the jiggly jello is still holding on.

DRACULA

Same as alvays...blood jello!

PANEL 3

A glob of the Jello finally, sloooooowly, droops off the spoon and splats back into the bowl. (Could be two panels.)

SFX

Shlurrrcchhh

PANEL 4

Dracula, looking forlorn, pushes the bowl away in disgust.

DRACULA

I vish I had something I could sink my teeth into!

162 • THE FUNNY BUSINESS

PANEL 5

Closeup of Dracula's dentures, with nice sharp fangs, sitting in a glass of water on the table.

PAGE 7

PANEL 1

On the patio of the rest home, the WOLF-MAN sits seemingly by himself at a small card table, hunched over a checkerboard. A game is in progress, with checkers scattered on various squares. Wolf-man looks mangy, much of his fur fallen out and leaving only a few wispy strands. His scalp and skin is covered with liver spots.

PANEL 2

Closer view. The Wolf-man studies the checkerboard intently, growling.

WOLF-MAN

Snnnrrrrrr

PANEL 3

His clawed hand grabs one of the black checkers and lifts it.

PANEL 4

His eyes light up, gleaming with delight. Wolf-man smacks down the black checker, taking one of the red pieces.

SFX(CHECKER)

Smak

WOLF-MAN

Arooo--haaa! Got you!

PANEL 5

Wolf-Man sits back in his chair, smug, furry arms crossed over his chest.

PAGE 8

PANEL 1

Looking down at the checkerboard from above. Nothing is happening.

PANEL 2

Side view. One of the red checkers lifts up all by itself.

PANEL 3

In a rapid motion, the red checker bounces in a zig-zag across the black pieces, seizing four of the Wolf-man's black checkers.

SFX

SMAK! SMAK! SMAK! SMAK!

PANEL 4

As all the seized black checkers seemingly move by themselves, taken off the board, the Wolf-man sulks like a pouting child.

PANEL 5

At the side of the card table, a pair of black-rimmed eyeglasses is picked up and a cane lifts up from the ground.

PANEL 6

As the eyeglasses and cane totter off, the Wolf-man shouts after them.

WOLF-MAN

I'll beat you next time, Invisible Man!

[LINK]

164 • THE FUNNY BUSINESS

... if you ever dare to show your face around here again!

PAGE 9

PANEL 1

From behind a sagging, worn sofa in the TV room, we see the silhouette of a squarish head looking at the television.

TV

All right, girls—left and right and...

PANEL 2

The television screen showing a group of spandex-clad babes jiggling and going through an exercise routine. It's an aerobics workout show.

TV

Feel those abs! I promise, this workout will give you buns of titanium. But most important—

PANEL 3

Closeup of FRANKENSTEIN'S MONSTER, grinning as he watches the sexy ladies on television. His face is sagging, the pieces starting to come loose, one of the bolts on his neck cocked at an odd angle.

TV

—is that we all have *fun*!

PANEL 4

One of the Monster's blunt-fingered hands picks at the unraveling stitches on his opposite wrist. Many of the loops are all coming loose.

TV

Now, raise your hands and streeeetch!

GRUMPY OLD MONSTERS • 165

PAGE 10

PANEL 1

Big panel, suddenly looming in front of the television, is NURSE WRENTCH. She is a scowling old battle-axe, every kid's worst nightmare of a teacher. She's not a monster, but the worst hard-ass drill sergeant the medical profession has to offer. In disgust, she shuts off the TV.

NURSE WRENTCH

That nonsense will burn ut your parts...again!

[LINK]

And Doctor F. isn't around anymore to install new ones.

PANEL 2

The nurse settles a pair of headphones over the Monster's ears as he still sits on the sofa.

NURSE

Here now, you just relax . . .

PANEL 3

Her fingers push the PLAY button on a portable CD player. Next to the player is a CD case labeled "Beethoven Violin Concertos"

NURSE (OUT OF PANEL)

And don't cause me any more trouble!

PANEL 4

The Monster closes his eyes and smiles to the music, swaying his head back and forth. He hums.

MONSTER

Hmmm mmmm mmmmm

PAGE 11

PANEL 1

Big panel, sudden action. Two nursing home orderlies running at full speed, pushing an empty gurney down the hall toward the set of patio doors. A nurse (not Nurse Wrentch) stands by the door, looking distraught. The shambling zombie with the walker reels to get out of the way.

CAPTION

Later...

CAPTION

It happens far too often, even here in the old monsters' home.

ORDERLY

Come on! Emergency out by the pond!

NURSE

Hurry!

PANEL 2

The Mummy comes out of the rest room, tucking the bandages around his waist. He looks down the hall as the gurney and shouting orderlies rush out the patio doors.

CAPTION

We no longer ask ourselves 'what happened?'

PANEL 3

Dracula and Wolf-man react, looking at each other with dread and alarm.

CAPTION

The only question is—*who*?

PAGE 12

PANEL 1

Dracula stands by the nearest window, holding up his cape to shade his face from the sun. He looks outside.

DRACULA

They've found the creature belly-up in the lagoon!

PANEL 2

The Invisible Man (nothing more than a cane, eyeglasses, and a robe) stands next to Frankenstein's Monster at the window. Wolf-man pushes close to the Invisible Man for a better view (Wolf-man and Invisible Man don't like each other very much.)

INVISIBLE MAN

Last week it was Hyde...The Phantom the week before that.

FRANKENSTEIN

Ah...remember poor Igor?

PANEL 3

Nurse Wrentch appears, glowering at the monsters by the window. She has her hands on her wide hips, her face in a sour scowl, looking like a bomb ready to go off.

NURSE WRENTCH

And just what do you think *you're* looking at?

[LINK]

Move along! Nothing to see here!

MUMMY

Yes, Nurse Wrentch...

PAGE 13

PANEL 1

The orderlies rush back in, pushing their gurney which now has a human-shaped figure on it, covered by a white sheet splotched with damp spots. Water droplets trickle down from it as they run along.

By now the walker-zombie has managed to reach the other side of the hall, and he's still in the way. He gets knocked against a potted plant as the gurney sweeps past.

ORDERLY

Out of the way!

PANEL 2

Suddenly from beneath the sheet the CREATURE FROM THE BLACK LAGOON sits up, thrashing and flailing. One big webbed hand smacks the nearest orderly aside, sending him sprawling.

SFX

Swakk

PANEL 3

The Creature sits up on the gurney, looking dazed and disgusted. He wipes his big fish lips.

CREATURE

Blecch! He gave me mouth-to-mouth!

PANEL 4

The indignant Creature stomps off down the hall, dripping slimy puddles of water, muttering to himself.

CREATURE (MUTTERING)

Can't even take a simple nap around here!

PANEL 5

The dazed and disheveled orderly picks himself up, rubbing his jaw. Nurse Wrentch steps up to him, glowering. She doesn't play favorites—she gets annoyed at everybody.

ORDERLY

But he was belly up! Just floating there—

NURSE WRENTCH

He's an *amphibian*, you idiot!

PAGE 14

PANEL 1

Big panel. A darling little girl, TIFFANY FRANKENSTEIN, comes skipping up the front walk to the Rest In Peace home. She is cute and spunky, wearing a pale blue dress. She has blond hair in two ponytails, very large blue eyes, and the face of a little angel. Just looking at her makes you want to go, Awwwwww.

PANEL 2

Tiffany climbs the steps to the porch, smiling. Over her arm is a wicker picnic basket full of goodies.

TIFFANY

Oh, I just love visiting day!

PANEL 3

She pulls open the front door of the nursing home, calling out.

								TIFFANY

Yoo-hoo?

PAGE 15

PANEL 1

Big panel. In the rec room, Wolf-man, Dracula, Frankenstein's Monster, the Mummy, and the Invisible Man are sitting around a table playing poker. A pile of chips is in the middle of the table, with stacks of varying sizes at each player's place. They each hold cards in their hands.

								DRACULA

I vill take two cards, Mummy.

								DRACULA

Did I ever tell you about the time I fought Jesse James?

PANEL 2

Dracula, holding his cards, keeps reminiscing.

								DRACULA

There I vas, out in the old vest —

PANEL 3

Scowling, Wolf-man scratches the fur on the side of his face. Maybe he has fleas.

GRUMPY OLD MONSTERS • 171

WOLF-MAN

Arrr, you've told us that one a million times, count! But it still doesn't change the facts.

[LINK]

Doc Frankenstein's daughter fought Jesse James—not you.

PANEL 4

The Mummy fumbles a new card into his hand. Wolf-man is grouchy, not having a good game.

MUMMY

I thought it was the daughter of Doctor Jekyll?

WOLF-MAN

Every time you guys come back from the grave, you lose more brain cells!

PAGE 16

PANEL 1

Frankenstein's Monster picks up a chip from his pile; the stitches around his wrist are very loose and unraveling.

FRANKENSTEIN

I call.

PANEL 2

When he tosses the poker chip into the pot, though, his whole hand comes loose and flops off, landing in the middle of the table.

SFX

Thwummp

PANEL 3

Looking very embarrassed, Frankenstein picks his loose hand from the table.

FRANKENSTEIN

> Sorry...

PANEL 4

In disgust, Wolf-man throws his cards down.

WOLF-MAN

> I fold! Rrrr!

[LINK]

> Never play poker with an invisible man.

PANEL 5

The invisible man's face—really, just his eyeglasses hanging there in empty air—stares back implacably.

PANEL 6

Bright and bubbly, Tiffany Frankenstein appears in the rec room, carrying her basket of goodies. She is grinning and absolutely adorable.

TIFFANY

> Hi guys! Did you miss me?

PAGE 17

PANEL 1

The monsters all brighten, delighted to see her. They talk at once.

GRUMPY OLD MONSTERS • 173

                    DRACULA

Ah, Little Tiffany!

                    MUMMY

Why, it's Tiffany Frankenstein!

                    FRANKENSTEIN

Ooooh

PANEL 2

Suddenly looming up behind the little girl like a wrathful priest, Nurse Wrentch scowls at her. Tiffany bats her eyelashes, contrite and innocent.

                    NURSE WRENTCH

Don't you disturb them, little girl!

                    TIFFANY

Oh, I won't be a bother, Miss Nurse. I promise.

PANEL 3

As Nurse Wrentch stalks away, looking for her next victim, Dracula looks over his shoulder, grumbling and making a face at her.

                    DRACULA

And they call *us* monsters! Hmmpff!

PANEL 4

Tiffany sets her picnic basket on the poker table and begins pulling out goodies: a hospital bag of fresh blood for Dracula, a roll of fresh gauze for the Mummy, hair tonic for the Wolf-man, a bottle of eyeballs.... Wolf-man looks happier than we've seen so far this whole issue.

174 • THE FUNNY BUSINESS

WOLF-MAN

Arrr, don't worry about Nurse Wrentch, Count. We've got a guest!

PAGE 18

PANEL 1

In the sitting room, Frankenstein's Monster sits calmly with his arm extended as Tiffany diligently stitches his hand back on.

CAPTION

Later...

MUMMY

We're glad you visit us, Tiffany. At least someone still remembers.

TIFFANY

I wouldn't miss this. You... you all—

PANEL 2

Now Tiffany is on the verge of sobbing. Her lower lip quivers, and an ocean of tears wells up in her eyes. Looking very concerned, Dracula pats her hand.

TIFFANY

—are the only friends I can turn to. Especially now!

DRACULA

There, there, little girl. Tell us vat is troubling you. Ve can help!

PANEL 3

Tiffany rummages in her basket and pulls out a stack of rolled blueprints and slick brochures, but we can't see what any of them are yet.

TIFFANY

I have terrible, terrible news, and I don't know what to do!

PANEL 4

Tiffany closeup, her face full of tears, her expression completely distraught.

TIFFANY

It's the evil *Van Helsing corporation*!

[LINK]

They want to tear down Castle Frankenstein!

TIFFANY

—And erect a set of luxury condominiums!

PAGE 19

Five panels, almost identical, like individual trading-card poses of the movie monsters. The funny punchline comes with the last panel:

PANEL 1

Frankenstein's Monster reacts to the news with shock and dismay.

PANEL 2

Dracula reacts to the news with shock and dismay.

PANEL 3

The Mummy reacts to the news with shock and dismay.

PANEL 4

Wolf-man reacts to the news with shock and dismay.

PANEL 5

A blank panel, showing only the invisible man's black-rimmed eyeglasses hanging in empty air. Presumably, he's also reacting to the news with shock and dismay, but of course we can't see anything.

PAGE 20

PANEL 1

Tiffany spreads out the brochures on the card table. They are bright and cheery and insipid, showing grinning yuppie homeowners standing in front of the condos. Headlines read: *Transylvania Shores*, a Gated Community of Exclusive Luxury Condominiums. The finest lifestyle in Old Eastern Europe!

TIFFANY

Just... look!

PANEL 2

Dracula picks up one of the brochures, scowling at a prominent logo on the back. "Another Fine Development Brought to You by the VAN HELSING CORPORATION." *[Note, we will use this logo again in later issues when they get to the construction site. I think it would be funny to have the Van Helsing logo look very much like the classic "VH" used by the rock group Van Halen. I can track down a copy of this logo, if needed.]*

DRACULA

Those Van Helsings! They have caused me plenty of trouble before.

PANEL 3

The Mummy looks at a site plan, which has been divided into dozens of crowded sardine-box plots, marked Unit 1, Unit 2, Unit 3, etc. Across the top are the words, "Former site of Castle Frankenstein [CONDEMNED]"

MUMMY

This is all just heiroglyphics to me.

GRUMPY OLD MONSTERS • 177

PANEL 4

Tiffany looks teary-eyed at a nostalgic snapshot of herself and a kindly-looking old man in a white lab coat. They are holding hands, standing in front of Castle Frankenstein.

TIFFANY

sniff My grandfather let me spend every summer at the castle. I really miss him!

[LINK]

What are we going to do?

PAGE 21

PANEL 1

Big panel. Dracula lurches to his feet and spreads his cape like a big vulture. He raises his voice, looking brave, intimidating.

DRACULA

Ve cannot let this happen!

PANEL 2

From across the room, Nurse Wrentch glares at him, and Dracula is immediately cowed.

NURSE WRENTCH

You! Sit down!

DRACULA

Yes, Nurse Vrentch...

PANEL 3

178 • THE FUNNY BUSINESS

The Wolf-man puts his chin in his hands daydreaming, looking off to one side (at Frankenstein's Monster, in the next panel).

WOLF-MAN

Ahhhhrr, Castle Frankenstein...I had some good times there.

WOLF-MAN

Remember, *we* had quite a tussle, eh Monster?

PANEL 4

Frankenstein's Monster grins.

PAGE 22

PANEL 1

Tiffany gathers up the plans and gathers her courage.

TIFFANY

We need a plan. You've got to help me—You're the greatest monsters ever!

PANEL 2

All the monsters look over their shoulders, furtively keeping an eye on Nurse Wrentch, who is currently scolding a nurse or an orderly. In the background, our shambling zombie is still trying to make his way across the floor with his walker.

INVISIBLE MAN

It's not going to be easy.

PANEL 3

The Mummy lifts a drooping bandage out of his eye so he can see. Maybe the cute little field mouse is just peeping out from between another gap in the windings.

GRUMPY OLD MONSTERS • 179

> MUMMY

Before we can save Castle Frankenstein—

PANEL 4

Outside shot of the Rest In Peace nursing home. Mummy's dialog balloon comes from one of the barred windows.

> MUMMY

—We've got to escape from *here*.

ISSUE #2

PAGE 1

PANEL 1

Big panel. Nighttime, we see the dark "Rest In Peace" care facility. Lights are burning in some of the windows. A bright crescent moon rides high in the sky overhead.

> CAPTION

Rest in peace, a retirement care facility... designed for "mature monsters with special needs."

> CAPTION

All of us are trapped here—the mummy, invisible man, frankenstein's monster, hunchback, volf-man, and plenty of others.

PANEL 2

Closeup of one of the barred, dark windows. Dracula is inside, looking out, sad and forlorn.

> CAPTION

Feh! I've been in *torture chambers* that vere more fun.

CAPTION

Good thing ve have an excuse to escape tonight!

PANEL 3

He sees two black bats flying past the window, outside and free.

DRACULAMY

Friends, I vill join you, soon!

PANEL 4

Dracula smiles as he hears a wolf howl out in the night.

SFX

Aarrooooooo!

DRACULA

Ah, the children of the night. Vhat music they make!

PAGE 2

PANEL 1

Big panel. Nurse Wrentch stands on the porch, hands on her hips and wearing a stern, ugly expression as she yells at the Wolf-Man, who is out on the grounds, head tilted up and howling at the Moon.

NURSE

Wrentch wolf-man, you come inside now. Enough of that yowling!

PANEL 2

Behind her, two orderlies (can make them like Abbot and Costello, one lanky, one chubby) twist earplugs into their ears. In the back of the panel, Wolf-Man shuffles toward the door, looking downcast.

CHUBBY ORDERLY

Jeez, it's not even a full moon tonight!

PANEL 3

Wolf-Man shuffles past Nurse Wrentch, but stops at a potted plant and lifts his leg, like a dog getting ready to pee.

NURSE

Wrentch, don't you dare!

PAGE 3

PANEL 1

Inside the rec room, sitting on the sofa, Frankenstein's Monster and the Invisible Man bend over a big open scrapbook that the Monster holds on his lap. He is grinning wistfully. Dracula comes up behind the sofa, looking interested.

MONSTER

Doctor Frankenstein took these pictures. Such good memories.

INVISIBLE MAN

Feeling nostalgic tonight, Monster?

MONSTEROH

Look, there's Igor!

PANEL 2

We see the open scrapbook full of corny photos, the Monster's hand (with black squarish fingernails) holding the page open: A grinning Igor carrying a torch, the Monster strapped on a table, the Monster putting his big arm over Dr. Frankenstein's stooped shoulder, both of them grinning for the camera. Typical "family vacation photos" with monsters.

MONSTER

Dracula, why aren't you in any pictures? You used to stay at the castle, too.

DRACULA

There I am, by the curtains. Vampires don't show up vell on photos, you know.

INVISIBLE MAN

Yeah, I know the problem . . .

PANEL 3

Frankenstein's Monster tilts up the book, turning a page, but he stares out at us, distracted and troubled. Dracula is behind him.

MONSTER

We just *have* to rescue Castle Frankenstein from the Van Helsing development corporation.

MONSTER

Tearing it down for luxury condominiums! Grrrrrr!

DRACULA

I have alvays hated those Van Helsings!

PANEL 4

Invisible Man (in his bathrobe and bunny slippers) at an open window, which he slams shut; the curtains are blowing inward from a cool breeze. We can see bars on the outside of the window.

INVISIBLE MAN

Blasted cold drafts!

INVISIBLE MAN

The escape is tonight. Will you miss this place when you get out?

PANEL 5

Dracula and the Frankenstein Monster look at each other in surprise. They answer in unison.

DRACULA & FRANKENSTEIN

No!

PAGE 4

PANEL 1

The Mummy is inside a supply closet, loading his arms up with rolls and rolls of gauze. An orderly opens the door, glaring at him.

ORDERLY

What's going on here? Even *you* can't use that much gauze.

PANEL 2

Mummy is flustered, trying to juggle his armful of gauze.

MUMMY

What? Oh, this? No, it's not for me.

MUMMY

The Invisible Man wanted to go out for a picnic tomorrow, and you know what happens when he gets too much sun.

PANEL 3

As the Mummy pushes past, still carrying the gauze, the orderly scolds him, wagging a finger at him.

184 • THE FUNNY BUSINESS

> ORDERLY

The Invisible Man wants to go outside, does he? To work on his invisible tan?

> ORDERLY

You know the rules! No unsupervised excursions. All patients must be accompanied. . . .

PANEL 4

The Mummy shuffles down the hall, still loaded with the gauze, as the orderly continues droning on about the rules and regulations.

> ORDERLY

. . . by a non-monster over the age of 18, and under the age of 65. Except on Tuesdays during autumn, in which case . . .

PAGE 5

PANEL 1

A frumpy nurse (how about the one from the redcross.jpg that Paco sent?) steps into a bath/shower room. There's a tub surrounded by a shower curtain. Steam billows up from the spray.

> NURSE

Why is that water still running?

PANEL 2

She yanks the shower curtain aside.

> NURSE

Yoo-hoo? Didn't you hear the bed call?

PANEL 3

Inside, we see the shower spray pouring down on the Invisible Man. He is visible only because of suds on part of his body, the deflected water spray, and the bristly scrub brush held in one invisible hand.

INVISIBLE MAN

Hey! A little privacy, please!

PANEL 4

The nurse turns beet red, horribly embarrassed, as she lets the shower curtain fall promptly closed again.

NURSE

Sorry! I didn't see a thing, honest!

NURSE

But please hurry up—lights out in five minutes.

PAGE 6

PANEL 1

Big panel. The night shift orderlies are herding all the monsters down the hall to their bedrooms. The focus of the panel, in the foreground, Dracula walks past the slow-moving zombie clicking along in his walker. They whisper to each other like prisoners in a jail-break movie, planning their escape.

ORDERLY

All right, Everybody get in your beds or coffins.

DRACULA (WHISPERING)

Pssst! It's tonight. Pass it on.

                             ZOMBIE

Tonight, yeah...

PANEL 2

As Wolf-Man walks past the Creature from the Black Lagoon, they both whisper to each other, sharing the same plans, keeping a surreptitious eye on the orderlies.

                            WOLF-MAN

Tonight.

                            CREATURE

Tonight...

PANEL 3

The orderlies open doors, herding monsters inside, looking at their watches. One hideous-looking demon (maybe with gorgon snakes on his head, long claws, big horns) snaps back at the orderly.

                            ORDERLY

Come on, you know the drill—this lockdown is to protect the public, not the patients.

                             [LINK]

It wasn't so long ago people were afraid of you old monsters.

                             DEMON

Hey, I never hurt anybody!

PANEL 4

Nurse Wrentch stands at the head of the hall like a Gestapo officer, hands on her ample hips. The monsters all answer in unison. Balloons come from various doors.

NURSE WRENTCH

Time for all good monsters to be in their beds.

MONSTERS (VARIOUS BALLOONS)

Yes, Nurse Wrentch. . . .

PAGE 7
Two panels

PANEL 1

Closeup of Nurse Wrentch's big mouth as she yells.

NURSE WRENTCH (SFX LETTERS)

Lockdown!

PANEL 2

Big panel, seen from outside, the quiet Rest In Peace home, dark and settling down for the night. Only a single light is still burning downstairs near the front door (presumably the office). Dialog balloons come from various spots on the house.

CAPTION

> Good night, Dracula.
> God night, Monster
> Did you take your sinus potion? No snoring tonight!
> Good night, Wolf-man.
> Good night, Hunchback.
> Where's my stuffed tarantula?
> Good night, zombies.
> Good night, Creature
> Good night, Invisible Man
> May I have a glass of water?
> Good night, John-Boy

PAGE 8

PANEL 1

Big panel. Nurse Wrentch opens the bedroom door, shines her flashlight to see that all the monsters are peacefully asleep. The rest of the room is dim, but in the wide beam of her light, we see Dracula's coffin snugly shut (engraved on the top are the words "COUNT DRACULA: R.I.P."), the Mummy's ornate sarcophagus is propped against the wall. One bed has only a lump in the sheets and an indentation on the pillow (the invisible man), with bunny slippers on the floor beside the bed. Wolf-Man is curled up like a dog on his bed, the sheet thrown off. Frankenstein's Monster is laid out on his back on a big lab-table slab, eyes shut.

CAPTION

    Later

PANEL 2

Small panel. Closeup of the bedroom door and knob as it shuts with a click.

SFX

    Klik

PANEL 3

All black panel, suddenly filled with several sets of bright, glowing eyes (like cartoons of wild animals lurking in the forest shadows). The monsters were only faking being asleep, and now they're all wide awake and ready.

PAGE 9

PANEL 1

The sarcophagus creaks open, and the Mummy pops out.

MUMMY

No time to lose.

PANEL 2

Dracula climbs out of his coffin.

PANEL 3

Wolf-Man bounces up and down on his bed, eager, like a puppy. Beside him, Frankenstein's Monster sits up stiffly on the lab table, arms stretched straight out in front of him.

WOLF-MAN

I'm ready! Let's go run around outside!

PANEL 4

Looking furtive, Dracula slips a bubbling, foaming test tube under his cape.

DRACULA

It's one of Dr. Jekyll's old recipes for a good night's sleep. Ve might find it useful, if ve run into trouble.

PAGE 10

This page is like the A-Team getting ready for a caper.

PANEL 1

Dracula pops his fang dentures into his mouth.

DRACULA

Fangs—check!

PANEL 2

The Mummy cinches his gauze tight around his forehead.

MUMMY

Bandages prepped!

PANEL 3

With his big blunt fingers, the Frankenstein Monster tightens one of the bolts on his neck.

MONSTER

Bolts—tight!

PANEL 4

As the Invisible Man's blanket is thrown aside, Wolf-Man is hopping on his bed, over-excited. He tilts his head back to let out a howl; he just can't contain himself.

WOLF-MAN

Ready! Ready! *AROOO—*

PANEL 5

All of the monsters round on Wolf-Man, scolding him.

MONSTER (ALL TOGETHER)

Sshhhhh!

PAGE 11

PANEL 1

Outside in a moonlit meadow, cute and adorable Tiffany Frankenstein is ready, also checking her supplies, as she waits for the monsters. She is kneeling on the forest floor, pulling things out of a wicker picnic basket, taking an inventory for their adventure. On the side of the basket, we can read, "This basket belongs to *Tiffany Frankenstein*."

CAPTION

In the woods nearby...

TIFFANY

The monsters said they'd meet me here...

TIFFANY

And together, we'll stop that developer from tearing down Castle Frankenstein!

[LINK]

My grandfather would be proud of me.

PANEL 2

Closeup, Tiffany starts pulling items out of the basket.

TIFFANY

I think I packed everything we'll need...

[LINK]

Maps... chicken sandwiches...

PANEL 3

Nonchalantly, still looking sweet, Tiffany removes a sharp and wicked-looking grappling hook.

TIFFANY

—grappling hook.

PANEL 4

Finished, she picks up her basket and skips off to the edge of the woods.

PAGE 12

PANEL 1

Inside the halls, one of the orderlies is on patrol strolling along by himself, like a prison guard.

PANEL 2

After he has passed, one of the doors pops open just a crack and the monsters crowd together, peering out to see if the coast is clear.

PANEL 3

With the orderly down the hall, the monsters sneak out, tiptoeing along.

PAGE 13

PANEL 1

Suddenly the orderly whirls, pointing a finger at them. The monsters cringe as they are caught in the act.

ORDERLY

Just what do you think you're doing?!

PANEL 2

Dracula leans forward, eyes narrowed, his hand extended, as he tries his Bela Lugosi hypnotic whammy.

DRACULA

Look deep into my eyes! You are getting very *sleepy* . . . you vill do anything Count Dracula commands!

PANEL 3

Not at all amused, the orderly crosses his arms over his chest.

ORDERLY

Would you cut it out? You try this on me every week.

PANEL 4

On the other side of the hall, another door opens up to reveal a very bitchy looking zombie woman with curlers in her hair. She appears very shrill. The orderly is distracted, looking at her.

ZOMBIE

You're making enough noise out there to wake the dead!

ORDERLY

What? Oh, sorry, ma'am—

PANEL 5

While he's distracted, Frankenstein's Monster grabs the orderly's shoulders, and Dracula pours his test tube of sleeping potion down the man's throat.

ORDERLY

Glurrrgggg

DRACULA

Ah, I haven't lost my touch...

[LINK]

vith a bit of help from Dr. Jekyll's chemistry set....

PAGE 14

PANEL 1

As the orderly falls snoozing to the floor, Frankenstein's Monster looks agitated.

MONSTER

We ought to split up—to cover more ground!

[LINK]

And somebody should create a diversion!

ORDERLY

Zzzzzzzznnnzzzz

PANEL 2

Wolf-Man scowls at him.

WOLF-MAN

You've been watching too much TV in the rec room again.

PANEL 3

Mummy leads the way as they all run down the hall toward a big door.

MUMMY

This way—to the exercise room.

PANEL 4

Mummy grabs the door handle with his bandaged hand, ready to pull it open.

MUMMY

We can get out the big window and make our way to the ground.

PANEL 5

As the door flies open, HORRORS!, Nurse Wrentch is waiting there inside, looking like death warmed over, scowling at them.

NURSE WRENTCH

Aha!

[LINK]

I *knew* you boys were up to something!

PAGE 15

PANEL 1

All the monsters shrink back in fear, cowering.

MUMMY

Curses!

FRANKENSTEIN

Oh no!

INVISIBLE MAN

Now what?

PANEL 2

The Mummy recovers first. He holds the drooping bandage out of his eye.

MUMMY

Wait a minute! Aren't we forgetting something? *We're* the real monsters here!

PANEL 3

Mummy closeup, as he gets angrier.

196 • THE FUNNY BUSINESS

                    MUMMY

We're supposed to be the scary ones.

PANEL 4

The other monsters get a backbone, standing taller, pressing closer to Nurse Wrentch.

                    DRACULA

He's right! How vill ve rescue Castle Frankenstein—

                    DRACULA

If ve can't even handle Nurse Vrentch?

PANEL 5

The Mummy holds out some of the thick rolls of gauze he took from the supply cabinet. Nurse Wrentch cringes backward.

                 NURSE WRENTCH

You stop right there! Just what do you think—

                    MUMMY

We know what to do with her,

                    [LINK]

don't we???

PAGE 16

PANEL 1
In a flurry of movement, Wolf-Man, Invisible Man, Mummy, Dracula, and Frankenstein's Monster roll out the gauze and wrap up Nurse Wrench. She looks like a cocoon made of bandages.

NURSE WRENTCH

Mmmfffff

PANEL 2

Trooping down the hall, the monsters carry Nurse Wrentch like a rolled up rug. Slumped on the floor, the snoozing orderly is still grinning, sound asleep.

PANEL 3

Inside the room, they prop her up inside the Mummy's sarcophagus, but she's rather hefty. They all try to wrestle her into position. Wolf-Man looks very smug and satisfied.

WOLF-MAN

There. She looks exactly like Mummy.

[LINK]

Nobody will ever know the difference!

PANEL 4

Mummy looks indignant.

MUMMY

I resent that!

PANEL 5

Frankenstein's Monster and Dracula struggle to close the lid, but Nurse Wrentch is just too bulky. They can't get it shut. Mummy stands off to the side, still miffed.

MUMMY

See? *I* never had trouble fitting inside.

198 • THE FUNNY BUSINESS

PAGE 17

PANEL 1

Back in the exercise room, the monsters all rush forward—only to be dismayed that the window has metal bars. Wolf-Man, though, is ready for anything. He cracks the knuckles on his clawed hands.

INVISIBLE MAN

I never noticed the exercise room window had bars!

DRACULA

But it's the second-floor!

WOLF-MAN

Just lemme at it!

PANEL 2

Wolf-Man grabs the bars with his paws, only to be zapped with electricity. Sparks fly, and his hair stands on end. Invisible man stands nearby.

SFX

Zzzzrrrtttttt

WOLF-MAN

Yow!

INVISIBLE MAN

It figures. A little more *planning* wouldn't have hurt.

PANEL 3

Frankenstein's Monster, though, is grinning, really looking forward to this.

                    MONSTER

Electricity? Let me! Me!

PANEL 4

He grabs the bars with his clunky hands. Even though it sparks and zaps and smoke curls from the bolts on his neck, his expression is one of pure joy.

                    MONSTER

Oooohhh!

PANEL 5

He finally bends the bars and tears them away from the window frame.

                    SFX

Screeekkk

PAGE 18

PANEL 1
The monsters whirl as an alarm bell begins ringing above the door to the rec room. They all look dismayed.

                    SFX

Klanng klanng

                    FRANKENSTEIN

Uh-oh.

                    INVISIBLE MAN

We don't quite have the knack of this escaping business. . . .

PANEL 2

Orderlies come running down the halls like commandos. One shouts into a walky-talky.

SFX

> Klanng klanng klanng

ORDERLY

> Perimeter breach on floor two, sector twelve!

[LINK]

> Intercept in progress!

PANEL 3

The Hunchback staggers down the hall, his hands clasped against his ears, weaving back and forth.

HUNCHBACK

> The bells! The bells!

PANEL 4

He careens into the scrambling orderlies, knocking them sprawling.

SFX

> Clunnnkk

ORDERLY

> Hey!

PANEL 5

Closeup of the hunchback, grinning. He did it on purpose!

HUNCHBACK (MUTTERS)

Glad I could help...

PAGE 19

PANEL 1

The shambling zombie is out for a night's walk, painstakingly moving down the hall in his rickety walker. Even though the alarms hammer through the speakers, the zombie doesn't seem to notice.

SFX

Klanng klanng klanng

PANEL 2

Floor-level closeup of the walker legs moving forward, then the bare rotted zombie feet shuffling to catch up.

SFX (WALKER)

Klikk

SFX (FEET)

Shuffle shuffle

PANEL 3

Nurses, including the one from the shower scene on p. 5, also come running down the hall, responding to the emergency. The zombie is in the middle of the hall, totally oblivious as the nurses shout at him.

NURSES (VARIOUS)

Out of the way!
Coming through!
Watch out!

202 • THE FUNNY BUSINESS

PANEL 4

The zombie sticks out his foot to trip the oncoming nurses. (Closeup of foot.)

PANEL 5

The nurses go sprawling like a football team in a pileup.

PANEL 6

Same as panel 2. The zombie moves on. Floor-level closeup of the walker legs moving forward, then the bare rotted zombie feet shuffling to catch up.

SFX (WALKER)

Klikk

SFX (FEET)

Shuffle shuffle

PAGE 20

PANEL 1

Now that the Frankenstein Monster has torn away the framework of bars and set the bent and twisted grid against the wall inside the room, the Mummy is at the window, ready to climb out.

MUMMY

Hurry! With those alarms, we won't have much time to escape!

PANEL 2

The Invisible Man hesitates, his sunglasses turned toward the floor, as if he's downcast. The monsters are all shocked when he says his news.

INVISIBLE MAN

Sorry . . . won't be coming with you.

MUMMY

What?

DRACULA

Vhy?

PANEL 3

Closeup shot of the Invisible Man's face -- in other words, we can't see *anything* except for his glasses hanging in the air.

INVISIBLE MAN

You can see by my expression that I feel really bad about this...

PANEL 4

The Invisible Man fumbles for an explanation. Wolf-Man growls at him.

INVISIBLE MAN

But to be of any real help, I have to be *naked*. And it's cold out there! My rheumatism. . .

WOLF-MAN

Fine time to tell us.

PANEL 8

The Invisible Man's robe lies in a pile on the floor after he has shucked it off. His cane floats in the air in front of the open door, held in his invisible hand.

INVISIBLE MAN

Go on without me! I'll stay behind and . . . and cover your escape!

PAGE 21

PANEL 1

As the Mummy scrambles over the windowsill, not looking very balanced, Dracula turns into a seedy-looking old bat.

SFX (DRACULA)

Pooof!

MUMMY

I'll go fir—

PANEL 2

The Mummy falls out head first, but one of his bandages catches on a nail on the windowsill. He unravels as he drops.

MUMMY

Aahhhh!

PANEL 3

Wolf-Man stands at the window sill, frowning at the long strip of bandage that dangles toward the ground. Beside him, the Dracula-bat flaps his wings, also looking.

WOLF-MAN

Who does he think he is? Rapunzel?

DRACULA/BAT

I vas afraid this escape vould be his undoing!

GRUMPY OLD MONSTERS • 205

PANEL 4

Dracula's bat wobbles in the air as Frankenstein and Wolf-Man climb down the strip of unraveled bandage, as if it's a fire-escape rope. The Mummy lies sprawled face-first on the ground, stunned silly and trying to recover.

DRACULA/BAT

Hurry! Tiffany is vaiting for us.

MUMMY

Curses!

PAGE 22

PANEL 1

With the Dracula bat flying above them, Mummy, Wolf-Man, and Frankenstein's Monster run toward us, away from the Rest In Peace home, in the background. Add that the Mummy is grabbing great loops of his unraveled bandages, carrying them wadded in his arms like a whole roll of loose toilet paper.

Inside the building behind them, all the lights are on now, alarms keep clanging into the night. Someone shouts from a window.

SFX

Klannng klannng klannng

PERSON

Monsters on the loose!

DRACULA/BAT (TO MUMMY)

Shamble faster!

206 • THE FUNNY BUSINESS

PANEL 2

A grinning Tiffany stands waiting for them at the edge of the woods.

TIFFANY

You made it! I knew you'd come!

WOLF-MAN

Hmmm, you look just like a girl I used to know—Little Red Riding Hood!

PANEL 3

The gang is all together now, with Tiffany carrying her basket and the monsters trotting after her into the trees.

TIFFANY

Next stop, Castle Frankenstein!

ISSUE #3

PAGE 1
Full page

In the middle of the page is cute little Tiffany, all alone with her basket of goodies. She's out in the dark woods, seemingly by herself. Everything is dark. The branches of the dead trees look like witches claws. A beetle and a centipede are crawling along the ground. A big ugly spider dangles from a web on a branch very close to her. From the dark patches in the forest, we can see glowing predatory eyes, four sets of them. Tiffany is looking around, seemingly worried. This should be a very scary page.

CAPTION

Sometimes things look almost too dark. Maybe even impossible...

CAPTION

The evil Van Helsing corporation wants to tear down Castle Frankenstein to make luxury condominiums!

CAPTION

That was my grandpa's home—I've got to save it!

CAPTION

But I'm just a kid, and Castle Frankenstein is so far away!

CAPTION

I can't do it alone.... I'll need all the help I can get.

PAGE 2

PANEL 1

Smiling now, Tiffany calls over her shoulder, toward the sinister glowing eyes in the forest.

TIFFANY

All right, guys! The coast is clear!

PANEL 2

The gang of grumpy monsters comes scrambling out of the underbrush, looking silly.

PANEL 3

The flustered Mummy, still trying to retuck his bandages, tie knots, and wrap his withered bones, now has to pick dried leaves, twigs, and cockleburrs out of the wrappings.

MUMMY

Curses! Back in Egypt I never had to worry about cockleburrs!

PANEL 4

Frankenstein's Monster has wide eyes, looking up in alarm as an owl hoots on a branch overhead. Dracula stands nearby, holding his cape up to cover the bottom half of his face (in classic Dracula pose), but it looks more like he's trying to hide instead of appear frightening.

> MONSTER

These woods are scary! There could be . . . *anything* out here!

> DRACULA

Even Nurse Vrentch!

PANEL 5

Close up shot, very sweet, of Tiffany's little hand taking the monster's big hand to comfort him.

> TIFFANY

Here, I'll hold your hand.

PAGE 3

PANEL 1

Wolf Man grins, showing his fangs.

> WOLF-MAN

Don't be a bunch of sissies! We're *free*!

PANEL 2

Using one of his back legs, he scratches himself vigorously in the ear, looking like a big dog. His expression is one of pure bliss.

> SFX

Skkttch skkttch skkttch

> WOLF-MAN

Ooh, wait a minute. Aaaahhh, that's better.

PANEL 3

Wolf Man bounds off into the underbrush, diving through shrubbery. We can only see his back half as he charges away in glee.

WOLF-MAN

We're out in the open! The wild! Let's make the most of it!

PANEL 4

Wolf Man on the prowl, sniffing, looking for prey.

WOLF-MAN

Ah, freedom! Eunning loose — hunting prey!

PANEL 5

Near his clawed foot, a cute field mouse dives for shelter in its hole.

MOUSE (SFX)

Eeeeep!

WOLF-MAN

This is how life was meant to be!

PAGE 4

PANEL 1

Big panel, atop a hill in a clearing, Wolf Man turns his head up to the full moon in the sky, his eyes closed in ecstasy, as he howls at the moon.

WOLF-MAN

Aaarooooooo!

PANEL 2

Huddled in the bushes, a very cute and scrappy little stray puppy (which looks something like a wolf cub) pokes his nose out of his shelter.

> PUPPY
>
> Yiip!

PANEL 3

Nearby, the Wolf Man looks at the puppy, glaring at it, while the puppy stares back, hopeful.

PANEL 4

Small panel. The puppy starts wagging its tail.

PANEL 5

Now side by side on the top of the hill (maybe in silhouette), the puppy and the Wolf Man both howl at the moon.

> WOLF-MAN
>
> Arrrooooooo!

> PUPPY
>
> Yiip!

PAGE 5

PANEL 1

Dracula stands in a clearing, where the monsters have met up. He is adjusting his fang dentures. The Mummy shoves drooping bandages out of his eye. Frankenstein's Monster is also there.

GRUMPY OLD MONSTERS • 211

DRACULA

Now that ve have escaped from the rest in peace home, ve must decide how to get to the castle.

[LINK]

I am not a young bat anymore. My vings von't carry me that far.

MONSTER

So much for the unflappable Count Dracula.

MUMMY

You don't expect us to *shamble* all the way there, do you?

PANEL 2

Tiffany, looking tough, stands with her hands on her hips, grinning in defiance.

TIFFANY

Don't worry—we won't need to flap <u>or</u> shamble.

PANEL 3

Dracula, Frankenstein's Monster, and the Mummy all look insufferably pleased at what Tiffany is saying to them. Tiffany doesn't need to be in the panel; her dialog can continue from previous panel.

TIFFANY

Do you monsters know how famous you are?

[LINK]

You may have been retired for a long time, but lots of folks remember you.

PANEL 4

Wolf Man comes crashing back through the bushes, happy to hear what Tiffany is saying. The faithful puppy is accompanying him. Either Tiffany's back is to us, or she isn't even in the panel.

TIFFANY

You scared a whole generation of people, and they're still grateful.

[LINK]

We can count on some of them to help us!

PAGE 6

PANEL 1

The little puppy seizes the loose end of one of the Mummy's loose bandages, tugging on it. The Mummy flails at the puppy, alarmed, but the puppy thinks he's playing and keeps tugging.

PUPPY (SFX)

Grrrrrr

MUMMY

Hey, stop that! Who let the dogs out?

PANEL 2

The puppy bolts, the gauze still clutched in his teeth. He runs fast, taking the bandage with him.

MUMMY (OUT OF PANEL)

It is the vengeance of Anubis, the jackal god!

PANEL 3

GRUMPY OLD MONSTERS • 213

The Mummy spins around in a blur, unraveling as the puppy keeps running. Wolf Man watches, grinning, like a proud father.

> MUMMY

Curses! Aaaahhh!

> WOLF-MAN

Isn't he cute? Can we keep him?

PANEL 4

The Wolf Man picks up the puppy, holding it, like a proud owner. It wiggles and wags its tail in his arms, squirming to get back down.

> WOLF-MAN

Just a stray, but he's kinda scrappy—do you think we should name him?

PANEL 5

The puppy dives into Tiffany's picnic basket on the ground. All we see is its butt and wagging tail as it noses around in the goodies there.

> WOLF-MAN

How about... gobblin'?

PANEL 6

Dracula and Frankenstein's monster help to rewind and reassemble the Mummy. Tiffany brightens as she hears a car horn honk nearby.

> DRACULA

Get yourself together, Mummy!

> MONSTER

Over and under, keep the lines neat...

                        SFX

Honnnk!

                      TIFFANY

Oh, here they are! Our friends have arrived!

PAGE 7

PANEL 1
Big panel. The monsters and Tiffany emerge from the forest to see a beaten-up old Volkswagen van parked and waiting for them. It has plenty of stickers and signs. Two stickers say "EQUAL RIGHTS FOR VAMPIRES" and "HAVE YOU HUGGED YOUR WEREWOLF TODAY?" A sign in the front windshield reads, TRANSYLVANIA OR BUST!

A big sign taped to the side of the VW bus says "H.A.R.M."

                      TIFFANY

It's a group called *Humans Assisting Retired Monsters*. I found them on the internet.

                       [LINK]

They'll take us to Castle Frankenstein.

PANEL 2

The group emerges from the VW bus for introductions. There are four of them, all halfway between long-haired hippies and Goths, wearing black lipstick, leather, chains, but also peace signs. Two in particular are the leader/driver, and and one wide-eyed fanboy hippy who will pester the Wolf Man.

                    HIPPY DRIVER

Wow, real monsters! Dude, we're like *so* honored to help!

PANEL 3

The fanboy hippy comes close to Wolf Man, wide-eyed and adoring, but the Wolf Man is a little chagrined.

FAN HIPPY

Hey, man, weren't you in *The Howling*?

WOLF-MAN

Uh, no . . . that was a different werewolf.

PANEL 4

The driver gestures for them to come on, and the monsters all scramble on board the VW bus.

LEADER

Man, you guys are *classic*! Welcome aboard!

PAGE 8
Five panels

PANEL 1

Seated on board the VW bus, which is driving along now, the fanboy is crowded uncomfortably close to the Wolf Man.

FAN

Wait—it was *An American Werewolf in London*, wasn't it?

WOLF-MAN

There are lotsa werewolves in the entertainment business.

PANEL 2

Frankenstein's Monster and Dracula are next to each other in the middle seat.

MONSTER

How can we get all the way to the castle in this bus?

DRACULA

There are mountains, and oceans —

LEADER

No worries, dudes! This bus has special modifications.

PANEL 3

Wolf Man, bored and annoyed, tries to concentrate on looking out the van's window as the fan keeps pestering him. The puppy sits on Wolf Man's lap, frisky and squirming.

FAN

I remember a werewolf from *Buffy the Vampire Slayer*! Was that you?

WOLF-MAN

Naw, I don't do television...

PANEL 4

Sitting next to one of the female Goth hippies, the Mummy digs in a big paper bag he found at his feet by the seats.

MUMMY

Oh look—snacks!

HIPPY CHICK

We've got raisins, dried fruit, and beef jerky.

MUMMY

Yum! Anything desiccated is fine with me.

PANEL 5

From the outside, we see the van driving along. The word balloons come from the van, but we should be able to figure out who's talking.

VAN (FAN)

Okay, how about *Teen Wolf*—I'm sure I recognize you from that!

VAN (WOLF-MAN)

Grrrr. This is going to be a long drive....

VAN (PUPPY)

Yiiip

PAGE 9

PANEL 1

Big panel; we see Castle Frankenstein in the distance, scary and haunted-looking, rundown, bats flying around the towers, dark trees all around it.

CAPTION

Meanwhile, at Castle Frankenstein...

BALLOON (FROM CASTLE)

I tell you, Mr. Gorr, this place is a *mess*!

PANEL 2

Inside the castle's huge, roomy main hall, Brad Van Helsing stands beside his simpering clerical assistant E. Gorr. Van Helsing is dressed in fine style, a new suit, the ultimate slimy yuppie. Next to him, E. Gorr has a clipboard on which he's busily jotting down words. On the pad maybe we can read the heading ACTION ITEMS. E. Gorr is pop-eyed, crouched over, with a hunchback, but he's also dressed in a business suit (though his doesn't fit as well as Van Helsing's).

218 • THE FUNNY BUSINESS

The interior of Castle Frankenstein looks like a wreck. Some of the ceiling beams have fallen in, giant spiderwebs lace the ceilings and doors, rats scuttle across the floor, and cockroaches crawl up the walls. (These cockroaches will be important in the end.)

VAN HELSING

We're doing civilization a favor by tearing it down!

[LINK]

You'd think any self-respecting mad scientist would take a little more pride in his home....

E. GORR

Yes, yes, Master Van Helsing!

VAN HELSING

I want to see real progress here. How am I doing so far?

E. GORR

Action item seven: demolish castle. Scheduled to begin on the 13th, Master.

PAGE 10

PANEL 1

Van Helsing frowns in disgust as he plucks a long spiderweb from the sleeve of his nice suit. E. Gorr takes down another note.

VAN HELSING

Ugh! This place is absolutely *infested*!

E. GORR

Action time eight: fumigate the rubble.

PANEL 2

Closeup as Van Helsing's fancy polished shoe comes down to squash one of the cockroaches on the floor, while other roaches scuttle out of the way. Guts and goop splurt out from the sole of his shoe.

SFX

Splurrrt

PANEL 3

Leaving the castle behind, Van Helsing and E. Gorr walk down the hill toward the construction trailer, which has the stylized "VH" logo and is marked, "Construction Headquarters."

VAN HELSING

The Van Helsing Development Corporation arrived not a moment too soon. We'll have the site in shape before long.

E. GORR

Yes, yes Master Van Helsing.

PANEL 4

They walk past a large, flashy sign erected just at the boundary. E. Gorr is still checking off items on his clipboard. The sign fills most of the panel. The sign has a pretty picture of an idyllic community, young couples holding hands and smiling, kids flying kites. TRANSYLVANIA SHORES: A PLANNED COMMUNITY OF NEW LUXURY CONDOMINIUMS.

E. GORR

Action item nine: evict peasants. Check.

PAGE 11

PANEL 1

Big panel. Inside the trailer offices, Van Helsing leers over an extravagant tabletop model of the planned Transylvania Shores development. There are lakes, parks, playgrounds, and hundreds of tiny identical condominium buildings.

VAN HELSING

Aaahhh, a *planned* community of identical pretentious houses, where all the people are content to be the same. . . .

PANEL 2

Closeup of Van Helsing grinning maniacally.

VAN HELSING

Free to lead planned lives on planned streets with planned yards.

PANEL 3

Sitting at his desk, E. Gorr jots down notes. A name plate sits prominently on the front of the desk, E. GORR, ADMINISTRATIVE ASSISTANT.

E. GORR

Yes, yes, Master Van Helsing. The perfect plan.

PANEL 4

Van Helsing stands at the trailer window, looking out dreamily, envisioning his grand plan.

VAN HELSING

They will shop only at our overpriced convenience stores, designer gas stations, trendy coffee bars, and barely affordable fast-food restaurants.

> VAN HELSING

In other words, civilization at last!

PAGE 12

PANEL 1

Big ominous panel as two giant wrecking ball cranes arrive, accompanied by heavy construction trucks, grinding their way past the headquarters trailer. A sign on the side of one of the cranes reads, MO'S DESTRUCTION SERVICE. And (in script below) "IF IT AIN'T RUBBLE WHEN WE'RE DONE, THEN IT'S FREE!" Van Helsing and E. Gorr step outside, smiling.

> VAN HELSING

Ahh, here they are. Only a week behind schedule.

> E. GORR

That's pretty good for construction workers, Master.

PANEL 2

Closeup of the ominous wrecking ball dangling from its chain on the crane.

> VAN HELSING (OUT OF PANEL)

It won't be long now until My dreams come to fruition.

PANEL 3

Standing at the door of his trailer, Van Helsing cracks his knuckles.

> VAN HELSING

We'll level the castle . . . and then we can really have fun!

PAGE 13

PANEL 1

The H.A.R.M. Volkswagen bus drives along. It's dripping water and has a few strands of seaweed clinging to the antenna and the windshield wiper (to imply that they've just driven over and through the ocean. The Wolf Man and his puppy both have their heads humorously stuck out the window, tongues lolling out.

CAPTION

Meanwhile...

VAN/DRIVER

Hey, man, almost there, dude according to this map.

[LINK]

"See the homes of the classic monsters."

PANEL 2

The van screeches to a halt at the sign on the edge of town. The sign reads, WELCOME TO DARKENHEIM, GATEWAY TO CASTLE FRANKENSTEIN. *BEWARE!!!*

VAN/DRIVER

Awesome! I can see why you love the place.

PANEL 3

Inside the van, the fanboy hippy keeps pestering Wolf Man, who pulls his head in from the window, glaring at him.

FAN HIPPY

What about *WOLFEN*? Or that old classic, *Curse of the Werewolf*? Were you in either of those?

WOLF-MAN

No! That was my cousin Leon. Now, will you please drop it?

PUPPY

Yiip!

PANEL 4

The doors open up and the monsters scramble out as the driver calls after them. The Goth hippy chick also leans out the window.

DIVER

Gotta let you all out here, Man. Sorry we can't stay, but we'll come back if we can.

HIPPY CHICK

Yeah, the *Black Lagoon* is being drained for a new theme park—unless H.A.R.M. can stop it!

TIFFANY

Let us know if you can help prove my little theory.

PANEL 5

The VW van drives off as the monsters watch after it. Tiffany and Dracula wave, while Wolf Man growls.

DRIVER

We won't let you down, man!

TIFFANY & DRACULA

Goodbye! Thanks for your help!

WOLF-MAN

Good riddance. I hate fanboys!

PAGE 14

PANEL 1

As they are heading into town *at dusk*, the gang encounters a group of peasants with overloaded suitcases, horse carts, and heavy packs on their backs. They all look forlorn. Tiffany is very disturbed.

TIFFANY

Wait. Where are you all going?

PANEL 2

One of the peasant men holds up an official-looking notice, disgusted. Tiffany sees it, horrified. Wolf Man growls, and his puppy growls beside him.

PEASANT

Evicted! Van helsing's tearing down our hovels to make a golf course!

WOLF-MAN

Grrr, we'll see about that. the boys are back in town!

PANEL 3

Big panel. They all look toward the silhouette of Castle Frankeinstein on a hill outside of the village. The monsters have wistful expressions on their faces. Tiffany, more determined than ever, takes the lead and stomps toward the village.

MONSTER

Ahhh, Castle Frankenstein. So many good memories there.

DRACULA

Yes, good times ve had . . .

MUMMY

Curses on Van Helsing!

TIFANY

No time to lose. Come on!

PAGE 15

PANEL 1

The gang stands in front of the town tavern, THE SLAUGHTERED LAMB, with a particularly scary and unpleasant sign showing a dangling sheep. Tiffany smiles brightly at it.

TIFFANY

This looks like a nice place to start. Let's go make friends.

PANEL 2

Inside, all the townspeople in the tavern stop and turn toward the door, eyes wide, mouths open, staring in astonishment at the group of monsters who have arrived.

PANEL 3

Finally two of the men turn back to their mugs of ale.

PEASANT 1

Well, at least they're not as scary as that Van Helsing bloke!

PEASANT 2

Now maybe things will get back to normal around here.

PANEL 4

Swaying between the tables with a full tray of beer mugs in her hand, we see the Bride of Frankenstein (as described in previous e-mail to Jeff). She stops and stares wide-eyed toward the door.

PANEL 5

Her tray of beer mugs crashes and spills to the floor.

> BRIDE
>
> Monster!

PAGE 16

PANEL 1

Grinning like a schoolboy, the Monster goes bounding across the room toward her, his arms outstretched.

> MONSTER
>
> Bride!

PANEL 2

As soon as he gets there, though, she slaps him a good one across the face, knocking one of his bolts loose.

> BRIDE
>
> And that's because you left for "boys' night out" and never came back!

PANEL 3

Pointing one finger at him, the Bride resoundingly lectures him.

> BRIDE
>
> How dare you shamble in here after all these years—Expecting me to take you back, no doubt! Hmmmph!

BRIDE

We were *made* for each other! Like any other mad scientist could have done better!

PANEL 4

The monster hangs his head meekly.

MONSTER

I, uh, but, uh, I'm here now. I came to save Castle Frankenstein!

PANEL 5

The Bride turns her back on him and struts toward the bar, calling over her shoulder.

BRIDE

About time you did something useful with yourself!

PAGE 17

PANEL 1

Face off, Brad Van Helsing and the construction boss are glaring at each other, faces close, snarling.

VAN HELSING

What do you mean your men won't work up at the castle after dark???

CONST. BOSS

Exactly what I said!

PANEL 2

Big panel, with the castle in the background and the looming demolition cranes and heavy equipment standing idle, the rest of the hard-hatted construction crew sits down and opens their lunchboxes and coffee thermoses.

PANEL 3

E. Gorr, looking very nervous and worried, comes up to the two men, who are still glaring at each other. E. Gorr holds a clipboard.

E. GORR

But this delay isn't on my schedule! We didn't account for any unforeseen difficulties.

PAGE 18

PANEL 1

Very angry, Van Helsing stands with his face in a grimace, ready to spit nails. His hands are clenched into fists.

VAN HELSING

Ridiculous superstitions! You're as bad as those peasants in town! What are you afraid of?

PANEL 2

The workers are sitting back on crates and in the backs of their trucks, calmly chatting, looking content. Two are playing cards. One of them munches on a sandwich.

CONST. BOSS (OUT OF PANEL)

Afraid? You've got it all wrong, Mr. Van Helsing!

PANEL 3

The construction boss is indignant. His shifts his hard-hat back on his head. Van Helsing, helpless, slaps his forehead.

CONST. BOSS

I'm talking 'bout *union rules* here! Ain't nobody messing with those!

PAGE 19

PANEL 1

View is from low to the ground. The puppy is close to an ornate wagon wheel, sniffing it. Maybe horses' hooves are in the front of the panel.

CAPTION

Outside the slaughtered lamb...

PANEL 2

Puppy lifts his leg, ready to pee on the wheel.

PANEL 3

Big panel. We see now that this is a big gypsy wagon, loaded with sacks, boxes, furniture, odds and ends all tied down with twine. A gypsy clan leader sits on the buckboard, yelling to his horses. Other gypsies can be seen inside the wagon. Everyone looks grim, not happy at all to be leaving.

GYPSEY LEADER

Yo! Ready to go! Nothing for us to do here.

[LINK]

Let's get out of this town and on to browner pastures!

PANEL 4

Wolf Man picks up the puppy, getting him out of the way as the carts rumble off.

WOLF-MAN

Must be bad if even the gypsies don't want to stick around long enough to curse somebody!

PAGE 20

PANEL 1

Inside the tavern, Frankenstein's Monster sits at a small candlelit table, across from the Bride. They are leaning close to each other, obviously well on their way to making up.

BRIDE

Oh, Monster . . . if only things could have been different.

[LINK]

Do you ever wonder . . . what if we'd made other choices?

PANEL 2

The Monster is starry-eyed as he stares at her.

MONSTER

Even after all these years, you're still a looker!

PANEL 3

The Bride is looking at him, but her gaze is far away, contemplative, dreamy.

BRIDE

Oh, but we wanted such different things. . .

[LINK]

You wanted to rampage. . .I wanted a family. . .

PANEL 4

She gestures to the seedy bar, the depressed and drunken peasants, the many empty seats.

> **BRIDE**
>
> And now just look at us!

PANEL 5

Earnestly, now, the Monster clutches her hands in his.

> **MONSTER**
>
> Give me a chance! I've really straightened myself out this time.

PAGE 21

PANEL 1

Dracula sidles up to the bar, leans over it, and signals the bartender.

> **DRACULA**
>
> Bartender! I vill have a goblet of fresh bludd! Type 'B Positive,' if you have it.

PANEL 2
The hardened bartender leans toward him, scowling.

> **BARTENDER**
>
> I'm gonna have to see some I.D.

> **DRACULA**
>
> I.D.? Vat? I am four hundred years old!

PANEL 3

Taken aback, Dracula opens up his empty wallet. A moth flies out and a spider crawls out.

DRACULA

Nurse Vrentch at the R.I.P. care home has my identification. Surely you can make an exception in this case —

PANEL 4

The bartender, unimpressed, points to a sign above the bar. The sign reads, "NO I.D., NO FRESH BLOOD, NO EXCEPTIONS."

PANEL 5

Sighing in defeat, Dracula slumps onto a barstool.

DRACULA

All right... ice vater, then.

PAGE 22

PANEL 1

Scappy little Tiffany has climbed up on one of the plank tables in the bar, raising her hands for attention.

TIFFANY

Listen up, everybody! We're here on a mission — to save Castle Frankenstein!

[LINK]

That castle is part of your history! Are you going to let some greedy developer just tear it down?

PANEL 2

Two peasants at a small table mutter about the prospect. Use same two guys from Page 15.

PEASANT 1

What can we do? It's not the good old days anymore.

PEASANT 2

Old Doc Frankenstein wasn't really so bad. His power bills were colossal, but at least he had a vision.

PEASANT 1

He even put in new street lights.

PANEL 3

At the bar, the bartender wipes a glass as he comments.

BARTENDER

And back then we did a brisk business in unsavory sorts— vampire hunters, and the like . . . .

PANEL 4

Tiffany continues her rousing speech as the peasants finally get to their feet and cheer.

TIFFANY

We can't let Van Helsing incorporate our monsters out of existence! We're fighting for your heritage!

PANEL 5

The peasants cheer and run for their pitchforks and torches, while the grumpy old monsters grin. This just may work after all.

                        TIFFANY

It's time to take up your torches again. This time we march *for* Castle Frankenstein!

ISSUE #4

PAGE 1

PANEL 1

Big panel. A line of peasants carrying torches and pitchforks are marching up the winding road toward Castle Frankenstein looming ominously in the background.

                        CAPTION

Near Castle Frankenstein

                        CAPTION

The peasants, carrying torches, march on their enemy, eager to eradicate the mark of evil that the Van Helsing corporation has made on their town.

PANEL 2

Closeup of an angry peasant's face. He is holding a torch.

                        PEASANT

Destroy! Burn it down!

PANEL 3

Another peasant carrying a pitchfork stands by the TRANSYLVANIA SHORES sign, shouting and pointing toward the well lit construction trailer off to the side. The "VH" Van Helsing logo is prominent on the side of the headquarters trailer. Another peasant in the line (the one from panel 2) looks sheepish.

GRUMPY OLD MONSTERS • 235

PEASANT

Hey guys, Over here! That's the wrong way!

SHEEPISH PEASANT

Sorry! Force of habit, I guess....

PAGE 2

PANEL 1

Inside the Van Helsing Corporation headquarters trailer, Van Helsing and E. Gorr are looking out the window at the line of torch-carrying peasants. E. Gorr looks intimidated, while Van Helsing is just annoyed.

VAN HELSING

There go the peasants again. Seems like they're always riled up about something or other....

E. GORR

Yes, yes, Master!

PANEL 2

Van Helsing turns away from the window to stand at his elaborate model of his "Transylvania Shores Planned Community." He is practically drooling with anticipation.

VAN HELSING

Soon, all the peasants will be evicted anyway, and my planned community can proceed.

[LINK]

Once dawn comes and a new work shift starts, the union destruction crews will tear down Castle Frankenstein!

PANEL 3

E. Gorr stands at the window. His eyes are nearly popping out of their sockets with his alarm.

> E. GORR
>
> Master Van Helsing! They're coming this way! Heading for our trailer — *With torches!*

PANEL 4

Outside, the peasant mob waves their torches and pitchforks, shouting.

> PEASANT
>
> Van Helsing, go home!

> (RANDOM)
>
> We want our village back!
> Save the castle!
> Down with corporate greed — up with mad scientists!

PANEL 5

Van Helsing looks angry but not fearful. He grabs a legal-looking document from his IN box.

> VAN HELSING
>
> Sigh. I wish people bothered to read their contracts—it would save so much time and trouble.

PAGE 3

PANEL 1

Van Helsing steps out onto the porch of the headquarters construction trailer with E. Gorr crouching behind him. The peasants set up a resounding shout of disapproval, but Brad Van Helsing just sneers.

SFX

Boo! Boo! Boooo!

> VAN HELSING

Boo? Is that supposed to scare me?

PANEL 2

Small panel as one of the peasants makes a snide comment.

> PEASANT

Not *that* kind of boo.

PANEL 3

Closer shot of Van Helsing as he holds up a detailed, official-looking document with ribbons and official seals.

> VAN HELSING

You forget that if you proceed, I own this town, free and clear. All of the streets and business buildings, even your hovels.

> VAN HELSING

It's completely legal. You signed away your right to protest when you all accepted a tiny fortune in zlotys.

PANEL 4

Out in the crowd, E. Gorr dutifully hands out photocopies of the contract to everyone in the audience. Van Helsing keeps talking (but he doesn't have to be in the panel).

> VAN HELSING

The proof is in the perfectly clear definitions and contractual terms in the fine print. You forfeit *everything* if you stand in my way.

ANGRY PEASANT

Fine print! Who reads fine print?

VAN HELSING

Why, hardly anyone. That's why civilization itself is based on fine print.

PANEL 5

Looking downcast, the peasants read their copies, grumbling and frowning.

PEASANT

I don't see any loopholes.

PEASANT 2

I knew I should have had my lawyer review all the terms....

PEASANT 3

Well, Tiffany Frankenstein and the monsters are up at the castle. Maybe they can find a way to save it.

PAGE 4

PANEL 1

Tiffany stands on the doorstep of Castle Frankenstein, big gates behind and above her, a rickety portcullis and a heavy wooden door. But our view is from behind her, looking over her shoulder, toward the construction trailers, the cranes, the headquarters trailer, with all the tiny lights of the peasants' torches.

TIFFANY

We'll make our last stand here.

TIFFANY

The peasants are down there right now with their torches . . . but I have a feeling that *this* is the real battleground.

PANEL 2

The Dracula bat flaps in front of Tiffany's face, returning from a long flight and giving his report. Beside her, Mummy looks forlorn on hearing the news.

DRACULA

Van Helsing has trapped them vith contracts and legalities.

MUMMY

Curses! They didn't stand a chance!

PANEL 3

With a POOF the bat transforms back into Dracula. Beside him the Wolf Man and his faithful puppy Gobblin both stand with nearly identical growling expressions.

WOLF-MAN

We'll have to fight Van Helsing ourselves, then! Grrrr!

DRACULA

Bluuhh! I am too old for such a long flight!

PANEL 4

Tiffany puts walkman headphones over the Monster's ears (identical to the ones he was wearing in Issue 1). In her hand is a CD case with the clear words "METALLICA: ST. ANGER" on it. Listening to the music, the Monster is angry and growling.

240 • THE FUNNY BUSINESS

> TIFFANY
>
> Here, Monster. This will put you in the right mood.
>
> MONSTER
>
> Aaarrrrrrrr!

PAGE 5

PANEL 1

Tiffany looks toward the wooded horizon, where the full moon is setting in the trees.

> TIFFANY
>
> Look, the moon is setting. The dark before the dawn . . .
>
> [LINK]
>
> It won't be long before the destruction workers begin their morning shift.

PANEL 2

In a very languid and lazy scene (in start contrast to Tiffany's words) the group of burly hardhatted destruction workers sit around in lawn chairs near their trucks and cranes. Some are snoozing, others playing cards, one is playing a harmonica, others digging in open lunchboxes in their laps. They do not look at all ambitious or threatening. *Tiffany's dialog either continues from the previous panel, or is included in a caption.*

> TIFFANY
>
> Once they start, the castle is doomed. Nothing will stop them.

PANEL 3

Big panel, poster shot, the last stand at the castle door. Tiffany stands in front, while Mummy, Wolf Man, Dracula, and Frankenstein's Monster look tough behind her.

WOLF-MAN

We can't let Van Helsing get past us, no sir!

MUMMY

Yeah, he'll only get through over our undead bodies!

PAGE 6

PANEL 1

A big ominous panel of Brad Van Helsing looming right next to them. He has come up the path to face the monsters, and now he stands there looking demonic. Behind him, the sky is dark and cloudy, with a crack of thunder and lightning bolts dancing around. Very terrifying.

VAN HELSING

That would be an acceptable resolution.

SFX (THUNDER)

Kkkraakkkkkk

VAN HELSING

Everything's perfectly legal and contractual.

PANEL 2

The scrappy puppy Gobblin dashes forward and latches his teeth on Van Helsing's pants cuff, tugging and growling.

SFX

Grrrrr

PANEL 3

Van Helsing looks down with an utterly withering look, as if he's just stepped on gum.

PANEL 4

The puppy dives away in terror, hiding at Wolf Man's hairy feet.

SFX

Yiiip!

WOLF-MAN

Good boy, Gobblin!

PANEL 5

A birds'-eye view from above, showing Van Helsing facing off with the monsters on the landing in front of the castle gate. Tiffany is in front, defiant.

TIFFANY

We won't let you tear down the castle, Mr. Van Helsing!

VAN HELSING

I assure you, there's nothing you can do to stop me.

VAN HELSING

Even though the destruction crew is still on break between shifts, I have other resources.

[LINK]

Mr. Gorr!

PANEL 6

Closeup as Van Helsing whistles shrilly.

SFX

Fwheeeet!

PAGE 7

PANEL 1

Tiffany and the monsters look at each other, wide-eyed in fear and confusion, as a loud rumble and clanking noise approaches.

SFX

Rrrrmmmmbbbblllle klannk clankk

DRACULA

Now vat?

TIFFANY

Stand strong, everyone!

PANEL 2

Big dramatic panel. The giant wrecking-ball crane arrives, looking like a terrifying dinosaur. On the side is the sign from last issue, MO'S DESTRUCTION SERVICE. And (in script below) "IF IT AIN'T RUBBLE WHEN WE'RE DONE, THEN IT'S FREE!" Riding in the cab of the crane, holding the control levers and grinning, is hunchbacked E. Gorr, still wearing his business suit. The monsters look up in awe at it.

E. GORR

Here I am, Master!

PANEL 3

Van Helsing crosses his arms over his business suit, insufferably smug. Mummy and Dracula look at him.

VAN HELSING

Why bother standing in the way of progress? I intend to knock down the castle and bring this place out of the 18th century!

> DRACULA

I *liked* the 18th century...

> MUMMY

I preferred 2000 B.C.

> VAN HELSING

Mr. Gorr, throw the switch!

PAGE 8

Note, the page breaks in the action sequence from pp. 8–11 are not set in stone. Can be flexible, if artist prefers different panel sizing.

PANEL 1

E. Gorr in the cab of the wrecking-ball crane, yanking levers, maniacally intent.

> SFX

Vvrrrroooommmm

PANEL 2

Tiffany, distraught, yells. Wolf Man crouches, ready to spring at the uneven stone-block wall of the castle. He looks over his shoulder; clearly he has an idea.

> TIFFANY

We've got to stop them! What can we do?

> WOLF-MAN

This calls for bold and ill-considered action!

PANEL 3

Climbing like an agile orangutan, Wolf-Man scrambles up the wall.

From below the Monster mutters a comment.

MONSTER

Ill-considered plans are his specialty.

DRACULA

He's trying to get closer to the wrecking ball!

PANEL 4

Reaching his position, Wolf Man hangs onto a stone block ledge and reaches out his hand, calling down to the Mummy. The Mummy tosses a loose end of his wrappings.

WOLF-MAN

Mummy! Throw me the end of one of your bandages.

MUMMY

Catch!

PANEL 5

Wolf Man yanks the bandage and swings Mummy up into the air like a ball on a string. Flailing and yelling, Mummy goes flying toward the ominous wrecking ball dangling on the end of the crane boom.

MUMMY

Curses! Aaaaaaaaaaaa!

PAGE 9

PANEL 1

With the long bandage dangling like toilet paper behind him, Mummy slams into the wrecking ball like a bug on a windshield. Far away on the castle wall, Wolf-Man cheers.

>   MUMMY

Ooooof!

>   WOLF-MAN

Good catch, Mummy.

PANEL 2

On the ground, Van Helsing yells up at the crane cab.

>   VAN HELSING

Mr. Gorr, what are you waiting for?

PANEL 3

With a poof of smoke, Dracula turns into a bat and flies toward the crane.

>   SFX

Pooofff

>   DRACULA

I vill help!

PANEL 4

Clutching the loose end of the Mummy's gauze, Wolf Man launches himself toward the wrecking ball, swinging like Tarzan on a vine.

>   WOLF-MAN

Coming, Mummy!

PANEL 5

The Mummy is straddling the chain of the big wrecking ball, while Wolf Man climbs up the gauze, hauling himself up beside him.

> WOLF-MAN

Ahhh, that wasn't too hard.

> MUMMY

Great... but now what do we do?

PAGE 10

PANEL 1

The Dracula bat flaps and flies in E. Gorr's face, making it impossible for him to see.

> DRACULA

Vatch the birdie!

PANEL 2

E. Gorr flails at the bat, knocking the controls.

> E. GORR

Go away! You're messing up my designer varmanti suit!

PANEL 3

Silhouette of the tall crane with the wrecking ball swinging wildly. Silhouettes of Wolf Man and Mummy clinging for dear life onto the wrecking ball.

> WOLF-MAN

Hey! Hold this thing steady!

PANEL 4

Closeup of the wrecking ball, with Wolf Man and Mummy clutching each other, trying to hold on. Both have eyes wide and mouths open as they yell.

WOLF-MAN & MUMMY

Yaaaaaaaahhhhh!

PAGE 11

PANEL 1

Frankenstein's Monster tugs at the stitches on his wrist, pulling them loose like the thread of an unraveling sweater.

MONSTER

I can lend them a hand!

PANEL 2

The Monster throws like a baseball pitcher hurling a fast ball. At the end of his throw, his hand comes off (like it did during the poker game in Issue 1) and flies.

PANEL 3

The Monster's hand slams into the crane's control levers.

SFX

Thwapp

PANEL 4

Closeup of the pulley and winch at the top of the crane boom. The chain has been released and is whirring through the block and tackle.

SFX

Klacketa klacketa klacketa

PANEL 5

The wrecking ball slams into the ground with enough weight and force to make a crater. Wolf Man and Mummy are still sitting on it, very shaken.

SFX

Kkkrrunnnch

MUMMY

Ouch! You call *that* a plan?

WOLF-MAN

Well, it was one way to stop the wrecking ball.

PAGE 12

PANEL 1

The foreman of the destruction crew looks at his watch on his thick, hairy wrist, then shouts.

FOREMAN

All right, men! Break's over! Time to clock back in.

PANEL 2

Big panel as all the workers begin to stir from their work site. One man pours steaming coffee from his thermos. Others pick up their hardhats and put them on their heads. One man cracks his knuckles. One burly man is still snoozing in his lawnchair, and the foreman kicks it to wake him up.

FOREMAN

Come on, Burt! You can snooze on the job!

ANOTHER WORKER

I can't wait until morning break.

WORKER 3

I knew I shoulda been a brain surgeon....

PANEL 3

The workers line up by the time clock, punching their cards to get started.

WORKER

Another day, another destruction....

PANEL 4

The foreman and his cheerful destruction crew come whistling up to stand behind Van Helsing.

VAN HELSING

Ah, reinforcements!

[LINK]

Mo, a bonus for you and your men if you finish the job today.

FOREMAN

You got it, boss!

PANEL 5

The bedraggled monsters look defeated and disheartened, seeing themselves vastly outnumbered. The situation is very bad indeed. Frankenstein's Monster hangs his head, patting Tiffany on the shoulder. We should see a few cockroaches crawling around.

MONSTER

Now what are we gonna do?

WOLF-MAN

I hope Van Helsing gets fleas....

MUMMY

Wouldn't that be cruel to the fleas?

PAGE 13

PANEL 1

Outside shot of the tavern, the Slaughtered Lamb. Sun is rising in the background; maybe there's a coffin or two propped up against the side wall.

CAPTION

Meanwhile, at the *slaughtered lamb*....

PANEL 2

The Bride and the bartender are cleaning up. Bride is lifting an overturned heavy plank table (to show how strong she is). As the bartender is wiping a glass at the bar, he looks up, hearing the fax machine ring.

BRIDE

The peasants sure make a mess whenever they go on a rampage....

SFX

Beeep whirrrrrr

BARTENDER

That's our fax machine! Who would be sending us a fax at this time of the morning?

252 • THE FUNNY BUSINESS

PANEL 3

The Bride stands over a very sophisticated-looking high-tech fax machine (very out of place in this old medieval tavern), holding a piece of paper as it curls out of the fax. On the heading we can read, "H.A.R.M., *Humans Assisting Retired Monsters*, Attention: Miss Tiffany Frankenstein." The Bride grins.

BRIDE

Finally! This is what Tiffany has been waiting for.

PANEL 4

Clutching a handful of papers that have come off the fax machine, the Bride races out the tavern door.

BRIDE

No time to lose!

PAGE 14

PANEL 1

The foreman holds up a plunger/detonator connected to long wires that run into the castle. Other destruction workers carry shovels, pickaxes, crowbars.

FOREMAN

Planted all the dynamite last night, Mr. Van Helsing. Above and beyond the call of duty.

WORKER

I love smashing things in the morning!

PANEL 2

Tiffany hasn't given up yet, though. She rallies, raising her hand and rousing the monsters.

TIFFANY

Wait a minute! We can't just give up!

[LINK]

You're *monsters*. Nobody threatens, shambles, gives the creeps, raises goosebumps, or *inspires terror* better than you!

PANEL 3

The monsters all look surprised, as if the thought hasn't occurred to them before.

WOLF-MAN

Hmmm, she's right.

MUMMY

The best part of being a monster is *scaring* people!

PANEL 4

Big panel -- Monsters on the loose! Mummy shambles toward the destruction workers, Frankenstein's monster staggers forward with arms stiffly outstretched (like Karloff), Wolf Man snarls as he bounds forward, Dracula has his cape in front of his face, peering over it in classic Bela Lugosi pose. In the lead of the group of oncoming monsters, we can see the cute puppy Gobblin also snarling and ready to fight.

MONSTER

Urrrr urrrrr

WOLF-MAN

Raaaahhrrrr! Let's strut our stuff!

DRACULA

Yes, ve can still chill their blood!

254 • THE FUNNY BUSINESS

PANEL 5

Bug-eyed, the destruction workers are terrified and they scramble, running so fast that their hardhats go flying.

WORKERS

>Yiikes!
>Those are real monsters!
>And they look pretty grumpy!
>Run away!

PANEL 6

Small panel. Closeup of Frankenstein's monster as he grins with delight at what they've just accomplished.

PAGE 15

PANEL 1

E. Gorr has grabbed the dynamite plunger and holds it up to Van Helsing. With a diabolical expression on his face, Van Helsing grabs the plunger, ready to blow up the castle. Tiffany cries out in horror as she sees what they're doing.

E. GORR

>We don't need those cowards, master. you can do the honors!

VAN HELSING

>There's more than one way to destroy a castle....

TIFFANY

>No!

PANEL 2

Spitting gravel and smoking tires, a hearse drives up and comes to a stop right next to Van Helsing and the destruction crew. The side of the hearse says R.I.P. The Mummy looks hopeful, but Dracula is intimidated.

SFX

Screeeech

MUMMY

Maybe that's somebody who can help us!

DRACULA

I don't think so....

PANEL 3

Nurse Wrentch climbs out of the passenger side of the hearse, her face stormy, her uniform crisp. She looks like she's ready to take on every monster from every movie ever made.

NURSE WRENTCH

So there you are!

NURSE WRENTCH

If you thought you could get away with this? Some of you need new brain transplants!

PANEL 4

Nurse Wrentch closeup as she holds out a scolding finger.

NURSE WRENTCH

Mark my words, once we get back to the nursing home there'll be no treats and no shuffleboard for a week!

NURSE WRENTCH

And you, little girl — I don't care if you *are* the granddaughter of Doctor Frankenstein. Your visiting privileges are permanently revoked!

PANEL 5

The monsters all look sheepish and cowering. Again, we should see a cockroach or two.

WOLF-MAN

We can explain!

MONSTER

Sorry, Nurse Wrentch.

MUMMY

We had to do something!

DRACULA

I am glad ve tried at least....

PANEL 6

Nurse Wrentch stands beside Van Helsing, and both look like evil incarnate, both utterly victorious.

WOLF-MAN

Talk about our worst nightmare...

PAGE 16

PANEL 1

The Bride runs up, breathless, her hair a mess. She extends the papers as she shouts. In unison, Nurse Wrentch and Van Helsing both spin their heads to look at her in surprise.

BRIDE

Wait! I've got a court order for you to stop!

PANEL 2

Tiffany takes the paper, reading and grinning. Ven Helsing pushes close, angry and curious.

TIFFANY

H.A.R.M. came through on my request. Castle Frankenstein is saved!

VAN HELSING

What are you talking about, pipsqueak?

PANEL 3

Dracula and Wolf Man stand next to the moss-covered blocky wall of Castle Frankenstein. Several cockroaches are crawling up the stones.

TIFFANY (OUT OF PANEL)

It seems this castle is a breeding ground for a very rare and endangered species of cockroach. Their habitat is protected by law.

PANEL 4

The Mummy holds up his bandaged finger. A cockroach is perched on it, waving antennas in the air.

TIFFANY (OUT OF PANEL)

It is illegal for the Van Helsing corporation to damage their home, or disturb them in any way!

PANEL 5

Dracula "helpfully" offers Van Helsing a large magnifying glass. Tiffany is very happy.

> DRACULA

Perhaps this vill help you read the fine print.

> TIFFANY

Civilization itself is based on fine print, Mr. Van Helsing.

PANEL 6 (could be combined with Panel 5)

Van Helsing, using the magnifying glass, scowls. E. Gorr is next to him, looking very antsy.

> E. GORR

Everything seems to be in order, Master.

> VAN HELSING

Cockroaches?! But... my investment! My planned community!

PAGE 17

PANEL 1

Frankenstein's Monster and the Bride stand next to each other, arm in arm. The Bride looks at his loose wrist stitches.

> BRIDE

Just look at these stitches! you're falling apart! You obviously need *somebody* to take care of you.

PANEL 2

While Van Helsing continues to read the court order in stunned disbelief, we see a shot from near ground level as the puppy comes up to his fancy shoes and pants cuff and lifts his leg to piddle on Van Helsing.

> VAN HELSING

This... this doesn't leave me any room to appeal!

PANEL 3

E. Gorr and Van Helsing turn around and begin to leave, grumbling. As a surprise, the Creature from the Black Lagoon pokes his head up out of the murky water in the castle moat, spitting water.

> E. GORR
>
> Cheer up, Master. Maybe we can find a nice swamp to drain.

> SFX CREATURE
>
> Sppaff!

> CREATURE
>
> Oh, no you don't!

PANEL 4

It's not over yet. Nurse Wrentch stands beside the R.I.P. hearse, determinedly holding the back door open and waiting for the monsters to join her.

> NURSE WRENTCH
>
> I've had enough of this nonsense. Now get into the vehicle so we can go back to the nursing home.

PANEL 5

Nurse Wrentch stands like a battle-axe, her plump arms crossed over her chest.

> NURSE WRENTCH
>
> No whining, now! It's not as if you have much choice — you've got no other place to live, and no one else to take care of you.

PAGE 18

PANEL 1

The monsters are all dejected and forlorn. The Bride holds onto the Monster's arm. Tiffany stops them, standing in the way.

MUMMY

At least we saved the castle. . . .

DRACULA

It vas fun vhile it lasted. . . .

TIFFANY

Wait a minute, Nurse Wrentch. They do have a choice. They can stay here at Castle Frankenstein — with me.

[LINK]

I volunteer to take care of them.

PANEL 2

From low to the ground, we see Nurse Wrentch's plump leg, with sensible nurse shoes and suport hose. Two cockroaches are crawling up it.

NURSE WRENTCH

Don't be ridiculous! You're just a child.

[LINK]

These monsters are retired. They have special needs. Nobody knows better than —

PANEL 3

Nurse Wrentch sees the cockroaches on her dress now and looks at them in angry disgust (she's not afraid of them). With a swat of her meaty hand, she smacks one into goo.

>   NURSE WRENTCH

Yeechhh! Filthy things.

>   SFX

Sppluttt

PANEL 4

Suddenly a handcuff clicks onto her wrist, and the other end dangles in the air, seemingly attached to nothing. (It is hooked to the Invisible Man's wrist.) We don't see his sunglasses or slippers yet.

>   SFX

Klik

>   VOICE (INVISIBLE MAN)

Breaking the rules, Nurse Wrentch? Shame on you! I'm shocked — not to mention disappointed.

PANEL 5

Nurse Wrentch is shocked, looking in surprise at the Invisible Man, seeing only his sunglasses at her eye level and his bunny slippers on the ground.

>   NURSE WRENTCH

How — ? What is this?

>   INVISIBLE MAN

I hitched a ride. You never even noticed my bunny slippers in the car.... or the fax I got from H.A.R.M.

PAGE 19

PANEL 1

Suddenly behind her and on either side are two "men in black" wearing impeccable black business suits, ties, sunglasses. They have seemingly appeared in an instant.

MAN IN BLACK

Excuse me, ma'am. We can't allow you to harm those insects.

M.I.B. #2

These endangered cockroaches are protected by law. I'm afraid you have just committed a rather serious crime.

NURSE WRENTCH

Who — who are you?

PANEL 2

Closeup of one of the grim men as he holds out a heavy official-looking badge.

MAN

B.I.P., ma'am. Bureau of insect preservation. We're going to have to take you in.

PANEL 3

In the background, the men in black each take one of Nurse Wrentch's arms and haul her off while she sputters and struggles. Meanwhile, the monsters — happy now — are looking back at the castle. Tiffany is beaming. (Could be two panels if that works better.)

NURSE WRENTCH

But they're just a bunch of bugs! Disgusting Roaches!

BIP MAN

Protected roaches, ma'am. That's all the B.I.P. needs to know.

TIFFANY

It sure looks like we're going to have a lot of house work.

MUMMY

A little dust never hurt anybody.

MONSTER

We'll help out, Tiffany.

BRIDE

Help with housework? You bet you will!

WOLF-MAN

I'm sure we could find some friends to lend a paw....

PANEL 4

Closeup of the invisible man's face (all we see are his cool black sunglasses).

INVISIBLE MAN

And I tipped them off. I'm an honorary member of the B.I.P.

[LINK]

I... really liked their sunglasses.

PAGE 20

PANEL 1

Large panel. A full moon hangs over Castle Frankenstein. Bats fly in front of it. But instead of looking ominous, this appears celebratory: Banners and pennants hang from the turrets (some can say "Go, Monsters!") Ropes with streamers and colorful flags, like a used-car lot, dangle from towers. Two different monsters are speaking from the castle.

CAPTION

Later...

CASTLE

I'm glad we didn't go back to the R.I.P. retirement home...

CASTLE

I'd much rather live out my sunset years here.

PANEL 2

Inside the castle, on the long curved staircase in the cobwebby front foyer, a gleeful Tiffany Frankenstein comes sliding down the bannister, her hands up in the air.

TIFFANY

Wheeeee!

PANEL 3

At the bottom of the bannister, looking very paternal, Frankenstein's monster holds his arms open and catches Tiffany as soon as she reaches the bottom. He is grinning, as is the little girl. In the background, though, the Bride looks worried.

MONSTER

Got you!

BRIDE

Be careful, Monster! Remember that little humans break so easily!

TIFFANY

I'm fine!

PAGE 21

PANEL 1

The Mummy is being luxuriantly wrapped in brand new white gauze by one of the young cute nurses from the RIP home. He has a few Egyptian gold necklaces and bangles, looking very spiffy.

MUMMY

Ahh, this is the life. . . .

MUMMY

Sweetie, did I ever tell you about the lost treasure of the pharaohs? Maybe I'll save you a trinket or two. . . .

PANEL 2

Wolf Man is sitting at a table holding a hand of cards, scowling across at a pair of sunglasses and another hand of cards floating in the air (the invisible man).

WOLF-MAN

You got any sevens, Invisible Man?

PANEL 3

Closeup of the Invisible Man's "face" — we just see his sunglasses in mid-air.

INVISIBLE MAN

Go fish.

WOLF-MAN (OUT OF PANEL)

Grrrr, I can never tell when you're bluffing!

PANEL 4

The puppy, Gobblin, is playing at their feet under the card table (furred and clawed feet for the Wolf Man, empty bunny slippers for the Invisible Man). The puppy is chasing after the scuttling cockroaches.

INVISIBLE MAN

Just play your cards!
 Werewolves (out of panel) are so distractible.

PANEL 5

Dracula looks out one of the castle windows to the moat, where the Creature from the Black Lagoon (from Issue 1) is happily swimming, doing the back stroke.

DRACULA

Even if it isn't the Black Lagoon, the creature likes our moat vell enough.
. . .

PANEL 6

Outside, in the castle's moonlit courtyard, a large group of rotting zombies have strung up a long net and are playing a game of volleyball.

DRACULA (OUT OF PANEL)

In fact, all the monsters like it here. . . .

PAGE 22

PANEL 1

In one of the towers, the Hunchback dangles from a rope, swinging and grinning as he rings the castle bell.

SFX

Bonnnng klonnnng!

HUNCHBACK

Dinner time!

PANEL 2

Tiffany and all the monsters sit at a long elegant dinner table in the castle's banquet room. The chandeliers are still decked with cobwebs. Candelabras adorn the table. The monsters are eating appropriate meals — blood jello for Dracula, a dog food dish that says "Wolf Man" for Wolf Man and another one that says "Gobblin" for the puppy beside him; Monster and Bride sit next to each other, with Bride tucking a napkin into Monster's collar. Mummy is lifting the metal warming cover from his plate, and scarab beetles scuttle out and away.

TIFFANY

Now that all you monsters are settled in and happy here, I want to ask you a favor.

PANEL 3

Tiffany, closeup, smiling.

TIFFANY

I want you to help me set up a brand new lab—just like my grandfather's. For special experiments...

PANEL 4

Group shot of all the monsters in the dining room, cheering as they hear her news. Good times ahead!

TIFFANY

I want to take up a new . . . hobby.

                    MUMMY

Great idea, Tiffany!

                    DRACULA

Hooray! Just like old times in Transylvania!

                    WOLF-MAN

Arrooooo!

                    PUPPY

Yiip!

PREVIOUS PUBLICATION INFORMATION

"Frog Kiss," copyright © 1991 by WordFire, Inc., first published in Marion Zimmer Bradley's Fantasy Magazine, Fall 1991.

"Special Makeup," copyright © 1991, WordFire, Inc., first published in The Ultimate Werewolf, ed. Byron Preiss, Dell Books, 1991.

"Memorial" © 2018 WordFire, Inc. First published in Reflections, 1978.

"Bump in the Night" copyright © 2022, WordFire, Inc., originally appeared in Pulphouse Fiction Magazine, Issue #19, August 2022.

"Quest Prize" © 2022 WordFire, Inc., first published in Animal Magica: A Fantasy Coloring Book, Volume 2, art by Tanya Hales, Mythic Mongoose Press, 2022.

"Paradox & Greenblatt, Attorneys at Law" © 2005 WordFire, Inc. First published in Analog, September 2005.

"Eighty Letters, Plus One," with Sarah A. Hoyt, © 2005 WordFire, Inc. and Sarah A. Hoyt, first published in The Mammoth Book of New Jules Verne Adventures, ed. Mike Ashley and Eric Brown, Carroll & Graf, 2005.

"Short Straws," copyright © 1995 WordFire, Inc., first published in The Ultimate Dragon, ed. Bryon Preiss, John Betancourt, and Keith R.A. DeCandido, Dell Books, October 1995.

"The Sacrifice," copyright © 2018 WordFire, Inc., first published online in Daily Science Fiction, 2018.

"TechnoMagic" copyright © 1996 by WordFire, Inc. First published in David Copperfield's Beyond Imagination, ed. David Copperfield & Janet Berliner, HarperPrism, 1996.

"Age Rings," copyright © 1988, WordFire, Inc., first published in Grue Magazine #7, revised 2017.

"Letter of Resignation," copyright © 2018, WordFire, Inc., first published in Selected Stories: Fantasy by Kevin J. Anderson, WordFire Press, 2018.

"Rude Awakening," copyright © 2017, WordFire, Inc., first published in Pulse Pounders II: Adrenaline, ed. Kevin J. Anderson, WMG Publishing, 2017.

"The Fate Worse Than Death," with Guy Anthony de Marco, copyright © 2014, WordFire, Inc. and Guy Anthony de Marco, first published in Unidentified Funny Objects 3, ed. Alex Schvartsman, UFO Publishing, 2014.

"Time Zone," copyright © 2018 WordFire, Inc., first published online in Daily Science Fiction, 2018.

"Dark Carbuncle," with Janis Ian, copyright © 2010, WordFire, Inc. and Janis Ian, first published in Blood Lite II: Overbite, ed. Kevin J. Anderson, Gallery Books, 2010.

"Tea Time Before Perseus," copyright © 2018, WordFire, Inc., first published in Selected Stories: Fantasy by Kevin J. Anderson, WordFire Press, 2018.

"Santa Claus Is Coming to Get You" copyright © 1991 by WordFire, Inc. First published in Deathrealm, Fall/Winter 1991.

"Cold Dead Turkey" copyright © 2015, WordFire, Inc., originally appeared in Naughty or Nice: A Holiday Anthology, Jennifer Brozek, ed., Evil Girlfriend Media (2015).

"Loincloth," with Rebecca Moesta, first published in Pandora's Closet, ed. Jean Rabe & Martin H. Greenberg, DAW Books, 2007.

"Grumpy Old Monsters: The Original Comic Scripts," with Rebecca Moesta, copyright © 2023, WordFire, Inc. Previously unpublished.

Read All the Cases of Dan Shamble, Zombie P.I.

Death Warmed Over

Unnatural Acts

Hair Raising

Working Stiff

Slimy Underbelly

Tastes Like Chicken

Services Rendered

Double-Booked

Don't miss the next exciting Dragon Business adventure!

About the Author

Kevin J. Anderson has published more than 170 books, 58 of which have been national or inter–national bestsellers. He has written numerous novels in the Star Wars, X-Files, and Dune universes, as well as unique steampunk fantasy novels *Clockwork Angels* and *Clockwork Lives*, written with legendary rock drummer Neil Peart. His original works include the Saga of Seven Suns series, the Wake the Dragon and Terra Incognita fantasy trilogies, the Saga of Shadows trilogy, and his humorous horror series featuring Dan Shamble, Zombie P.I. He has edited numerous anthologies, written comics and games, and the lyrics to two rock CDs. Anderson is the director of the graduate program in Publishing at Western Colorado University. Anderson and his wife Rebecca Moesta are the publishers of WordFire Press. His most recent novels are *Gods and Dragons*, *Dune: The Heir of Caladan* (with Brian Herbert), *Stake*, *Kill Zone* (with Doug Beason), and *Spine of the Dragon*.

For information on upcoming projects, appearances, free books and stories, and general fun stuff, sign up for Kevin's newsletter at wordfire.com.

facebook.com/KJAauthor
twitter.com/TheKJA
instagram.com/TheRealKJA

To Order Autographed Print Copies

of this book and many other titles
by Kevin J. Anderson
please check out our selection at

WFS
WordFire Shop

wordfireshop.com